MojaVe GReeN

DIMENSIONS IN DEATH. BOOK 2

First Paperback Edition: October 2014

For information on subsidiary rights, please contact the publisher at rights@jollyfishpress.com. For a complete list of our wholesalers and distributors, please visit our website at www.jollyfishpress.com.

For information, write us at Jolly Fish Press, PO Box 1773, Provo, UT 84603-1773.

Printed in the United States of America

THIS TITLE IS ALSO AVAILABLE AS AN EBOOK.

Library of Congress Cataloging-in-Publication Data

Mojave green / The Brothers Washburn. -- First paperback edition.
     pages cm. -- (Dimensions in death ; book 2)
  Summary: In an isolated mining town deep in the Mojave Desert, an unearthly creature once preyed upon the town's folk for decades and now eighteen-year-old Camm Smith must battle unearthly monsters and outwit dangerous government agents to rescue the friends she placed in danger.
  ISBN 978-1-939967-85-5 (paperback)
  [1. Horror stories. 2. Mojave Desert--Fiction.] I. Brothers Washburn.
  PZ7.M7284 2014
  [Fic]--dc23
                              2014020745

10 9 8 7 6 5 4 3 2 1

To Clara B. Washburn, our loving mother, who told some of the scariest stories we have ever heard. Thank you for opening our eyes to the wonders of the universe of imagination.

Praises for *Pitch Green*,
Book 1 of the *Dimensions in Death* Series

"The Brothers Washburn are masters at writing for young adults. Every character is believable, every description is vivid, and every moment is a surprise. The story was the perfect mix of frightening and intriguing that made it impossible to put down."
—Celese Sanders, columnist, *The Daily Independent &
Taft Midway Driller*

"[The Brothers Washburn] know their way around horror stories and suspense fiction . . . Books like this will spur young readers to become enchanted with the whole realm of literature. Parents and teachers alert!"
—Grady Harp, *Top 50 Amazon Reviewer*

"The Brothers Washburn quickly draw the reader into their horrific realm . . . *Pitch Green* is a zestful new entry in the Stephen King, blood-and-squishy-eyeballs school of horror."
—Elaine Lovitt, *Top 100 Amazon Reviewer*

"*Pitch Green* is a very fast paced YA horror story that will keep you on the edge of your seat, you will not want to put it down."
—Jody Joy, *Jody's Book Reviews*

"*Pitch Green* is full of not only horror but a mystery aspect that leaves you glued to the pages."
—Kayla Shirley, *Kayla's Place*

"If you love a scary story, *Pitch Green* is sure to satisfy . . . I would recommend *Pitch Green* to any fan of YA horror."
—Alice Anderson, editor, *Bella Online*

"Although this is basically geared towards young adults, I admit I got the heebie jeebies and goosebumps reading it . . ."
—Jennifer Jordan, *Gimme The Scoop Reviews*

THE BROTHERS
WASHBURN

Mojave Green

DIMENSIONS IN DEATH, BOOK 2

JOLLY
FISH
PRESS

Provo, Utah

I

Camm shook her head in frustration. "Come on, guys! It's already Sunday morning. I cannot believe it is almost three a.m." Peering nervously into the dark shadows looming on every side, she tried to hustle her two girlfriends back to their dorm.

Ever since her brush with death the year before in the abandoned Searles Mansion, Camm felt vulnerable in the dark, especially after midnight. Sometimes, in the wee hours of the morning, she awoke drenched in sweat, tormented by vivid nightmares that always ended in a deep stone dungeon piled high with the skulls of small children.

Camm had learned to work through the sleepless hours doing homework and anything that could be done while locked away in her private dorm room with all the lights on. She did not come out until the sun was up and daylight again ruled the world.

Right now, all she wanted was to be back in the dorms, safe and warm in her little room, where the lights all worked and the air smelled fresh and clean. She had no patience for a casual stroll through a dark, abandoned corner of the Yale campus, but her friends, Sally and Martha, were difficult to hurry. Both were inebriated and a little unstable on their feet, especially Sally.

Sally, a freshman like Camm, was short and shapely, on the plump side, with a pretty face and long, dark hair. She enjoyed life, laughed easily, and always looked for a reason to be happy. She and Camm had become friends because they complimented each other so well. Camm was the responsible one, who made sure they both studied and got to class on time. Sally made sure they both had fun along the way.

Martha was a first-year law student, but was only eighteen months older than Camm. She was extremely smart, even for Yale, but her appearance was quite forgettable: average height, average build, nondescript hair, and an honest, but unremarkable face. In social gatherings of more than two or three people, she was awkward and had little to say.

Martha had started college at a young age, and managed to graduate in two and a half years by going straight through. She had graduated from Brigham Young University—a Catholic at a Mormon school. She had come to Yale anxious to let her hair down and party a little.

Camm gently nudged her two friends along a sidewalk that cut across campus. They had just reached a small street lamp posted along the way, when it blinked twice and went dark. Camm scowled. She did not like it when lights went out for no apparent reason, not since the events in the Trona mansion.

It was spring in Connecticut, and the air still carried a chill. The night sky was thick with clouds and an oppressive dampness hung over them like a heavy shroud. Looking ahead, Camm saw another lamp twenty yards further down the sidewalk, in the direction of their dorm.

She pointed. "Hurry, head for that light. Let's get out of the dark."

"Why are we going home so soon? Things were just getting fun." Sally didn't sound upset, but then she never did.

Camm had reluctantly agreed to come with Sally to the fraternity party because she knew that once Sally started drinking, she would need someone to watch out for her—someone who didn't drink. It wasn't that Camm was morally opposed to drinking so much as she had witnessed how drinking caused Sally to lose her inhibitions as well as her ability to exercise good judgment. In Camm's opinion, there was no excuse for that.

"You were about to have more fun than you counted on." Martha laughed, then hiccupped. She was slightly drunk, but still acutely aware of what was going on around her.

Camm liked Martha because she had no hidden agendas and was one of the few people Camm knew who was smarter than she was. Martha had sought out Camm's friendship from their first meeting, and with Martha's easy-going personality, she was easy to like.

As they reached the safety of the next lamp along the sidewalk, it blinked twice before going out, exactly as the previous light had done. Camm's scowl deepened. Placing her balled fists on her hips, she twisted about, intently searching the deep shadows. A heavy sigh escaped her lips, sending curling, twisting vapors into the cold air.

"That's odd," Martha observed, "for lights to suddenly go out like that." Sounding remarkably sober, she watched Camm with increasing interest.

"Let's go back to the party," Sally whined with a smile. "It was just getting fun."

A group of boys had been escorting the tipsy Sally upstairs to show her "a big surprise," when Camm intervened, deciding it was time for them both to leave.

The boys had been clearly unhappy with the unexpected change in plans, but had been no match for Camm's will and determination. When Martha saw her dorm mates leaving the party, she decided to go with them since she was bored and just reading some old magazine she had found lying around the frat house.

Camm lifted her head and carefully sniffed the air. Seeing Martha's puzzled look, Camm asked, "Do you smell anything bad? Like rotten eggs?"

Martha raised an eyebrow. "Rotten eggs?"

"It's nothing." Camm shrugged it off. "I don't like it here in the dark. Let's keep going."

The darkness and cold seemed to conspire against Camm, surrounding and enveloping her in its icy grip. This was unpleasantly familiar to Camm. Staring around, her stomach clenched as nightmarish memories bombarded her.

"Let's move!" Grabbing both her companions by the hand, Camm pulled them toward a large brick building with a portico lit by several flood lamps. Upon reaching the building, all its lights blinked twice and then went black, leaving the trio in obscure darkness, deepened by cloudy skies that blocked the moon and starlight.

Martha's face filled with concern as she glanced nervously at Camm. Sally was still totally oblivious to the coincidence of the lights going out.

"Why can't we go back? I wanna go back to the party—it was warm there. Let's go back. Okay?" Sally held on to the last syllable, dragging it out into a long, plaintive whine.

Ignoring Sally, Camm glanced around for a stick, a rock, anything that could be used as a weapon, but then realized that if what she feared was happening was actually happening, a stick or rock would be of absolutely no use anyway. Their only defense was to stay in the light.

A row of spotlights gleamed from across the wide grassy quad where a distant building loomed out of the darkness. "Quick," Camm whispered, pointing across the quad. "Let's go there—those lights are still working."

Stepping off the sidewalk, she led them out across the grass, her friends struggling to match her pace. Their only light came from remote sources—barely illuminated buildings or faintly visible street lights. Making matters worse, a thin fog rolled in, silent and evil, as if intent on obscuring their vision even more. Camm was becoming desperate for light of any kind—anything but the hated darkness and what it might be hiding.

Their feet made a crunching noise on the frosted grass. There were no other sounds. The darkness and heavy mist combined to cast a deathly pall over the three girls and everything around them. Old, unpleasant feelings grew in Camm's gut, overpowering feelings of terror she had hoped never to feel again.

This can't be happening, she thought desperately. *Not here in Connecticut, not all the way on the other side of the continent. Besides, I saw it die—we watched it die!*

Grabbing each of the other girls by the elbow, Camm tried to quicken the pace. She felt a desperate need to get into the light.

As they approached some thick bushes growing in the quad, a man-like figure suddenly leapt out at them. Blocking their path, it crouched before them, arms upraised, legs spread and knees bent. The creature's face was hideous, half human, half predatory beast, with deformed eyes framed by thick, bushy brows. Below a large, distorted nose that appeared to be badly broken, its mouth gaped wide, showing immense teeth, pointed and unevenly placed. Though the creature made a loud growling noise, the grimacing face appeared paralyzed, barely moving.

Again, the thing sprang toward them, reaching out with both hands in a menacing manner as it swayed stiffly back and forth on unsteady legs.

Sally began to scream in a horrified, high-pitched voice that squeaked. Her legs danced up and down as if she were riding a stationary bike, while her arms fluttered back and forth in a helpless manner. Martha, her face white and taut, did not scream, but stepped behind Camm, seeking protection from her taller, albeit younger, friend.

Camm's whole body had gone stone cold, but she showed no outward reaction, except to take a boxing stance with both fists up in front of her face. Holding her left arm directly in front with the elbow pointing down, she used her left fist as a shield before her face. The right arm was cocked back at a forty-five-degree angle to the left arm, the right fist ready to lash out.

The horrid figure jumped forward again, thrusting its fixed face up close to Camm, continuing to growl through unmoving lips. Camm's reaction was instantaneous—she landed a right cross hard on the figure's big nose. The sound of crunching cartilage echoed through the quad. The creature stumbled backward, lost its footing, and fell with a plop on its rear end, the same horrid expression frozen on its face all the while.

The growling noise stopped. In its place, a muffled voice said, "What'd you do that for?"

Reaching up with its right hand, the figure grabbed itself on top of its ugly scalp and yanked its own head clean off. Sally stopped screaming and froze in disbelief at the act of self-decapitation. Martha watched, fascinated.

But instead of becoming headless, another head and face appeared beneath the horrid one. The new face belonged to Mark Zelbolski. He brought his left hand to his face to hold his nose. Blood flowed from both nostrils. Looking up at Camm with a pained expression, he repeated in a nasal voice, "What'd you do that for?"

Mark had been the best looking guy at the party. Tall and dark with perfect features, he was one of those guys who was almost too good looking. His face would have been pretty on a woman—would have been. His once perfect nose now pointed off at an obtuse angle. He sat in the frosty grass, legs splayed out, trying to stem the blood that flowed out his nose, past his mouth, over his handsome dimpled chin, and onto his expensive designer shirt.

The terrible mask he'd worn lay like a dead thing on the grass next to him.

Camm stared down at Mark's dejected form. He could not have known he was dealing with Camelot Mist Smith, who had been taught basic boxing moves by her best friend and next-door neighbor, California Gold Jones, or Cal for short— both Camm and Cal hated their formal given names. Mark also could not have known that Camm despised being scared or startled and did not tolerate threats from anyone, not even someone as popular and good looking as Mark. Even Cal had had to learn that lesson the hard way.

Another figure, wider and stumpier, now emerged from behind the thick bushes with a mask in hand and stomped toward Camm. "I can't believe you did that. Who do you think you are?" he demanded. "You can't just start slugging people in the face."

With exaggerated force, he flung his mask to the ground and kicked it away.

Camm, quickly recovering her composure, calmly replied, "It seems that I can."

She was talking to Dwight Pearlsmith, one of the boys who had been escorting Sally upstairs for the big surprise. He had been the most threatening when Camm pulled Sally away.

Martha raised a discreet hand to her face to hide a smile. Sally had stopped screaming, but looked around confused, trying to figure out what had just happened.

Dwight jabbed his forefinger in Camm's direction. "Who do you think you are? You just slugged Mark in the face! You probably broke his nose!"

Martha tried to suppress a giggle. "Oh, there's no doubt about it. His nose is definitely broken."

Camm noticed a small black box in Dwight's left hand. It had several buttons and a toggle switch on it, as well as a small radio antenna. Pointing at the box, Camm asked accusingly, "What's that in your hand?"

Dwight belatedly hid the box behind his back.

Martha responded for Dwight. "That is the remote-control device they were evidently using to turn off the lights as we walked by on our way home."

Ignoring Martha, Dwight tossed the box into the bushes behind him. Swearing and waving his arms, his face flushed red with anger, he advanced towards Camm. When she didn't back away, he planted himself right in front of her and shouted, "Who do you think you are?" Before she could answer, he leaned in eye-to-eye to yell accusingly, "You broke Mark's nose!"

"What'd you do that for?" It was more a plea than a question from Mark, who sat with blood flowing freely from his nose. His eyes were wide, like he was about to cry, and he looked confused as if he had no understanding of what had just happened.

Dwight resumed pointing his finger at Camm, now jabbing it directly into her shoulder for emphasis. "You can't just slug people in their faces, breaking their nose any time you want."

"Breaking their noses," Martha corrected, still trying to hide her smile. She sounded particularly tickled by the current turn of events.

Camm did not back away from Dwight's jabbing finger, but gave him a serious scowl. "Back off, cowboy," she warned. "Right now!"

"Or what? You think you can fight me? Get real! Just who do you think you are? Wonder Woman?" Dwight laughed and continued to jab her in the shoulder.

Camm smelled the sour odor of beer on his breath. His

eyes were bloodshot, bright red. She stepped forward with her left foot and resumed her boxer stance.

Dwight hesitated, and then, smirking, jabbed her hard one more time in the shoulder. "What?" he challenged with a snarl. "You gonna do something about it? Huh, girlie? I'd like to see you try. Come on! What ya gonna do?"

Camm had always been taught by her parents, teachers, and pastor that you never threw the first punch in a fight, but if someone else did, it was okay to defend yourself.

Cal gave different advice. He said if it became obvious a fight was unavoidable, then throw the first punch and make it count. If you took the other guy down first, fast, and hard, the fight wouldn't last long. Cal took his own advice and few people messed with him. Camm decided not to wait to see what Dwight was going to do next—she took Cal's advice.

She danced lightly from foot to foot, and then planted her left foot firmly ahead of the right as she leaned in with a quick left jab, punching Dwight solidly in the right eye.

Shocked by the unexpected jab, Dwight stumbled backward, but quickly recovered his balance, holding a hand over his smarting eye.

Mark watched in amazement. "What'd you do that for?" he asked plaintively.

"Owwww!" Dwight howled. "Who do you think you are? Man! You're out of control! Someone really needs to slap you hard up side your head."

He still wasn't down and was again moving in on Camm. But she was faster. Stepping forward with her right foot and leaning in with her body weight, Camm brought her right fist around in a combination roundhouse right cross, striking Dwight on his left eye.

This time his whole body lurched back. He staggered, trying to regain his balance, but stumbled over Mark and fell hard next to him on the grass. "Ouch, ouch, ouch!" Dwight shouted and rolled around on the grass, yelling and swearing as he covered both eyes with his hands. He looked like a small child throwing a temper tantrum.

A sharp pain throbbed in Camm's right index finger where her fist had struck Dwight's skull above the eye. She kept her expression neutral, not letting her face betray the pain.

Mark, Martha, and Sally all looked at Camm in awe, mouths hanging open.

Dwight finally quit thrashing around and peered up at Camm the best he could through swollen eyes. "You stupid ape! You are in so much trouble. I'm going to get you kicked out of school! I'm bringing criminal charges, too! You can't go around punching people like some big ol' hairy Amazon. I'll see that you're expelled, not just suspended!"

"I don't think so, Dwight." Martha calmly stepped out from behind Camm.

"What do you know? You little twerp!" Dwight snarled.

"I'm taking a criminal law class this semester—I actually know a lot. First of all, we did not attack you—you attacked us. It was an unprovoked attack, and you both brought masks to hide your identities. You could have been robbers or rapists, anything you wanted, hiding behind masks to take advantage of helpless girls."

She shrugged her slight shoulders. "Maybe, you really are rapists. But, Camm stopped you. Whatever you say, this was no joke. You heard Sally screaming—our fear was real."

"Yeah," Sally piped up. "You made me pee my pants."

As if making closing arguments, Martha continued. "Second, you made first offensive contact by jabbing Camm in the shoulder. That's assault and battery, and Camm had a legal right to defend herself. Sally and I are witnesses—you were becoming increasingly more violent. Camm had reason to fear for her safety and for our safety as well. Camm was also defending us."

"Yeah!" Sally added emphatically.

Martha held out three fingers for Dwight to see. "Third, if this goes to the dean, you're both in big trouble for messing with the school lights that are supposed to prevent these kinds of attacks. You can claim it was just a prank, but at this point, we are entitled to assume it was a real attack, and you blacked out the lights so that no one would see you attack us.

"I think you are right, Dwight. Someone could be expelled for this, but it won't be Camm. It will be you, the attackers, not one of your intended victims, who get expelled."

"And fourth!" Sally had sobered up in the excitement and decided to throw in her own two cents. "You both got your butts kicked by a girl—by a girl! Do you want the whole school to know? Once you start complaining, we'll make sure everyone hears the whole story."

They all eyed each other, no one speaking. Dwight and Mark kept glancing up at Camm, who scowled down at them, both fists still clenched. She hadn't retreated an inch.

Finally, Mark rolled onto his side and carefully stood up. The blood flow from his nose had abated a little, but he continued to gingerly press a blood-soaked hanky to his nose. Reaching down with his free hand, he helped Dwight to his feet, guiding him away from Camm.

With both eyes now almost swollen shut, Dwight staggered as he tried to find his footing. Supporting and pulling Dwight along, Mark led him back in the direction of the frat house.

"I can't believe I have to go through plastic surgery again." Mark sighed.

Camm and Martha looked at each other as if to say, *"Well, that explains a lot."*

The last thing they heard from the pathetic pair was Dwight grumbling, "Who does she think she is, anyway?"

With a big sigh, Sally smiled at Camm. "I guess you're right. It's time to go home."

She slid her arm through Camm's arm on one side, and Martha did the same on the other. The trio resumed their course to the dorms, Camm ignoring the throbbing pain in her right hand.

Soon, they walked under another small street lamp, and this one didn't go out.

Martha grinned up at Camm in the yellow light. "You're my hero," she whispered.

II

"Hey, guys! Wait up." Dylan struggled to catch up with the other two boys. He was a little shorter and heavier than Danny and Larry, and it took him longer to travel the same distance. This was true especially when the other two ten-year-olds purposely ran ahead in an effort to leave him behind. Not that they didn't like him—the trio went everywhere together. It was just their way of teasing him for being slow.

Staring after his friends as they jogged up the steep mountain trail, Dylan thought how some things never change, including how he had almost missed today's adventure. As he was sneaking out the back door that morning, his mom had spied him. "Dylan Justenough, where do you think you're going? And with your rifle, too? Does your father know?"

Luckily for him, a loud crash and the baby's wail from the

kitchen had sent his mom flying out of the room, and he had made his escape. With all the kids in the Justenough family, he knew it would be awhile before she gave him another thought.

Meeting Danny and Larry where the pavement ended on the northern side of Pioneer Point, they had hiked across the open desert to the foothills of Argus Peak, northwest of Trona, and then up a narrow canyon to a natural spring called Indian Joe's.

Down in Searles Valley, the soil was so alkaline and filled with chemical salts that very few plants could survive. Only a few desert plants grew at all, and then not well. Not even grass would grow. Of course, those same minerals and chemicals created jobs for the valley's residents. Trona's largest employer was a mining operation that extracted minerals from the dry lake bed and shipped them all over the world.

Up at Indian Joe's, however, the soil was mostly free of the chemical salts. Over a hundred years earlier, John Searles, Trona's founder, had planted garden vegetables near the spring. Some of the plants still grew wild in the protection of the canyon's shade where they could drink all year long from the life-giving spring waters. Fig and other non-native trees that Searles had planted also still grew along the steep canyon floor below the spring.

After prowling around Indian Joe's, enjoying the cold spring waters and resting in the shade, the boys had decided to hike farther up into the mountains in search of jackrabbits, road-runners, ground squirrels, and other worthy prey. They were anxious to shoot the new box of long-rifle ammo that Dylan had brought along for their .22 rifles. Dylan was always able to get more ammo from his older brothers.

"Maybe, we can even find a rattlesnake or scorpion," Danny said as he sighted in on an empty beer can.

The hot desert sun beat down on them as they trudged along the upper mountain trail. Dylan was sweating profusely and struggling to keep up. When he finally asked for a rest stop, the two faster boys hooted as if it were a funny joke.

"See you on the other side of that ridge up there," Larry had called, and the two sprinted off laughing. It was no joke to Dylan.

Drawing a shaky breath, he squared his shoulders and set off, chubby legs pumping the trail as he vainly tried to close the distance between himself and his friends. He hadn't gone far before he was forced to stop, out of breath and lightheaded. Hands on his hips, he worked to suck in enough dry desert air to replenish his lungs.

Feeling suddenly strange, Dylan shivered, as if cold, though ahead of him the air shimmered with heat. An otherworldly feeling clung to this place. Giant boulders, some bigger than a house, littered the mountainside. Dry, suffocatingly hot air engulfed him, and the deep, deep silence of the desert settled over everything like an ancient blanket. He felt like an explorer who had left earth and gone to an alien planet.

Without warning, his vision wavered and the strange sensation passed through him again. Feeling like he might throw up, he carefully leaned his rifle against a big rock and bent forward with his hands on his knees, taking regular, deep breaths like his mom had shown him. As quickly as it had come, the strange feeling faded. He straightened to look around. Danny and Larry were already almost to the distant ridge and still running.

Dylan's shoulders slumped. *I'm never gonna catch those guys—not as long as they're trying to stay ahead of me.*

Numbly, he watched their shrinking forms grow more distant. Heat waves rising from the dirt gave their images a glimmering mirage appearance, as if they were disconnecting from him and his world. Suddenly, they vanished from sight.

At the same time, a strange noise drew his attention to the big rocks up the mountainside above him. He spun around, seeking the source of the noise, but there was nothing new to see. The noise stopped.

"You guys, knock it off!" he hollered, angry now, certain the noise was part of a joke they were playing on him. His harsh yell wandered out into the open desert air, disappearing without even an echo in response. Then, he remembered. Larry and Danny were a long way up the mountain trail ahead of him—he was down here alone.

Another chill traveled up his spine, once more in defiance of the overwhelming heat. Involuntary shivers vibrated throughout his body, leaving him shaking with the strange sensations. Again, he felt nauseated, almost seasick. Bending over like before, the sensation quickly passed, but now he was worried.

Why did he keep feeling so strange? Was he getting sunstroke? Would he be able to make the long hike back home across the open desert to Pioneer Point?

He heard the strange noise again. It sounded like rocks

rattling around in a plastic five-gallon bucket. He looked behind him and to each side—nothing. Wait. There was something, a shimmering dull emerald color, like a wave, gliding along just visible behind the large boulders to his right. He closed his eyes, worried he was seeing things. He was sure now he was suffering from the early symptoms of heatstroke.

Keeping his eyes closed, he leaned back into the shadow of a huge rock and took long, slow breaths. The rock's surface felt cold against his hot skin.

He thought longingly of the cool shade back at Indian Joe's, but decided to continue up the trail after his now-long-gone companions. If he kept in the shade of the bigger rocks as much as possible, he should be all right. He didn't want to give his friends any more cause than they already had to ridicule him.

Feeling better, he opened his eyes and turned up the trail, only to come to an abrupt halt. Something lay on the path that hadn't been there before—a large, peculiar rock. More greenish in hue than the other rocks around it, it was thick and flat, shaped like a giant arrowhead, pointing downhill toward him.

Large, perfectly round black disks sat on either side of the wide top, with two holes, perfectly placed, under the disks. A large crack ran evenly along the bottom of the rock, under the two holes. The markings were amazingly symmetrical, appearing exactly on one side as on the other. Like a statute, carved and placed in the middle of his path, it sat there twenty feet in front of him. More than a foot tall, it was at least three feet across at its widest point. Strange he hadn't noticed it before.

He took a step forward when something on the rock moved—or did it? He wasn't sure what he'd just seen. As he continued to watch, it moved again. A long black ribbon, forked on the end, shot out of the crack, then was sucked back in. It was barely there, less than a second.

Suddenly, the rock started rising off the ground, up, up, up, high into the air.

Fighting an overwhelming sense of disbelief, Dylan realized it was not a rock. Turning to run, he opened his mouth to yell for help.

He never got the chance to yell, let alone run. Everything went dark. Momentarily, his feet kicked wildly, but in no time at all, he descended head first into pitch black.

"What's taking Dylan so long?" For the last half hour, Danny had been practicing his baseball throw using the round, smooth rocks from a dry creek bed.

"I bet he's hiding along the trail somewhere to jump out and scare us," Larry muttered.

Keeping a sharp eye out for an ambush, they trudged back down the trail in silence. Not far from where they had last seen him, they were surprised to find Dylan's .22 rifle lying across the trail in the dirt.

Danny frowned. "Dylan wouldn't ever drop his .22 in the

dirt like this. He waited too long to finally get his own." Picking up the rifle, Danny carefully brushed off the dirt and blew the dust out of the barrel.

"What's that?" Larry ran further down the trail and bent to pick something up. "Look at this," he yelled, waving a lone hiking boot. "This is Dylan's. It has his name on it."

Together they stared at the boot in disbelief. The laces were knotted tight as if the boot was still tied to Dylan's foot.

"Is he playing a joke on us?" Larry almost whispered.

"That doesn't seem like him."

They scanned the rugged mountainside, hoping Dylan would pop up at any second yelling, "Got ya," but nothing moved. All was quiet.

Danny blew out a slow breath. "What's he doing out here in the mountains, all by himself, no rifle, and wearing only one boot?"

Though they searched for him the rest of the morning, they never got a chance to ask.

Like so many of Trona's lost children before him, Dylan had disappeared without a trace, never to be seen again.

III

Cal's roommates were all out, so he had the apartment to himself, at least for now. He decided to whip up a pot of baked beans—California Gold style. He began by cooking four strips of bacon in the bottom of a sauce pan. As the bacon sizzled and sputtered, Cal sang himself a bean song that he made up on the spot:

Eating beans is always smart.
Lovers eat beans to strengthen their heart.
Hunters eat beans to sharpen their dart.
Athletes eat beans by the shopping cart.

Here he was distracted momentarily while he focused on the preparation of his meal. As the bacon cooked, he peeled and diced a Granny Smith apple. Removing the cooked bacon, he broke it into small pieces, and then fried the diced apple in the bacon grease. After the apple bits were fried crispy and

placed on a paper towel, he poured out most of the grease
(pouring it directly down the sink, which his best friend Camm
had said he should never do, so he did it with hot water and
lots of dish washing soap).

Next he poured in a whole can of kidney beans, and then
added the bacon and apple bits. He sliced in copious amounts
of onion and added sliced jalapeño peppers from a jar, pouring in some of the juice for good measure. He added brown
sugar, ketchup, and vinegar with a little mustard to up the
flavor ratio. Finally, he up-ended a bottle of hot sauce over
his concoction. He used Tapatio, his favorite brand.

He loved the smell of Tapatio, and in most of Cal's recipes,
it was the most important ingredient.

Surveying his work with satisfaction, he thought, *Take it
from the boss. Don't risk a loss. You may win the toss, but don't skimp
on the hot sauce.*

It occurred to Cal that should he ever need a mantra, it
would be: *Don't skimp on the hot sauce!* He could see applications
of that bit of wisdom in all areas of life.

While the savory-smelling pot of beans simmered, he went
back to his happy bean song:

You can get your beans at the closest Walmart,
Or make your own—it's a real fine art.
Simmer beans slowly, keep ingredients tart,
Plan your meal wisely, keep the horse before the cart.
I'm not one to boast, but for my own part,
A dish of good beans will always make me . . .

His cell phone rang, playing a Katy Perry tune, interrupting his song just as he spooned the hot beans into a large bowl. He had a box of rainbow-colored Goldfish crackers to go along with the beans, and, in the freezer, an extra-large ice cream sandwich for dessert. He sighed, not wanting an interruption to his feast, but he knew who was calling—he had a girlfriend.

Cal's girlfriend, K'tlynn, had asked to see his phone a few weeks back and, without his permission, had programmed it to play the Katy Perry tune when she called him. Cal was not a big Katy Perry fan, but he left it on his phone, so as not to offend K'tlynn.

The idea of having a girlfriend had been appealing at first. Cal had not really had a girlfriend before, one he could kiss and hug, and be amorous with. Oh, he had a best friend, who was a girl—that was Camm. He had grown up next door to her and been attracted to her as long as he could remember. When he had tried a few romantic moves in high school, she had quickly put him in his place—sometimes painfully.

Last summer, he thought she might be starting to like him in the same way he liked her. But, then they'd both headed off to college, and Camm had grown distant. While calls and texts kept them in touch, she was all business and said nothing about her social life, even when Cal talked about some of the things he was doing with K'tlynn. Of course, he would much rather be dating Camm, but he couldn't judge her feelings about him. If Camm was bothered by Cal dating K'tlynn, she didn't show it in their phone calls. He decided he would have to see the whites of Camm's eyes to know when it was safe to go after her again.

In the meantime, he was finding that a girlfriend was a fulltime occupation. He had not really known how to go about getting a girlfriend, but that had not been a problem, since he was tall, good looking, and played on the freshman football squad.

Several girls had been interested in him, but K'tlynn had been the one who had landed him. After all, she was extraordinarily pretty. With platinum blond hair, large blue eyes, and a petite, but curvy figure, Cal thought she was pretty enough to be a model or even an actress.

It was pretty cool, in the beginning. They went to dances, plays, and sporting events together. She even took him home for Sunday dinner. Lately, though, Cal had begun to worry about their relationship—a small, but nagging worry.

Two things had happened to cause him concern. First, he had walked up to her while she was talking with her friends. They had been giggling about something, but got very quiet when Cal approached. He hadn't been paying close attention to what they were saying, but became suspicious when they all got quiet.

Later, he played it back in his mind and became convinced that K'tlynn had been talking about her wedding day with her friends. She had been discussing her colors, her wedding gown, and who her bridesmaids would be. Cal wasn't sure he wanted to be dating someone who was so anxious to get married.

The second thing that concerned him was a conversation he had with K'tlynn's father. Her father was a high-powered attorney with a prestigious national law firm. He mainly practiced white-collar criminal defense in federal court. One night after dinner, he had asked Cal what his plans were after he graduated.

"Son," he said. He always called Cal *son*. "What are you going to do with yourself after you get that sheep skin?"

Truthfully, Cal had not thought about it much. He was just enjoying being on the football team and going to his classes, which were mostly general education courses.

"I dunno, I'm still thinking about it," was his honest reply.

"Well, son, it's time to start making decisions. And, I'm going to be frank, my boy. You're tall and strong, but you don't have what it takes to play professional ball. You can't depend on the NFL to pick you up after college. You need to decide what you are going to do with your life after football, and start preparing now for a good career."

Cal had been a little offended. Every player at Florida State held out some hope of going to the NFL. No one, especially a freshman, wanted to hear that he didn't have what it takes. Cal still hoped the NFL would be his career after college.

Stammering as he searched for a non-offensive response, Cal had finally said, "I dunno. I was thinking of maybe teaching phys-ed in high school if I don't get picked up by the NFL. One way or another, I was thinking I could make football my career."

K'tlynn's father had put his arm around Cal in a patronizing manner before responding, "Oh, don't do that. There's no money in teaching high school. You'll be poor your whole life.

"You want to go to law school, that's what you want to do. Change your major to English. English majors do the best in law school. That's what I did. Go to law school, and I will get you on with my firm when you graduate. You'll make a lot more money. Trust me on this."

Cal had squirmed out of the man's grip and made an excuse to get away, but had quickly made up his mind about a few things. He was not ready to be dating someone who was thinking about marriage and whose father wanted to guide his career. And, if he didn't get into the NFL, he was going to teach high school physical education, no matter how much it paid.

Katy Perry began playing again. Cal sighed, seriously considering not answering his phone, but then decided his feast could wait a few minutes longer. His mouth was watering like a waterfall, so he swallowed a mouthful of saliva and answered his phone.

"Yello." He tried to not sound disappointed at the inconvenient interruption.

"Hey baby, what cha doin'?" Being from Florida, K'tlynn had a slight southern drawl.

"Uh, nothin'. Uh, you know, just thinking of you."

"You're not eating are you? We're eating at my parents tonight. I don't want you to lose your appetite. Remember, I told you to not eat before we go."

Cal didn't understand her concern. He had never lost his appetite in his whole life.

"I'm not eating," he lied, but then thought, *At least, not at this very moment.*

Cal knew that a little bowl of beans would not make him lose his appetite, and he liked his own cooking better than he liked K'tlynn's mother's cooking.

"I'll pick you up in about an hour, you know, like we agreed."

"I know, but I finished my homework early and thought maybe we could go now."

Cal was not going to miss out on his fresh, hot bowl of home-cooked beans.

"I'm still doing stuff, you know, here. I'll see you in about a half hour. Okay?"

"Okay." K'tlynn sounded disappointed. "I just thought maybe you wanted to see me, too."

Cal sighed to himself. "I do. I do. I just need to finish some stuff here. See you in about twenty minutes. Okay? I'll call you when I'm on my way."

"Okay, baby." She still sounded disappointed. "See you then."

The call had been annoying, but nothing was going to get between Cal and those beans. He pushed K'tlynn out of his mind and sat down to eat with gusto. However, before he could start, he was interrupted again. In walked one of Cal's roommates, Lenny.

"Dude," Lenny said as a form of salutation.

"Hey," Cal responded with a nod, trying to hide the bowl of beans behind the box of Goldfish crackers.

Lenny eyed the beans, and then looking at Cal with a question on his face said, "Dude?"

This time it meant, *Can I have some beans?*

Cal sighed and spooned half the beans into another bowl for Lenny. As Lenny began to stuff his face, he smiled at Cal and said, "Dude!"

The meaning now was, *These beans are great, thanks!*

Half of Lenny's vocabulary consisted of that one word: "Dude." The way Lenny said it could mean a thousand different things, anything from, "How's it going?" to "Hey, come here" to "Toss me a Coke" or "You annoy me, get lost!"

Halfway through the first semester, Cal had determined that Lenny's name was not really Lenny, but was Sebastian Cornelius Humanistaid. Lenny was the youngest son in a politically prominent, old-money family, and he had been named after great grandfathers from both his father's and mother's side of the family tree. Cal had asked him why he went by Lenny if that wasn't his real name. Lenny replied with an intense, almost painful, look on his face. "Dude!" This time it meant, well, this time Cal didn't know what it meant.

Lenny and Cal had become good friends. When Lenny heard that Cal was from California, he had assumed Cal was a surfer, which he wasn't. Lenny, who was from New Jersey, was a surfer. He belonged to a small cadre of New Jersey surfers who lived near the shore. Lenny had never even been to California, though he had been surfing in Hawaii.

Lenny was taller than Cal, which was pretty tall, and sported a long, sun-bleached-blond ponytail. He was a top-notch physics major and a talented basketball player. He was not on the basketball team, though, because he had no competitive spirit. He never cared what the score was. He just loved playing basketball. He was always as happy after a loss as he was after a win.

While Lenny was an "A" student, he never studied. He also never slept, except in class. Most of the time, he didn't seem to be paying attention in class. If he was, he didn't seem to understand what was being taught. Sometimes in class he would look at Cal with a furrowed brow and shake his head from side to side, whispering, "Dude?" which meant, *What?*

But then, without any more effort, he would ace the next test. Cal thought it would be to his advantage to study with Lenny, except for the fact that Lenny never studied.

Most people avoided Lenny because he was odd and didn't bathe much. Lenny considered a trip to the beach with a couple hours surfing as a sufficient substitute for the week's bath. Cal didn't mind his roommate's eccentricities and enjoyed his unique view of life.

After wolfing down his half bowl of beans, Cal rushed over to pick up K'tlynn. While driving her to her parents' home, K'tlynn interrogated Cal. "Were you eating, Cal? You smell like bacon and baked beans. Really, Cal! I asked you not to eat."

K'tlynn had an unnaturally high, cartoon-like voice that made her sound like she was whining no matter what she said. Sometimes, it got on Cal's nerves.

"Oh, you know me," he joked. "I always smell like beans. Besides, Lenny was eating baked beans when I left the apartment." He sniffed his shirt sleeve. "You know, sometimes your clothes can pick up smells."

She didn't smile, but studied him a moment. "Cal," she asked, "did you change your major to English, like Daddy told you?"

No, I freakin' did not! he thought, but instead, said calmly, "Not yet."

"Why not? You know Daddy is just trying to help. He's real smart. You should change your major so you can go to law school, like Daddy said."

"You know, I'm still just a freshman. There's plenty of time. Let's not worry about that now. Between football practice and homework, I got a lot going on right now."

"Well, don't take forever. Next year you'll be a sophomore, you know."

No kidding, he thought sarcastically.

They pulled up in front of K'tlynn's home, a large Mediterranean style home with rose-colored stucco and a red-tile roof. Being from a small desert town, Cal was still getting used to Florida's opulent communities. K'tlynn's parents lived in a particularly expensive neighborhood.

As Cal opened the car door for his girlfriend, his cell phone went off. This time with just the normal ring. Juggling the phone with one hand, Cal pulled K'tlynn up with the other. He glanced at his phone while K'tlynn slid out of the car.

"Uh, hey, this is my mom. I better get this."

"Oh," K'tlynn whined, "let it go to voice mail. We're with *my* parents now."

Cal gave her a penetrating look. "This is my mother. I'm taking this call. You go ahead. I'll meet you inside in just a minute."

Cal answered the phone as K'tlynn stomped her tiny little feet up to the front door with a pouty expression on her face.

Camm and Sally had just left their dorm building on their way to a freshman writing class when a friend from their dorm came running to catch them from behind.

"Camm!" she yelled. "The phone is for you, back at the dorm."

Camm glanced down at her cell phone, which was on, but quiet. "What phone?"

"The phone in the super's office."

Camm and Sally whirled around to hurry with her to the dorm administrative offices.

"Why would someone call me on that phone?"

Their friend shrugged. "He said he's from the dean's office. That's all I know."

Camm looked at Sally, who gave her a worried look. Camm felt sick to her stomach. This was not something she wanted to hear. It was only weeks to finals and the end of the school year.

Camm's late-night encounter with the two frat boys had

been several weeks ago, but it had been all the talk around the dorm. Overnight, Camm had become a celebrity. Mark's broken nose had been obvious to everyone, and Dwight was still wearing sunglasses to hide two black eyes. Everyone teased Camm about never being invited to another frat party. That was actually okay with Camm, though she didn't make a big deal about it.

Initially, Camm had worried the incident would get her kicked out of school. But, when nothing happened, she had convinced herself that nothing would. Surely those two idiots were too proud to tattle on her, and in truth, they had started the fight.

But now this call. Camm was doing well in school—she didn't need this. She jogged back to the dorm so as not to keep the dean waiting. Pausing to calm her breathing and fast-beating heart, she picked up the handset with trepidation and answered, "This is Camm Smith."

An unnaturally deep voice responded, "Young lady, have you been fighting again?"

It was Cal, trying to make his voice sound like how he thought a dean would sound.

"You moron. You scared the crap out of me."

Camm was more than annoyed. Cal laughed, sounding very pleased with himself.

Of course, Camm had told Cal all about the late-night incident with the lights going out and the masks and everything. She and Cal talked or texted almost daily.

"You are, without a doubt, a total drooling moron."

"You're a big ol' hairy Amazon." Cal shot back. To Cal's great amusement, Camm had reported all the names Dwight had called her.

"This Amazon is going to kick your drooling moron butt as soon as she gets the chance!"

Cal was still laughing. Camm noticed the girl who had called her to the phone was giving her a funny look. This was an odd way to talk to someone from the dean's office.

Camm felt better after trading insults. She always felt better after talking to Cal.

"Why did you call me on this phone anyway?" They had agreed to use a landline in certain emergency situations. She was now afraid of what Cal's answer might be.

Cal got serious. "I'm on a landline, too, at a pay phone. Camm, we have a *Code Red.*"

"Oh, no!" Camm's heart sank. She and Cal had agreed before leaving Trona what and how they would communicate with each other if certain things happened in their home town. *Code Red* was their agreed upon term for "another child has gone missing in Trona."

They suspected their cell phones were bugged, so if they needed secrecy, they decided to find other ways to talk, like third-party landline phones, which they thought were harder to tap for eavesdropping, since no one would know in advance which phones they were going to use.

"How do you know?" She asked.

"My mom called yesterday. A friend from Trona called her in Houston. It happened a couple weeks ago, but she just heard about it now."

"Who was it?"

Cal whispered, "Dylan Justenough."

Camm rolled her eyes. Whispering over the phone didn't help. She vaguely knew who Dylan was. She certainly knew the Justenough family.

"Okay," Camm decided. "Let's do plan B."

"I forget, what's plan B?"

Camm sighed. What was the point of creating advance plans if she had to tell him over the phone what the plan was?

"We each buy prepaid phones. I text you on your old phone, in code, the number of my new phone. From then on, we use our prepaids to communicate any private information."

"Okay. What was the code again?"

"Oh, for heaven's sake, Cal. Forget the phones. I'll come see you in Houston in about a month, after school gets out. We will decide from there."

"Cool! Stay out of trouble in the meantime. You know, quit beatin' up the frat boys."

As Camm walked to class, her heart ached for Reverend Justenough's family. She remembered when Cal's younger brother, Hughie, went missing. The thought was still painful.

If only it had been a call from the dean's office, instead of this.

IV

The man sat frowning in his dreary Washington D.C. office. There were no pictures on the walls, no mementos on the shelves, no personal items on the desk. There were books, dozens and dozens of books, but no warmth, no personality to his surroundings. He sat slumped forward, staring out his office window at the colorful cherry blossoms. The cheery spring view did nothing to dispel his foul mood.

He ran his fingers through his long, white hair and sighed. He had some of the smartest scientists in the world working for him, but still there were too many gaps in the latest theory they were working on.

Theory! If only it was just theory. That was the problem. It was reality. It was actually happening, and they couldn't explain it—they couldn't control it. As a theoretical physicist, he could handle theory, but reality was kicking his butt.

The intercom on his phone buzzed and the receptionist said, "Excuse me, sir. An Agent Allen from the FBI is here. She is asking to see you. She doesn't have an appointment."

The darkness to his mood deepened. He remembered Agent Allen from the Trona incident. His face looked as if he wanted to swear, but he did not use profanity. He considered it a waste of time and a sign of a weak intellect.

"Show her to the conference room. I'll meet her there in a few minutes." No one was ever brought to his office. Every piece of paper on his desk was top secret. Since his desk was covered in papers, it was just easier to see people somewhere else when it became necessary—which was not often.

He did not immediately get up to go see her. He would let her wait—partly as a power ploy, partly out of sheer rudeness. He justified the latter with the thought that maybe he could discourage such unannounced visits in the future.

When he finally did get up to go see her, there was pain in every step he took walking down the hall. He wore expensive, supposedly comfortable shoes, yet it felt as if he were walking barefoot on sharp rocks. His doctors told him he had idiopathic neuropathy of the lower extremities, which meant his feet hurt, and they didn't know why.

Idiots!

The man himself had two PhDs and an MBA. He was tired of people with all the right degrees but none of the right answers. Whether in his work or personal life, he thought very little of doctors who didn't know why. He paid people to know why!

He also had a severe pain in his lower back, which radiated down both legs when he moved. As a result, he walked slowly, never hurrying. He knew he should use a cane when he walked, to help relieve the pain, but he eschewed the idea. He was afraid it would make him look feeble. Though he was starting to show the signs of age, he was far from weak. He didn't want anyone getting the wrong idea.

The FBI agent stood up as he entered the conference room. The look on her face said she was annoyed at having to wait, which pleased him. She extended her right hand in an offer to shake his. He ignored it.

With his hand, he indicated her chair. "Sit."

He sat opposite her and waited for her to talk. She was studying his face, so he studied hers. She was young with clear, confident eyes—she showed no fear. It didn't seem so very long ago he was like her, thinking the world was a logical place, and he had it all figured out. He almost wished he could go back to that simpler time in his life when his self-confidence over-powered all doubts, and he had no chinks in his armor.

After several moments, when she didn't say anything, he began to wonder what kind of game she was playing. He didn't like games, unless he was setting the rules, so he lowered his chin and raised an eyebrow as if to say, *"Well?"*

"I don't know if you remember me," she began. "I was the FBI agent in Trona, you know, when all that stuff . . ."

He interrupted, "I remember you very well, Special Agent

Linda Allen. I remember the incident in Trona. I remember everything."

The way he said it made it sound as if he literally remembered everything, not just what happened in Trona.

He continued tersely, "What do you want?"

Agent Allen scowled at him, crossed her legs, and folded her arms against her chest. "I think you already know what I want. Another child is missing from Trona. Like the others, he has just completely disappeared with no evidence as to what might have happened to him. I want to know what is going on. I thought your people had the situation under control."

The last sentence sounded like an accusation. It was an accusation.

If the man had been in the habit of using profanity, he would have used an obscene response. He should have been told of this before now—what was he paying his people for? He did not like hearing things for the first time from the FBI. He did not like being caught off guard.

As upset and annoyed as he was, his face showed absolutely no response to her comment. There was no trace of emotion or even acknowledgment. He did not reply to her either. To reply would either demonstrate his ignorance or admit responsibility, neither of which he wanted to do. He simply looked at her with a level gaze, his eyes unflinching.

The agent shifted nervously in her chair. "Well, what do you know about it?"

Although he did not show it, this question angered him more. She knew who she was talking to and had no right to accuse him or question him. From the beginning, she had been in way over her head, and now, she was walking on thin ice. He was tempted to just send her away without further discussion, but in this case, the truth wouldn't hurt—she wouldn't believe it anyway. Leaning forward, he almost smiled. "Nothing."

"I can't believe that," she shot back.

"I don't care what you believe."

He remained calm and impassive. He was actually enjoying this conversation—it was always a relief when the truth suited his purposes.

"How do we know it wasn't your creature out and about again?" This was another accusation, but again the truth suited his purposes.

"It was not." He felt like sighing, but consciously restrained it.

"How can you know?" She was becoming angry.

"I know." His face did not change expression—it was none of her business how he knew.

Her face hardened. "There is another child missing. No one knows how or why. We've been through all this before. This is no coincidence. Now, I have to go back to Trona to make another investigation. But this time, I know so much more. This time, I will start with a search of the mansion. I know right where to search, too. Is that what you want me to do?"

She sat straighter in her chair. "I'm just asking for a little help here. You know something, but you won't tell me anything. I can't believe this. If this goes to the media . . ."

The man finally showed an inkling of emotion. He leaned

forward and with deliberate intent interrupted her. "This will not go to the media."

"But, if it did . . ."

"You're not listening to me. It will not." Although his voice was flat and his face impassive, there was no doubt as to the seriousness of his intent. He cocked his head slightly and raised an eyebrow. The expression said volumes—more than her career was on the line.

"I don't know what you expect me to do then if you won't—"

"I have no expectations of you or the FBI, except that you will do your job. I am not your superior." Oh, but he really was. "Go to Trona and investigate the missing child. That is *your* job."

She opened her mouth to protest, but he held up his hand and stopped her. He had said all he was willing to say. It was time to cut the conversation short before she could ask any more impertinent questions.

"You will do your job. I will do my job. Now, this interview is over. See yourself out." He got up and left the room without another word.

He always made an effort to walk so that no one could tell he was in pain. However, on occasion, he could not hide a slight limp, especially when he was angry, as he was now. When he got back to his office, he picked up the phone and dialed a familiar extension.

The tall white-haired man on the other end of the line knew who was calling. "Yes?"

"We have to go back to Trona. Tonight."

"Why?"

"I believe there has been another cross over."

"Impossible, we have it under constant electronic surveillance and the chain is on it twenty-four-seven now. The phase device has been stopped. We would know."

"Not it. I believe something else has crossed over."

"Oh, no! What?"

"I don't know, but another child is missing."

"Has this ever happened before, where something else crossed over?"

"I don't know. As you are aware, the records are spotty."

There was hesitation. It went without saying that neither one wanted to go back to Trona.

"We must go tonight. The FBI have already started their investigation. Either the device is working again or something new is happening—either way, we don't want to be surprised."

"Very well."

After a long pause, they both hung up without another word.

The man gazed out his window again. The signs of a bright and beautiful spring were everywhere, but he didn't see them. His face was as dark and cheerless as always.

He knew he needed to hurry home to get his travel bag packed, but he was reluctant to get up. He didn't want to face the impossible reality that existed in Trona.

Why was this happening on his watch? This was not his fault.

The whole thing began long before he was even born. No one knew for sure what was really happening. Even with the best scientific minds leading the way, even with the federal government's deep pockets funding the research effort, still no one knew.

The science used in the old mansion was apparently ancient, and yet so far advanced it could not be explained with any of the current scientific theories. The applications used by the Trona chemical plant went beyond what anyone now living had ever dreamed of and his team of scientists was being forced to rewrite even the most fundamental principles of science in an effort to explain what was happening. So far their efforts had been fruitless.

The US Federal Government was trying to control a technology that for all practical purposes should not exist—a technology that defied all rational attempts at explaining its logical basis, at least in this world.

This was not his fault, but he knew he would get the blame if things got out of control again. It was his job to control the uncontrollable. Whatever was going on in Trona, he would take care of it—even if it killed him.

V

ob woke with a huge headache. His mouth felt like it had cheek-to-cheek carpet. He was sitting in the sand, leaning against the bumper of his car. The sun was up, and the light felt like needles pressing into his eyes. He must have had a good time last night (though he didn't remember most of it) because he had a very bad hangover. And he really had to pee.

He struggled to his feet and peered inside his car. Three of his buddies from Trona High School were comatose inside. They had parked several miles north of town, east of Valley Wells, on an old dirt road that appeared to go nowhere. Beer bottles were strewn across the sand around the car, and only cold ashes remained from what had been a fire the night before.

Bob limped, his right foot asleep, over to some mesquite bushes a few yards from the car. The acrid smell of strong urine wafted through the air. Bob gave a loud sigh of relief, and then shivered, as if with a chill, though the morning air was already getting warm.

Before he could zip up his pants, his vision wavered, and he suddenly felt dizzy and nauseated. Trying to step back while pulling his zipper up, he lost his balance and fell into the puddle of his own urine. Rolling onto his side, he jumped to his feet, swearing as he went. There was a wet patch on his right pant leg covered in sand. He brushed off the sand, and then scooped up another handful to rub over the wet patch, trying to clean it off.

This will give the guys a good laugh, he thought as he turned to see if anyone in the car was watching him. He froze in place, and then whirled to look in every direction. The car was gone. His car was gone. It had been right . . . there. He walked over to the spot.

His first thought was that his buddies had left him. But he hadn't heard the car drive off. He had walked only a few feet away. Besides—he patted his pocket—he still had the keys.

He spun around again, looking in every direction. No car. Nothing. Only bushes and sand. He closed his eyes tightly and rubbed his temples with his forefingers. His head throbbed! The pain made it difficult to think.

What is happening? Am I still asleep? Think!

He opened his eyes, hoping the car would have reappeared, but was disappointed. Still no car. Nothing. *NOTHING!*

Staring in dumb amazement, Bob finally noticed that not only was his car gone, but so were all the empty beer bottles that had been strewn on the ground around it. In fact, he saw no litter anywhere. Even the ashes from their fire last night were gone.

Hardly daring to look, Bob searched for the dirt road they had driven out on last night. It was missing, too.

How can a dirt road just disappear?

Another sudden chill passed through him in spite of the hot desert sun.

He closed his eyes again and slowly lifted his head, facing south. When he opened his eyes, he didn't see what he was afraid he wouldn't see. The whole town of Trona with its chemical plants and suburbs was gone. His mouth fell open. "Holy . . ."

He didn't finish. Somehow there were no words to express his dismay.

Ouch! His head ached. *Man! I need to think.*

Something had just happened that had never happened before. Without warning, the world had suddenly changed. He needed his brain to start working now. Something was happening, and he needed to figure it out—his life might depend on it.

Bob looked to his right. With a sigh of relief, he saw something he recognized. There was Argus Peak, the most prominent mountain bordering Searles Valley, right where it should be. In front of him, there was the dry lake bed right where it should be. He looked to his left. There were the Slate Range Mountains where they should be.

He looked back to his right and expelled his breath in

disappointment. He should have been able to see Trona Road, the highway back to town. A mile or two to the west should have been a ribbon of asphalt running north and south. Instead, he saw nothing but sagebrush and sand.

Bob realized that while he was still in the Searles Valley, all vestiges of civilization and humanity were missing. Anything man-made—his car, the beer bottles and litter, the whole freaking town—was gone.

The morning breeze was cool, but the sun was hot. Already thirsty, Bob checked around again, shrugged his shoulders, and, not knowing what else to do, started walking in the direction where Trona used to be. He still had the wet urine stain on his pant leg.

Jim jerked awake, then regretted the sudden action. Movement intensified his headache. He was sitting in the front passenger seat of Bob's car. The sun shone mercilessly through the car windows, and with his hand, he tried to block the glare from his eyes.

Gazing vacantly out the window, Jim saw Bob, facing the other way, taking a leak in some nearby bushes. As Jim watched, Bob's image wavered and blurred, like a mirage or when a view is obscured by heat waves rising off a distant hot-road surface. Bob stumbled—the wavering intensified. Bob was falling, then he just evaporated into the desert air. Bob was gone.

Jim sat up straight and stared out the window for a better look. No Bob. He blinked his eyes several times and looked again. No Bob. He scoured his eyes with both fists, trying to rub away whatever was blocking his vision. Still no Bob.

"Hey!" he cried. "Hey, wake up back there!" He reached over the seat and slapped the knee nearest to him. The only response was a slight moan and some shifting in the back seat. Jim tried again, slapping the knee as hard as he could. "Hey, wake up, man, wake up!"

"What!" This came from an angry Sean. "Stop with the slapping! What's the matter with you? And stop yelling! You're hurting my head."

"Bob's disappeared!"

Sean adjusted himself in the seat, frowning as he tried to get comfortable. He reclosed his eyes. "He'll be back. I mean, where can he go?" The words trailed off into a mumble.

Jim whacked him again. Now Sean came wide awake. Jumping forward in his seat, he socked Jim in the side of his head, which did not agree with Jim's hangover headache.

Jim held up his hands. "Stop, man, stop! I have to tell you somethin'."

"Dude!" Sean shouted. "What's wrong with you? Why are you slapping on me?"

"Just listen, man, just listen for one minute and stop yellin'."

Jim held his head in both hands, trying to get his thoughts together. The third boy in the car, Dave, was blinking his eyes rapidly as he started to wake up.

Jim continued, "Bob was right there, by those bushes. I was looking right at him, right there, peeing in those bushes. And then, all of a sudden, he went all fuzzy or something. I mean, he looked all squiggly like, and then he wasn't there no more. He was right there, and then he was gone. Like, poof! He just disappeared."

Sean looked intently at Jim—his expression was half scowl, half question mark.

Dave shook his head as if trying to straighten out his brains. "What are you yapping about? And why are you talking so loud? You're hurting my head."

Sean's scowl deepened. "What do you mean, 'he looked all squiggly'?"

"I was looking straight at him, and then he went . . ." Jim made squiggly motions with his hands. "And then he just vanished." Jim's fingers made a motion like a small explosion. "You know, like into thin air!"

Sean frowned. "Dude, you're still loaded."

Dave rubbed his tongue with his fingers and gagged. "Yuck, tastes like I ate a whole jackrabbit, fur and all." He shuddered, then opened his car door and stepped out.

"No, man!" Jim started to panic. "Where are you going?"

"You know, water the shrubbery. Just doin' my part for the planet." Dave slammed the door behind him as he shuffled off towards some nearby sagebrush.

Dave stood facing south, head tilted back, eyes closed. A look of relief washed over his face. Jim watched from the car, his whole body tense, waiting for Dave to disappear. Sean watched Jim with an angry expression that said he might slug him at any moment.

Both Jim and Sean froze as a strange sound seeped into the car—a sound like a baby rattle on steroids or rocks tumbling around in a dryer. Still staring at Dave, Jim's eyes suddenly widened and almost popped out of his head. He pointed toward Dave, yelling in a high squeaky voice, "What's that, man? What's that?"

Sean turned his head to look at Dave, and his jaw dropped open. Staring bug-eyed, his mouth moving soundlessly, he finally emitted a whispery noise that sounded like, "Oh! Oh! Oh!"

Without thinking, Jim moved his finger over to a switch on the armrest and pushed it, locking all the doors in the car.

Dave heaved a huge sigh of relief. He felt so much better. *Now,* he thought, *let's go home and get a huge carb-loaded breakfast with lots of OJ, and we'll all feel better.* He finally opened his eyes. *That wasn't there before.*

Directly in front of him was what appeared to be a huge snake head, raised and cantilevered out on a huge snake body. If it was a snake head, it was enormous, the size of a fifty-gallon barrel. The eyes were perfectly round and perfectly black. There were symmetrical markings under the eyes, and two dark holes made the nostrils. The long slit of a mouth opened and a forked tongue shot out, wisping across Dave's face. It wasn't wet with saliva, but dry and raspy like sandpaper.

It's freakin' alive! Dave realized.

He turned, and was back at the car in two quick steps. He pulled frantically at the door handle, but it was locked.

"Open the door! Open the door!" he gasped in full panic mode. Looking through the car window, he saw Jim and Sean petrified, looking past him at . . .

Dave glanced over his shoulder and saw that the head had pulled back, waving side to side. The mouth gaped open, the black tongue flickering in and out, two long fangs thrusting down. The head tipped back ever so slightly in anticipation of a strike. Dave did not wait, but jumped onto the roof of the car and rolled over to the other side, landing on his belly in the sand.

A split second after Dave leaped out of the way, the enormous head struck forward, striking the side of the car so forcefully it lifted up onto two wheels. Both windows on that side of the car shattered into thousands of pieces, but remained in place. As the car bounced back down on all four tires, Jim and Sean started screaming.

Peering under the car, Dave watched an enormous figure slither out of sight. Pulling himself into a crouching position, he peeked over the hood. He saw nothing. Breathing heavily, he tried the front passenger door—locked. His fist smacked the door, causing Jim to jump and hit his head on the roof of the car. All color had drained from Jim's face and his mouth was still stretched wide in a scream.

Dave pleaded, "Open the door! Please open the door! Jim, please open the freakin' door!" Dave's voice reached a frenzy as he pounded the door with the palm of his hand. Jim continued screaming, shaking his head from side to side, while pointing at the shattered safety glass.

Clearly, Jim and Sean were not about to risk opening the door to let Dave back into the car. Checking around, he could not see the snake. Still in a crouching position, he scurried away from the car toward some large mesquite bushes. After about twenty feet, it occurred to him there was no good cover anywhere, except under the car. He was moving away from the car when he should have slid underneath it.

Starting back toward the car at a run, he saw the snake again. It had flanked him around the back of the car and was now headed directly toward him. With its head raised several feet above the desert floor, its body moved back and forth in classic snake fashion. It was gigantic and moving surprisingly fast.

Bob had walked about a hundred yards away from the car—well, from where the car used to be. The day was getting hot, and he was already so thirsty.

His footsteps slowed. Where was he going anyway? He

knew he had been able to see the town from where they had parked the car the night before. He had easily seen the lights of the Trona chemical plant.

It's not like the whole town could have slipped out of sight. Could it?

To his right was a small rise capped by large boulders. He could get a better view from there. He hustled up the rise, climbing onto the highest boulder. Shielding his eyes from the sun, he looked in every direction. No Trona. No Trona Road. He should be able to see Valley Wells, the old swimming pool, but it was gone, too. He looked back the way he had come—still no car.

Turning toward Trona again, he squinted into the bright sunlight.

Is there something there? It was too far away to tell for sure, but it looked like a single large structure stood where the center of town used to be. *Is it just a rocky hill? Is it that creepy old mansion? Why would everything else be gone except for the old mansion?*

Bob couldn't tell what it was for sure from where he was standing. It could be man-made, or it could be nothing at all. Whatever *it* was, there was nothing else there.

What was the point of walking to where Trona was supposed to be, if it wasn't still there? Bob sat down on the boulder and began to think in earnest. He would have to sort the whole thing out, but in the meantime, he needed to find a place to survive.

First of all, that meant water. He was out in the middle of the desert in late spring. The days would get hot. He wouldn't last much more than forty-eight hours without water. Going to where the town should be, but wasn't, was not going to get him water.

He could see the large outcropping of rocks where Great Falls should be. The name "Great Falls" was misleading because it referred to the great distance the water fell, not to the amount of water falling. Usually, only a trickle of water flowed over the massive rock formations that created the falls. Sometimes it was completely dry, but at least there was a chance of water there. And if there was no water at the falls, he could climb up to the water's source, a spring several miles farther back in the mountains.

Hopefully, he would find water there and shelter from the sun in the natural caves around the falls. Bob figured he should be able to get there before the day got too hot because it was only a few miles away.

He scurried down the rise, across a dry wash, around another rise, and then came to a dead stop. He had almost bumped into two Indians.

Indians? Where did Indians come from?

They stood still, apparently just as surprised to see him as he was to see them. They wore nothing but skimpy breech cloths and some sort of hair decoration. They were shorter than Bob and much thinner. Their skin had been bronzed a deep brown, and their black hair hung in braids down to the middle of their backs.

One of them pointed at Bob and said something to the

other. The look on their faces switched from surprise to menace. One pulled a shiny obsidian blade, attached to a crude leather and wooden handle, from the waist of his breechcloth.

This can't be good, Bob thought.

Dave had two choices. He could try running away from the giant snake, but there was no cover as far as he could see, and he didn't know if he was faster than it was. Or, he could head for cover under the car, but that would take him closer to the snake.

In a flash decision, Dave sprinted toward the car. It was a race to see who reached it first. They arrived at the same moment, not giving Dave time to slide under the front end of the car.

Instead, Dave stepped onto the front bumper, and then the hood, vaulting himself to the other side of the car, opposite the snake head. Out of the corner of his eye, he saw the snake strike, barely missing him, but coming close enough for him to smell its foul breath, stinking of rotted meat. Absentmindedly, he wondered, *Why is it chasing me if it is still digesting its last meal?*

He fell to the sand and rolled to the back of the car, bumping up against a moving wall. When Dave came to his knees, he realized he had rolled into the body of the snake, which was now wrapping itself around the car to come back at him. Moving through the sand, the snake's body glistened in the light. Along its length, an intricate pattern of diamonds-on-diamonds in pale shades of green accented with black and white markings played in the desert sun.

Dave crawled on his hands and knees as fast as he could toward the rear of the car, panting as he went, "Oh crap. Oh crap. Oh crap."

Reaching the back bumper, he slid on his stomach, squirming underneath military style. The body of the gargantuan reptile bumped against the car on three sides, causing it to bounce and twist. Above him, Dave could hear Jim and Sean screaming in the car like little girls.

He clenched his jaw, disgusted. The snake was coming after him because they had locked him out, and now *they* were screaming like little girls.

Dave had almost wiggled completely under the car when he felt a large, cavernous mouth clamp down on his left foot. He dug his fingers as deep as he could into the soft desert sand, but it did no good. The snake pulled him thrashing and kicking from underneath the car, leaving long claw marks in the sand. As he came out from beneath the car, it hoisted him upside down into the air well above the car. The snake had him just barely by his left foot.

Dave squirmed violently at the same instant the snake shook its head to the side, opening its mouth to get a better grip on its intended prey. Dave's squirming combined with the snake's head shaking caused him to lose his left sneaker in the snake's mouth, and he was simultaneously thrown aside.

Landing on his side in a clump of sagebrush, Dave rolled

painfully across a small cactus. Springing to his feet, he saw his only choice now was to run away from the car. He only got three steps away.

Bob ran as fast as he could. He thought he was headed back in the direction where his car used to be, although he didn't know what good that would do. He was being followed by two nearly naked natives armed with stone knives. While he sprinted with all his might, he sensed they were no more than loping along, just keeping up with him. He figured they were probably waiting for him to run out of breath. He'd be easy to overpower then.

Bob didn't know what else to do other than run. He couldn't fight both of them. He probably couldn't even fight one of them. They had knives. Bob had no weapons other than his fists, and he had never been a good fighter. He was quickly getting winded.

To make things worse, he was starting to feel nauseated and dizzy again. His vision was going fuzzy. *Not now!* he thought. *Please, not now!*

Watching through the car window with blanched, horror-stricken faces, Jim and Sean continued screaming as the snake began to swallow its latest squirming meal in one whole piece.

They were not aware of it, but they were holding hands

over the seat. Mesmerized, they stopped screaming and stared through the shattered glass windows at Dave's legs kicking as they stuck out of the snake's engorged mouth. The rest of Dave was a large lump lost down the snake's throat.

Too soon, the kicking stopped. Only Dave's ankles and feet, one foot missing a shoe, were visible when the snake's image, through the multifaceted glass, became blurry, then sinuous, then gone.

Just as Jim had seen Bob disappear earlier, the snake, with an almost-swallowed Dave, vanished while he and Sean watched.

In that exact same instant, Bob appeared suddenly from out of nowhere a few feet from the car, running hard while looking back over his shoulder. At top speed, he smacked into the side of the car and bounced back onto his rear end, landing on a beer bottle. Dazed and wheezing for breath, he blinked in astonishment at the car. Jumping off the crushed bottle, he lunged up to open the front car door, but it was locked.

Jim and Sean, startled by Bob's sudden appearance and collision with the car, went from silent amazement back to screaming like little girls.

Bob frantically worked the door handle. Realizing that Jim and Sean were not going to unlock the door, he remembered he had the keys in his pocket. Casting an anxious glance behind him, he unlocked the door and jumped inside, firing up the engine while ordering his passengers to shut up. He spun the car around, sending a billow of dust and dirt into the air, and headed down the dirt road, which had reappeared with the car.

Still catching his breath, Bob glanced around the car. "Hey," he panted, "where's Dave?" Jim and Sean eyed each other with expressions of incredulity and shook their heads.

Jim spoke up. "Dave's not here, man."

When they reached Trona Road, Bob took the turn too fast. The car fishtailed across the road before he got it back under control. They had barely gone a few hundred yards towards town when they saw a convoy of black SUVs coming up the road toward them.

One of the SUVs pulled into their lane and continued toward them alongside of an SUV in the other lane. Blue and red lights began blinking from behind the grills of the black vehicles. Cop cars were familiar to the three boys, but they had never seen anything like these. With nowhere to go, Bob slowed his car to a stop.

The two front SUVs stopped directly in front of him, blocking his travel in that direction. A third SUV circled around on the shoulder to come to a stop sideways across the road directly behind Bob's car. The boys were completely blocked in by the black cars. Considering what he had just experienced, Bob was relieved to see law enforcement. Glancing around the car, he asked again, "Where's Dave? What happened to Dave?"

Sean stared at the floor, but Jim solemnly replied, "Dave's not here, man."

Several men in dark suits and sunglasses got out of the SUVs, as well as two older men with white hair. The taller of the white-haired men began pointing and giving directions to the younger men in dark suits. The other man walked toward Bob's car. He had a slight limp and a very angry expression on his face.

Two very confused, nearly naked Indians crouched behind some large mesquite bushes watching flashing red and blue lights in the distance. They had been chasing a strange intruder, a tall white man, but he had escaped in the belly of a large beast that roared loudly and ran swiftly, kicking up towering clouds of dust. Though they were always cautious of the giant creatures roaming the land, they had never seen or heard of anything like this. Both feared the coming of a new kind of evil, and they didn't know the half of it yet.

VI

C al stood next to the open passenger door of his Camaro, waving a piece of cardboard like a fan in an attempt, per instructions from Camm, to air out his car. It was a half-hearted effort. He was more interested in the showdown that had begun between Camm and Lenny.

"You are not getting into that car until you go shower!" Camm stood with one hand firmly planted on her hip and the other pointing toward the showers. They had spent the night at a KOA near Flagstaff, Arizona, and they all wanted to get back on the road as soon as possible.

Lenny didn't even bother looking toward the showers, but held his hands out in a helpless manner and, by way of argument, said, "Dude?"

The furrow on Camm's brow deepened, and she stabbed her finger in the direction of the camp showers. "I've told you before, I'm not a dude! We are not getting back in that car with you until you shower! End of discussion! Now, move it! You're wasting time."

Lenny blinked at Camm, looking confused and helpless. He didn't seem to register why anyone riding with him on a long, cross-country road trip would want him to shower.

Cal sighed and glanced heavenward as if help might come from that direction. No such luck. He should have seen this coming. Camm had come out to see him in Houston after Yale let out for summer, and Cal was ecstatic to see her again. Though he had promised to stay in touch with K'tlynn over the summer, with Camm around, he could think of nothing but teaming up with Camm again. She was anxious to find out what was happening in Trona, so they told their parents they were going to Los Angeles to stay with friends for a while and wanted to drive through Trona on the way there.

Camm had brought a friend, who had just finished her first year in law school at Yale. Her name was Martha. Cal thought she was nice, in a quiet kind of way. Martha said almost nothing to him, but he had heard her talking with Camm about a summer clerkship in L.A. Cal didn't mind her coming along for the ride. If things had stayed like that, there wouldn't have been any special problems, and everyone would have been happy.

However, the day before they left Houston, Lenny, Cal's college roommate, showed up out of the blue. It was as if Lenny had just stepped out of the void into their world. He was on a full-ride academic scholarship and therefore felt he didn't need to work during the summer. Instead, he had decided to go on a "walk-about." Cal wasn't sure what a walk-about was, except maybe bumming around and living off friends for the whole summer.

To Camm's consternation, when Lenny heard that Cal, Camm, and Martha were headed to California, he could not be restrained from joining them. Lenny, the surfer, was counting on catching an awesome swell in So-Cal.

"Look," Cal had tried to explain, "we're going through Trona, where I grew up, and trust me, there are no waves in Trona. We're, like, two hundred miles from the ocean. It's all desert, man, just desert as far as the eye can see."

"Dude. I heard your old man," Lenny had retorted. "He said you're on your way to L.A! That's the bomb, dude. I'll find a board, live on the beach, get to know the local babes. You know, just let me hitch along."

Truth was, Cal didn't mind having Lenny along. However, Cal had a higher resistance to the odiferous emanations that wafted from Lenny's unwashed corpus than either Camm or Martha—especially Camm, who did all the complaining for both herself and Martha. Martha continued to say very little to anyone except Camm. Two days trapped with Lenny in Cal's car was more than Camm was willing to tolerate.

"Go. Wash. Do it now, or we are leaving you here! You can hitchhike from here for all I care." Camm looked like she meant it, and she probably did. Cal recognized that look on her face—there was no changing her mind at this point.

Lenny looked to Cal with pleading eyes. He had given

them a long, rambling explanation as to why he didn't shower more than once every ten days. It had something to do with hunter-gatherers, pheromones, and evolution. Cal was used to Lenny's ramblings. Martha looked bemused, but Camm was having none of it. She had actually snorted in disgust.

"Clean up or clear out! Now! Hit the showers or we're leaving without you! We're not going to wait much longer." Camm folded her arms emphatically.

Unfortunately, there was no way to reconcile Lenny's desire to live as much as possible like a modern-day hunter-gatherer with Camm's understanding of, let alone patience with, that concept. There was also no reconciling Lenny's incomprehension as to why anyone would take offense at his body odor, and Camm's intolerance for his rank smell. Both could be very stubborn, and Cal now saw that this clash had been inevitable from the start.

Lenny held out his hands. "Dude, I don't even have any soap or anything."

"Dude, yourself," Camm fired back. "Hit the showers, and we'll find soap."

Camm was not giving in. She glanced over at Cal with irritation. Cal knew she hated being called "dude." Lenny had been calling both her and Martha "dude" the whole trip.

Again, Lenny looked to Cal for rescue.

"Sorry, man," Cal said, shrugging his shoulders. He had known who was going to win this fight the second it started. "She's the boss. I take orders from her."

"It's your car, dude," Lenny pleaded.

"Yeah, I know, but, like I said, she's the boss. Get used to it. Just shower man, so we can get back on the road and not waste any more time."

Cal knew Lenny was stubborn, but he was no match for Camm.

Martha saved the day. She grabbed her shower packet that contained her soap, shampoo, and other hygiene items. Taking Lenny by the arm, she directed him off toward the showers.

"I know Camm, too," she explained with a knowing look in her eye. "Better do what she says before she punches your lights out."

Cal could hear Lenny still grumbling, but he went along with Martha, apparently willing to follow instructions from her, if from no one else.

After they had passed out of hearing range, Camm shot Cal an annoyed look and said, "Tell me again why we're bringing him along."

Cal held his hands up in a helpless manner. "He asked for a ride to L.A., just like Martha."

Camm scowled at him. "It's not the same thing, and you know it. Martha's helping pay for gas. Lenny's not helping with anything."

Cal's eyes widened. "Hey, Camm, don't move. There is something on your neck." He reached toward her, but she brushed his hand away.

"Don't try that with me! You're just trying to change the subject."

"No, Camm, really; there is something on your neck." Cal

reached out and plucked something off her neck. Holding up his palm, he showed her what he had found.

It was a small, brown, hairy spider, maybe a baby tarantula. Camm pulled back with an involuntary shiver. She hadn't known it was on her, but now rubbed her neck vigorously. Cal knew it was hard to spook Camm, but he also knew she hated spiders. From their earliest childhood, it had been Cal's job to get rid of spiders. Camm was so self-sufficient that she didn't let Cal do much for her, so Cal had always been glad to perform at least that small service.

She shuddered again. "Get rid of it. Just get rid of it." She turned her head away, refusing to look at it. Cal stepped over to some bushes and gently dropped it to the ground in a protected area, where it scurried to get away.

Camm was scowling when he returned. "I bet Lenny brought that thing into the car. He probably has insects and small rodents hidden all over his body."

Cal sighed. "Yeah right, like he's totally covered in spiders and rodents and stuff—just well hidden. Come on Camm, you are such a big, whiny baby."

Camm smiled in spite of both Lenny and the spider. The light came back into her eyes. Cal had thrown down the gauntlet. "You're a big, whiny baby with a poopy diaper."

Cal countered immediately, "You are the poopy diaper."

Camm pointed both index fingers at him and exclaimed, "You are the poop!"

Cal let her have the last word. This type of exchange was only a silly little ritual carried over from childhood, but for the moment, they both laughed, friends again. The tension had eased. They were, after all, lifelong best friends.

Camm sighed. "Cal, seriously, we have to talk to Lenny. He's got to pay his own way!"

At that moment, Cal's cell phone went off. Without looking to see who was calling, Cal said, "I'd better take this." Turning away, he wandered off with his phone.

Camm stayed by the car, muttering to herself under her breath. She picked up the make-shift fan and continued the fruitless effort to rid the *"odor de Lenny"* from the car.

When Cal came back, the expression on his face had changed drastically.

Camm read his expression instantly. "What's going on? Who was that on the phone?"

"A buddy from the Trona football squad. I told him to call me if anything else funny or weird happened. It looks like we have another *Code Red.*"

"Oh no!" Camm's shoulders drooped. "Another one so soon? Who is it?"

"Dave McCurdy, but it gets worse."

"How can it get worse?"

"Those old dudes in the suits are back. There are black SUVs and government agents everywhere. Even your old friend, Agent Allen, is there. Although, he said she doesn't seem to be working directly with the other guys. I guess that's government efficiency for you."

"Agent Allen can hold her own. She knows what she is

doing," Camm said, sticking up for the FBI agent. "Those other guys better watch out."

"I guess." Cal remembered the white-haired men and the very real threats they had made. He wasn't anxious to see them again.

He tilted his head. "But here's the weird thing. No one knows what happened for sure. Dave was out with his party crew—you know, Jim, Sean, and Bob—and they just kinda came back without him. No one's saying what happened to Dave, and no one, not even your sweet ol' Agent Allen, can get near the other three. They were hauled out of Trona, in a black helicopter, no less, with not so much as a 'by your leave' for their parents. No one has talked to them or seen them since. Their parents are fit to be tied.

"All we know is that Dave's parents have been told he met with a terrible accident and won't be coming home—not even a body to bury. Jim, Sean, and Bob's parents have been raising holy hell to find out what's going on, but the Feds won't even say where their sons have been taken. They could be at Guantanamo Bay, for all anybody knows."

Camm looked exasperated. "This is going to make things more complicated."

"Ya think?" Cal retorted sarcastically. "But wait, it's more complicated than you know. They have set up a guard post or something just south of town, near the West End plant. No one who doesn't already live in Trona is allowed to come into town, except to work at the plant. There's talk of evacuating the whole town, but it may be just talk. Anyway, they don't want to shut down the plant, so they are checking everyone's ID who comes in or out of Searles Valley.

"If we try to go back, they will spot us a mile away. I don't know what Jim, Sean, and Bob did, but I bet if the Feds catch us back in town, we'll get the same treatment they got. Our parents will never know what happened to us."

Camm put her chin in her hand and looked puzzled. Cal could tell she was thinking. For some reason, this brought back fond memories of a much younger Camm.

She finally asked, "Have they set up a road block on the north end of town, you know out by Valley Wells or Great Falls on the road that comes in from Panamint Valley?"

"I don't think so, why?"

"I guess we'll just have to use the back door then." She gave a quick nod of her head.

Suddenly, Cal was paying full attention again. "What?"

"You know, rather than come in from the south, let's head north to Vegas and Death Valley. We'll come in from the north. It will take a couple extra hours, but if we get there in the middle of the night, they will never know we're there, and we can find a place to hide out."

Cal scowled with concern. "The Feds aren't playing around, Camm. You know what will happen to us if they catch us sneaking around town, don't you?"

"Yes, of course, I know. Are you turning chicken on me?"

"No," Cal answered flatly. "I just wondered how you felt about spending the flower of your youth in a federal pen."

"Let's make contact with Agent Allen as soon as we can. She will help us think this through. We can trust her to not give us away to the NSA agents."

"She couldn't protect us from the NSA last time."

"I know, Cal. It's the best I can think of for now. We'll work on it as we go, but we can't just give up. There are innocent people in Trona, people we grew up with, and like you said, they are not being told the truth. They deserve a chance to protect themselves."

Camm laid her hand on his arm and peered earnestly up into his face. "Unless we do something, kids will keep on disappearing. Think of the Justenoughs. Think of Dave. We can't let this keep happening. We know things, important things, things that might save lives. At some point, what we know may be critical to those people. We have to go back."

While Camm talked, Cal contemplated her face. She was all worked up, preparing to take on the world again. It brought back visions of her chewing out the old white-haired man. Cal had wanted to kiss her then, and suddenly, he wished he could now. Staring down at her upturned face, all he knew was, wherever she was going, he was going, too.

"Okay, let's go do it, but, you know, I'm way too pretty for prison."

Camm laughed in spite of herself and gave Cal a friendly

punch in the arm. "Load up, pretty boy. Here come Martha and Lenny. Time to hit the road."

Suddenly, turning back to Cal, Camm gave him a quizzical look. "What did you say? The flower of your youth? When did you get to be so poetic?"

"Oh, you know, in college they make you read books and stuff. Don't be surprised. It won't be long and I'll be as smart as you, maybe even smarter."

Camm laughed, but her eyes considered him thoughtfully.

She was still distracted when Lenny walked up to her and held his arms out for inspection. His hair was wet, and his long, blond ponytail was pulled tight in back, but was uncombed. His t-shirt and shorts were damp as if he had washed them and used the hand dryer on the bathroom wall to mostly dry them out. Everything smelled like Martha's bath soap.

"There! You happy now?" he demanded with pain in his voice.

"Yes," Camm said as she guided him toward the car. "You smell like a rose."

That did not make Lenny happy. "Dude! I don't want to smell like a rose—that is so unnatural. I want to smell like a hunter-gatherer."

Camm rolled her eyes, "Whatever, caveman. We'll return you to the wild as soon as possible. Now, get in the car. There has been a slight change of plans."

Any relief Cal felt from the resolution of the Camm-Lenny conflict was washed away by the nervous anticipation of going back to Trona, and maybe to prison. Cal knew those white-haired guys meant business. Nevertheless, he slid into his Camaro and started the engine.

Martha and Lenny sat close together in the back seat, discussing the pros and cons of rose-scented soap. Cal was surprised by how much of the talking was coming from Martha. She was deeply involved in the discussion, making some strong arguments about the advantages of smelling like a rose if you were a modern-day hunter-gatherer.

Glancing over at Camm, seated next to him, Cal smiled. The air in the car was a lot easier to breath now. If he was going down, at least he was going down with Camm. For better or worse, Team One was back in business, and that was what was important. Whatever they had to face, they would face it together. Cal couldn't ask for more than that—at least for now.

Slipping the Camaro into first gear, he released the clutch and pressed hard on the gas. With a roar of the engine and a screech of the tires, they were on their way to Trona.

VII

Special Agent Linda Allen sighed, glancing between the paper in her hand and the two beefy young men standing guard outside the back door of the old Searles Mansion. It was true she had a court order giving her access to the mansion and everything inside, but when it came down to it, it was just a piece of paper. And those two very big guys had guns bulging conspicuously under their suit jackets. Of course, Agent Allen had her gun, too, but it was still two against one. Besides, a fire fight between different branches of the U.S. Federal Government, especially the NSA and FBI, was probably not a good idea.

The shorter guard noticed her standing by her car and scowled. After a quick head jerk to alert his companion, he talked into his shirt cuff, and then, cocking his head and holding a finger to his ear, listened to a response through his ear piece.

That's real discreet, Agent Allen thought sarcastically. At this point, she had nothing to lose, so she marched up and thrust the paper out for their inspection.

"Here is a court order signed by a federal judge giving me access to this property, the building on it, and any appurtenances hereto, and everything on the property, inside the building, and in connection with said appurtenances. Please open the door and step out of the way."

There were no appurtenances thereto, but she used the legal jargon, hoping to sound as official as possible.

The taller guard took the paper and quickly scanned it. "This was signed by a judge in Washington D.C. Does a D.C. judge have jurisdiction in California?" he asked flatly, obviously not expecting an answer. No one moved out of the way. No one opened the door.

Agent Allen set her jaw and stood a little straighter. "The D.C. circuit has jurisdiction over FBI investigations. I am here on an official FBI investigation. That order is effective. Unless you obey that order immediately, you *will* be in contempt of court."

Truthfully, she wasn't sure if the D.C. court had jurisdiction or not. Typically these sorts of orders were not served on other federal agents, and usually nobody questioned their authenticity. She had, in fact, used a judge in D.C. hoping to blind-side the other agents, who were probably monitoring the closest Federal Court for just this kind of order, so they could oppose it.

It was crazy the NSA would not assist a legitimate FBI investigation. They should be helping each other—after all, they were on the same side. But lately, she had felt they were her competition. They certainly acted like it.

"We were not given notice of the motion for this order. I don't believe the order is enforceable without proper statutory notice." This came from the tall agent who had brought up the issue of jurisdiction.

Agent Allen studied him. *Interesting. He seems to know his stuff.*

Under different circumstances Agent Allen might have considered him good-looking. He was tall, maybe six foot five, with dark hair, dark complexion, and brilliant blue eyes. Normally, his chiseled features would have been appealing to her. She was not, after all, made out of wood. Right now, however, she just wanted to kick him in the knee, or maybe somewhere else.

Agent Allen was prepared with a quick rebuttal. "This property is still owned by the same company that owns that plant over there." Agent Allen pointed in the direction of the large Trona chemical facility, spouting smoke and fumes. "The legal owners of this property were given the required statutory notice, and they chose not to respond. The order is based on de facto legal notice and is legally enforceable."

The two guards looked at each other, and the shorter one

shrugged. The other, the good-looking one, was not willing to give up so easily.

"The NSA has taken legal custody of this building and related property, ceded by its owners without objection or opposition. Therefore, any notice of a request for an order granting access to the building should have come to the NSA." The guard gave her a slight smile, indicating he thought he had won.

Agent Allen noticed, against her will, that his teeth were straight and very white. At the same time, she realized his aftershave smelled enticing. *I'm not familiar with that particular scent. Hmmmm.*

However, she was not willing to concede defeat, especially not based on his animal magnetism. If anything, she was now prepared to take off the gloves.

Her thoughts raced as she tried to remember what she had learned in her Federal Civil Procedure class in law school. "There was no public notice, statutory or otherwise, given of your agency taking custody of this property or building, and we, the FBI, were not given specific actual or statutory notice either. You cannot legally demand notice be given to you *in lieu* of the actual owners unless you have notified, pursuant to law, all interested parties of your action. Your failure to receive notice of our motion for this order is due only to your antecedent failure to follow proper notice procedures once having obtained custodial control of the premises."

She kept a straight face, but thought, *Could I sound any more obtuse?*

After a deep breath, she continued, "You must comply with this order or be in contempt of court. Open the door and step aside!"

The guards stiffened noticeably. Mr. Animal Magnetism cleared his throat as if he were going to say something, but instead glanced at his partner. Agent Allen knew what she was seeing—they were showing all the signs of defeat, at least on the legal argument front. But, they did not move out of the way. Finally, Mr. Animal Magnetism, after clearing his throat several more times, said, "We have to inform our superior first."

"Look, Mr. What-ever-your-name-is, just move out of the way."

"Roberts, my name is Roberts, and I still have to inform our boss."

"No need." Agent Allen deliberately emphasized each word in her next statement. "Just obey the court order and open the door. I will take it from there."

The other guard responded, "We don't have the key to the door, nor the code to turn off the alarm. We have to wait for Mr—"

Just then a black SUV roared into the dirt parking area, skidding to a stop and throwing a bellowing cloud of dust into the air. Agent Allen frowned. These guys had been playing her all along, stalling for time until their boss could arrive.

The door to the SUV flew open. Out stepped one of the old white-haired men. He was the taller of the two, the one with short hair. Agent Allen disliked this one the least. She still didn't like him, but she definitely disliked the other one—the one she had met with briefly in Washington D.C.—more, much more.

The white-haired man had shed his coat and tie, undoubtedly due to the very warm spring temperatures. Walking casually to where his guards were standing, he held out his hand for the court order, which was obediently handed to him by Mr. Roberts. The old man gave Agent Allen a smile devoid of all warmth, and then, without comment, carefully perused the paper. His face showed no expression, and he seemed to be reading every word in the whole document. She had served a lot of papers, but no one had ever stopped to read them while she waited. Tapping her foot impatiently, she was sure it took an ice age for him to read the whole thing.

She was prepared to resume her legal arguments, but when he finished reading, he considered her closely, and then smiled his humorless smile again. A slow burn ignited inside her. She recognized the smile for what it was—he was patronizing her. Few things made her more angry than being treated like a needy child.

"So, you want to see inside, do you? Let's go inside then. You'll not see anything different from what you've already seen. Boys, please excuse us."

The old man produced a key, and the two guards stepped smartly out of the way. Once the door was opened, he entered a long combination into a key code box just inside the door to turn off the alarm system. Stepping aside, he held out his hand in an exaggerated gesture, indicating that Agent Allen should enter first.

Inclining her head, she stepped up to the door and turned to the two guards. She flashed them a flirtatious smile. "Boys," she said in farewell, and then entered the mansion, followed closely by the white-haired man. With overt politeness, she held up her hand to stop him, "I won't need an escort. I'm sure I'll be fine on my own."

"I'm sure you will," he replied, "but there is nothing in the order that says I can't come along. And, anyway, perhaps it is time we had a talk—we do work for the same government."

She smiled again. "Perhaps it is." She hoped he wouldn't ask her why she wanted to search the mansion. She didn't know why. Once again, her investigation around town had come up empty-handed. Last time, it had turned out the mansion had been the key to everything. She hoped it still might be.

As soon as they entered the mansion, it knew they were there. It always knew when humans trespassed its safe hold, tainting its refuge. It felt stronger. As its strength grew, so did its anger, so did its hunger for human flesh—a hunger that was now all consuming.

Even trapped, locked away down deep, it could smell two humans. It knew who they were. It knew both scents. It remembered and fought the chain that bound it. It wasn't strong enough to break free yet, but still it fought the chain, still it hungered.

The mansion's back door opened into the massive kitchen. As they passed through, everything was as Agent Allen remembered from her very first visit, the one she had made with Camm. The brightly polished pots and pans still hung above the spotless work area, reflecting the clear light streaming down from the high windows. Along one wall hung rows of burnished steel knives and cleavers, all glinting wickedly. The marble countertops shone, and the massive sinks were free of dead flies and any tarnish.

Entering the huge dining room with its intricately carved baroque furniture, she again found the room spotless. Pausing, she ran a hand over the smooth, dark wood of the immense dining room table. She nodded. As before, not a speck of dust was to be found anywhere. The white-haired man cleared his throat, gesturing toward the door leading farther into the mansion.

Their footsteps echoed hollowly as they trod on the dark slate floor of the mammoth grand hall. Big enough to contain several ordinary Trona homes, the hall was perfect in its grotesque splendor. The woodwork covering most surfaces writhed with carvings of gargoyles, devils, goblins, and predatory animals of all kinds, frozen in various attack modes.

A massive fireplace stood at the back end of the hall, tall enough for her to stand in and set with three immense logs on its grates. Around the fireplace, snarling rodents, carved into the musty moss-colored stones, appeared ready to spring out into the hall at any moment.

Agent Allen glanced up at the two upper stories. To reach their balconies, one would have to climb the grand sweeping staircases situated on each side of the hall toward the front of the mansion. She knew each level was lined with museum-quality paintings, mostly of demons or fanged animals, often half-human, half-animal, all wildly tearing apart their prey.

What still interested her most was the macabre grandfather clock that stood near the front of the hall. The clock was huge and the workmanship was perfect. The shiny wooden layers of the clock face seemed to reflect an old man's face, while the clock's hands were shaped like bony fingers. The brass weights were sculpted, coiled snakes. The pendulum was fashioned of various metals in the image of a hanged man, his face distorted with agony.

"Hmmm," Agent Allen muttered to herself, suddenly aware of the older man's gaze. She had not favored him with her thoughts, preferring to keep them to herself.

Everything looked exactly as it had on her first visit to the mansion, but completely opposite from her last. On her last visit, she had discovered Camm and Cal in the great hall, armed with high-power weaponry and suffering from serious physical and emotional trauma. They had been in a fight for their lives. Pools of green slime had spread across the slate floor. A trail of sulfurous-smelling fluid had led to the cellar door, which had been forced open.

Camm and Cal had led her down through the cellar to a secret door. They had followed the putrid trail of slime down a winding stone staircase deep into the earth. In a stone dungeon filled with bones—many of them children's bones, they had watched the monstrous creature draw its last breath. Agent Allen shivered and shook her head to clear away the horrible image.

On that last visit, the mansion had been a wreck. Dirty, dusty, broken, stained, and tainted with a vile stench; it had aged fifty years in one night. Cobwebs hung from the damaged balconies. Splintered doors and gun blast holes told of violent struggles. Now, all was back spic and span, in perfect shape again without dirt or damage.

"Well," Agent Allen said, "you guys sure cleaned up from the last time I was here."

The old man smiled and asked, "What is it you want to see?"

Not wasting any time, she thought. "Is it?" She hesitated. "Is *it* still here?"

The man's smile faded. He nodded.

"Is it way down all those stairs in that little stone room?" Agent Allen glanced towards the wine cellar door.

He nodded again.

"Can I see it? I mean, is it safe to see it?"

With a wave of his hand, he led the way down to the empty wine cellar. Pulling on the hand-shaped candle holder, he opened a secret door. Down, down the narrow stone steps they descended toward the deeply buried stone room.

Since her last visit, the mansion had been wired for electricity. Bare, dimly lit light bulbs (which she had to duck to avoid) hung from the low ceiling, lighting their way down. The white lines on her shirt glowed with a bright luminosity indicating that the passageway was lit with black lights, emitting a long-wave ultraviolet light.

As she neared the small stone room, the sickening odor of sulfur assaulted her senses. The narrowness of the spiral stairway, the cold dampness of the stone walls, and the frigid air, so different from the warm air outside, combined to send a shiver through her spine.

Thinking of what lay ahead, her chest tightened with foreboding. Then, she narrowed her eyes. No matter her fears, she was determined to see the creature again. She had to find out what was going on now. If there was any way for this thing to get out and prey on children, she had to know. If it was not responsible for the recent deaths, what new danger did they face?

At the bottom of the stairs, there was something else new. A large, thick Plexiglas window or door had been affixed with large, steel bolts into the stone wall, blocking the passage and separating the bottom stair from the little room and its occupant. Small holes had been drilled through the shield to allow an exchange of air, which explained the overwhelming stench.

On the other side of the Plexiglas lay the monstrous, rodent-like creature with a thick chain attached to one of its hind legs. Its dank, olive-green fur was matted and nasty, glistening wetly in shades of rotting green that Agent Allen remembered in her nightmares. It lay in viscous pools of stinking, steaming liquids that oozed from festering wounds and other orifices that may have been natural or not. To Agent Allen, nothing about the creature looked natural.

"Is it alive?" she asked.

As if to answer her question, the rat took a deep breath and let it out in a long sigh of olive-colored vapors. Then, opening one puss-filled, blood-shot eye, it peered at her intently. The sense of evil was palpable.

Agent Allen backed up a step, hitting her head on a low-hanging light bulb. Instinctively, her hand went for her pistol. For a moment, neither agent nor rat moved.

VIII

The tall white-haired man looked amused at Agent Allen's reaction.

Turning toward the Plexiglas, as if talking to the creature, he said, "We were afraid that our young friends had killed it, but fortunately we were able to resuscitate it. The builder of this mansion left a few instructions—very few—but there was some information on this creature.

"I don't think the creature knows life and death the same way we do. While phosphorus is the basic building block at the cellular level of all life forms on Earth, this creature is built instead with the elements arsenic and sulfur. Its life functions are not like anything we've ever seen. By all normal criteria, it can be dead, but then still be reanimated.

"Although we were able to reanimate it after it was poisoned, it is not yet anywhere near its normal strength and vigor. Its healing processes are not fully understood, so we can only help it heal on a trial and error basis.

"For example, we were slow in realizing that it eats only fresh meat from its own kill, and then uses the bones from each kill in some kind of ritual that we don't understand. Its olfactory senses are incredible. It seems to identify everyone and everything by scent. We've also noticed that it never sleeps, not ever. It will lie down and close its eyes, but its brainwave activity never slows down—it never stops thinking. Ever since it recovered from the toxin, its brainwave measurements have increased geometrically. I wish we knew what it was thinking."

He shook his head, studying the creature closely. "Any normal injuries will heal within hours, but when Camm shot the alien toxin directly into its brain, the healing processes were directly impacted and have been slow to restart. We can't help because we don't know the difference between its dead flesh and its living flesh—it all looks dead to us. It may take considerable more time to bring it back to a hundred percent of its former strength."

Agent Allen stared at the man with confusion. "It is a killer, a monster that eats people, and then saves their skulls. Why would you resuscitate it, let alone want it at a hundred percent?"

The man hesitated and scratched his head. Finally, he said, "I'm not sure how to explain this, but this thing is the guardian. It has a job to do, a very important job. Even though it did terrible things, we need it to do a job that only it can do."

Agent Allen's confusion did not clear up. "The guardian of what? This mansion?"

He hesitated again. "Well, yes, of the mansion, but more, much more than that. It is the guardian—" He appeared to search for the right word to use. "Of the passage."

She glanced around. "Of this passage here?" she said, indicating the spiral stairway with a sweep of her hand.

"No, no, no," he said, shaking his head. "Much more than that." He stared down at the creature as if the right words might be there. "It is the guardian of the passage between here and somewhere not here, uh, like a door, a quantum link outside of space and time. I'm not making sense. Am I? I don't know how to explain what it does in layman terms."

"You certainly don't," Agent Allen replied with impatience. "And, I have another question. When I was down here last time, there was a large, empty picture frame, like those on the big pictures upstairs, hanging on the back wall of this stone room. It is not there now. Why was that picture frame there, and what happened to it?"

The white-haired man smiled. "I'm not sure this will be any clearer. The frame was not a picture frame, but a dimensional frame that harnessed the cross over energies of overlapping dimensions. Normally, dimensions don't touch, but apparently when they do, like here in Searles Valley, the dimensional overlap can cover many square miles. However, the dimensional energies can be exchanged only at a focal point that might develop anywhere within the range of overlapping or touching dimensional fields. One or more focal points can develop randomly at any time or place across the overlapping range of fields.

"However, the builder of this mansion, a Mr. Alberto Samuel, Sr., used a very ingenious dimensional frame to stabilize the focal point, allowing him to control the energy exchanges. With that frame, he could control both the place and time of the energy cross over. Now that the frame is gone, we're finding that energy will cross over at random focal points, developing at any time or place across the Searles Valley basin.

"And, when I say energy, I mean anything and everything. Remember Einstein's formula $E=MC^2$? Everything is energy. Even matter is a form of energy. Things like that green monstrosity in front of us can come through a focal point. And that's the problem. When you open up a focal point to bring through the untold mineral wealth from another dimension, how do you stop an unwanted life form from coming through at the same time?

"That was the other advantage of Alberto Samuel's dimensional frame—it could hold a guardian in limbo between dimensions, releasing the guardian when the focal point opened and recapturing the guardian when the point closed.

"We don't know where Alberto got a giant undead rodent with cells made of arsenic and sulfur, but it can exist between dimensions without apparent harmful effect. When the focal point was opened, this guardian was always right there in the passageway, challenging other life forms that might want to wander through.

"Unfortunately, we let the dimensional frame get away from

us. Like I said, Alberto's operating instructions were sparse and incomplete. We were operating mostly by trial and error, and we didn't get a second chance on some errors."

Totally overwhelmed with information, Agent Allen stared at the old NSA agent for a moment, but quickly recovered, not wanting him to stop talking. "Does this dimensional frame's disappearing act have anything to do with the mansion changing from the wreck I last saw into the mansion's current state of spotless perfection?"

The white-haired man smiled sourly. "Only incidentally. There are at least two mansions, one in this dimension and at least one other on the opposite side of a quantum passage that leads to who knows where. The mansions would switch places when the grandfather clock donged at midnight, releasing the guardian, and then switch back again sometime before dawn, recapturing the guardian. The grandfather clock controlled the dimensional frame, and the dimensional frame controlled the focal point and the guardian.

"When you were last here, the clock in the other world's mansion had been damaged by our young friend's gun fire, trapping the damaged house on this side of the passage. When we attempted to repair the controller, our man inadvertently opened a focal point, triggering an automatic switch-back, bringing the undamaged mansion back here. Apparently, this dimension is the normal or default state of rest for the spotless mansion."

He sighed. "We regret that occurrence. We had brought the dimensional frame up to the main hall, where we could study the frame and the broken clock together. When the damaged mansion switched back to its state-of-rest location on the other side of the passage, it took both the frame and the broken clock with it. We were left with the spotless mansion and an unbroken clock, but no dimensional frame, on this side.

"Unfortunately, the clock that needs to be fixed is now on the other side where we can't get to it. The clock on this side is still working. Until we turned it off, this clock tried to open the focal point each night at midnight, but couldn't because the broken clock on the other side wasn't able to open the opposite end of the focal point at the same time.

"Each time the end of the passageway opened on our side, the mansion partially phased out. When the focal point failed to develop, the mansion phased back in, always spotlessly clean and in perfect repair, no matter how big a mess we made during the day.

"We have decided there must be a default version of this mansion somewhere because, while it never completed the switch to the other dimension, it always came out of the attempted phase-through process in exactly the same unblemished condition."

For the first time, he smiled a real smile. "We no longer enjoy the luxury of having the nightly phase-through process to do our housekeeping for us. The risks of unwanted guests coming through even an incomplete focal point were just too great, so we turned the clock off.

"But, even when the clock was working, we had to clean up any mess made by that giant rodent. Without the dimensional frame on this side of the passageway, the clock didn't seem to know what to do with the rat, and we don't either. It doesn't make sense to waste it, so we keep it chained down here, hoping to use it again as a guardian someday."

Agent Allen stared at him, slowly shaking her head. "You know, in some crazy, demented way, that almost makes sense." Drawing a deep breath, she glared at the monster rat. "In the end, I don't think that anything you do with that monster will make sense."

The white-haired man coughed and cleared his throat. "Let's go back upstairs, where we can breathe fresh air and continue our discussion where that thing isn't watching us so closely."

Agent Allen nodded her head in assent. "Okay, just a second though. Let me get a good last look at that ugly thing."

Stepping closer to the Plexiglas, she placed both hands on the clear barrier and studied the rat. Its oozing wounds had streaked its fur with green slime, adding to its hideous appearance. Its hairless tail dipped in and out of the noxious pools surrounding it. Dangerous and revolting, it smelled as bad as it looked. It was still peering at her through the narrow slit of one eye. An olive-colored mist expelled from its mouth with each breath.

Those claws look sharp.

She shivered, watching as the claws flexed slowly back and forth. Her eyes were drawn to the fangs sticking down from each side of its upper lip. A thick, green foam was now dripping off the fangs as if the rat had started to drool.

How could they not want to destroy it?

The narrow slit of an eye opened wider. The eye watching her was not the dull window on an animal's brain she had expected, but instead, shone with intelligence. It was a knowing eye filled with hate and anger and something she didn't understand, couldn't understand.

"It looks at me as if it knows me," she managed through a tight throat.

"Of course, it knows you."

She glanced at the old man in surprise.

"Don't you remember? You two have met. Oh sure, it looks like just a large rat, but it is more advanced, mentally, than that. It is definitely macro-cephalic."

She raised a questioning eyebrow.

"Its head is larger proportionately than it should be for a rat, even of that size. Its head and its brain are both larger, and the brain is well developed."

"Does it have human-like intelligence?" she asked in alarm.

"We don't think so. We don't actually know. But, it is certainly at least as smart as a dolphin, or maybe a chimpanzee."

She studied the rat with newfound respect, and more than a little horror. It had moved up onto its curled legs and was now glaring at her with both eyes.

"Has it ever left this stone room since . . . since that day I was first down here?"

"No, it has been here ever since."

"You know that for sure?" She looked hard into his eyes.

"See the video surveillance system?" He pointed to small

cameras in each corner of the stone room. "That system has been operating twenty-four-seven since the last time you were here. Several pairs of eyes are watching this creature constantly, every second of every day. I assure you. It has never left this room at any time—not even for a second."

"Then why have the children of Trona started disappearing again?"

"That is a good question. Like you, I'm here to answer it. Unfortunately, we do not yet have the answer, except to say it is not the doings of this ugly creature. We can account for its whereabouts at all times."

She opened her mouth to ask another question, when the rat suddenly burst forward and jumped straight at her, throwing itself against the Plexiglas. Its claws and teeth scraped against the hard plastic-like surface, making a loud screeching noise. Rising up on its haunches, it clawed at the barrier, trying to dig its way through to the startled FBI agent. Greenish spittle flew from its mouth, staining the Plexiglas.

In spite of herself, Agent Allen screamed and stumbled backward, landing on her rear on the stone steps behind her. With relief, she saw the chain was still affixed to the monster's hind leg, preventing it from throwing its full weight against the Plexiglas. The shield was holding.

The white-haired man did not startle or move, except to bring a hand up to rub his chin. He raised one eyebrow. "Oh ho, it seems to be feeling better, much better. It may be stronger than we think."

Agent Allen got up, dusting herself off, and turned on the

man angrily. "I don't care what you say. There is no sane reason for keeping that thing alive!"

With his hand, he indicated they should go back upstairs. Agent Allen was glad to comply. Her heart still racing, she worked to slow her breathing. The rat was splayed against the Plexiglas, its blood-shot eyes trained on her, its jaw open in a snarl, dripping green ooze. She turned away.

"Let's get out of here."

Before they could start up the stairs, the lights above their heads dimmed, and then went out completely. Agent Allen swallowed her panic. Surely the Plexiglas would hold in the dark—the lack of light shouldn't make a difference. The darkness at her back was filled with menace.

"What just happened!" she called out, sounding more startled than she intended.

The man answered calmly, "Don't worry—it can't get to us. It just suppressed the lights."

"It can turn off the lights?" Agent Allen was incredulous, not just at the rat's abilities, but at the academic conversation she was having just inches away from a snarling monster rat.

"No, it can't turn off the power, but it can suppress the actual light so that it doesn't shine. It finds most common wavelengths of light to be painful. It has developed a defense mechanism that allows it to block or contain the radiation of photons."

"How does it do that?"

"We don't know yet, but we think it has internal organs that can generate and direct a powerful charge of dark energy through its nervous system at the quantum level. Think of an electric eel generating and directing a killer electrical charge at its prey."

This explanation did not calm her fears. Though she couldn't see a thing, she could hear both the man and the rat breathing in the profound darkness. Her own breathing was laboring under the stifling stench.

She heard the man's feet twist on the stone floor. His voice came at her more directly. "Nothing personal. It just prefers the dark. Take my hand and let's go back upstairs. There will be light there."

Agent Allen's fear turned to anger. She did not like being at a disadvantage to anyone, especially this man. "You go ahead. I can find my way. Thank you."

She heard his footsteps start up the stairs. Guiding herself with a hand on the wall, she carefully followed. Behind her, she could hear the harsh breathing of the rat.

Once they were back on the main floor, they went into the dining room and sat around a corner of the large dinner table. He asked her, "What else do you want to know?"

She was still upset at being startled by the rat and plunged into darkness. She couldn't help but feel he had intentionally failed to warn her. "I want to know everything you know."

He smiled. "Well, we both have law degrees from Yale. We already have that much knowledge in common."

She blinked, surprised he knew she had attended Yale.

"But, if you want to know everything I know, you will need

a master's degree in chemistry and a PhD in chemical engineering." He continued to smile to her annoyance.

"I don't mean like that, not everything about everything you know. I want to know what's going on here in Trona. What happens to the kids who disappear? Who or what is taking them? And why? How did all this start in the first place?"

The man leaned back in his chair and gazed up at the high ceiling, pursing his fingers together in front of himself. Agent Allen realized she didn't even know his name.

He began. "How long the 'phenomenon' that goes on in the Searles Valley basin has been happening, we don't know. Certainly for hundreds of years, maybe thousands of years. The government became aware of this place around the start of World War II. The plant ownership alerted the government to the fact that certain very rare elements could be obtained here."

"What rare elements?"

The man hesitated. "Plutonium."

"Plutonium? Plutonium isn't found in nature, it's manufactured."

"Actually, trace amounts of some isotopes are found in nature, but not enough to be useful. This place is different. There is no plutonium found in Searles Valley, but this place does provide access to plutonium and many other rare elements through the passageway."

Agent Allen shook her head. "I don't understand."

"Frankly, neither do we. But this mansion, along with the

chemical plant next door, were built specifically as a means of access to important elements that are available in other dimensions."

"They are not actually in this valley—not on this planet?"

He smiled. "Correct."

"It sounds to me like rare elements are taking priority over innocent lives."

His smile vanished. "You are being intentionally harsh."

"No, I don't think so. The mansion and chemical plant are still here and children are still disappearing. How many will have to die before the government admits it has lost control here? What makes that terrible rat and this old mansion so important?"

"You ask those questions as if they had simple answers. I'll give you a little history. When the government became involved during the second world war, the handling of the whole thing was given to the OSS."

"Military intelligence?"

"Correct. For obvious reasons, a great effort was made to keep all this secret. In fact, this is still a national security concern. That is why the NSA is now in charge. If you didn't have sufficient security clearance, I couldn't be telling you about it. Of course, what I do tell you is for your ears only."

Agent Allen nodded.

"Anyway, the mining of plutonium, while possible, proved to be impractical and was abandoned after the war. At that time, no one knew what to do with this place. When the OSS was done away with and the CIA created to replace it, it didn't fit under the CIA mandate. The military no longer wanted to be in charge of it, and since it was so secret, very few people knew about it. So it just got filed away and forgotten."

Agent Allen's mouth dropped open. "Forgotten?"

The white-haired man sighed. "I'm afraid so. Local plant management was tasked with securing the mansion. It was supposed to be overseen by the government, but there was no agency that was capable or had the correct mandate to oversee it. When those government agents who had been involved at the beginning either retired or died, well, it was just forgotten.

"When you came out here to investigate the disappearing children, the project came back onto the government's radar, so to speak. We were assigned to come out to see if the mansion was somehow involved. As it turns out, the mansion was involved, in more ways than we could have imagined. We have been trying to catch up ever since."

Agent Allen's eyes narrowed. "So, for all those years, they left a giant, green rat from another dimension to feed off the town's children while it supposedly protected this mansion?"

"Not exactly. The rat was to prevent anything from our side going to the other side, and especially, anything from the other side coming here. The rat is from over there, somewhere, and seems well suited to guarding the passage. Except for our young friends, no one and nothing has ever come close to killing it. Whatever happens, it keeps coming back, protecting the passage. In many ways, it acts possessive of, even territorial about the passage. It is the perfect guardian."

Agent Allen was still angry and very confused. "Where is

this other side you keep talking about? What is 'over there?' Do you even know what you are talking about?"

The man sat back and studied Agent Allen. He rubbed his chin as if reviewing what he had been or should be saying. After a moment, he suddenly changed the subject. "Look, before I tell you more, I want you to know there is a *quid pro quo* here. We need your help, too."

So, that is why he is so forthcoming. "What is it you want?"

"Our young friends, Miss Smith and Mr. Jones, are on their way here. In fact, they may already be in the valley. They evidently thought they could avoid our detection by coming in from the north, through Death Valley. They were wrong, of course. We believe they will try to contact you once they get here.

"If I have to deal with them, I will throw them in the slammer and throw away the key, which is what I told them I would do. If you will see to them, and get them out of here before they get into trouble, I'll pretend they never came back. I think that would be best for everyone."

Truthfully, Agent Allen had been wishing she had Camm's help during this most recent investigation. She had been missing Camm and didn't need additional incentive to help keep her out of trouble. But that was no business of the NSA.

"Okay, let's be sure we are clear. If I keep Camm and Cal out of trouble, you will continue telling me everything you know about what's going on here?"

The man nodded. "If you get them out of the valley, without going to jail, I will give you as clear a picture as I can. And by the way, they have two friends from college with them—a young woman and young man. Neither of them is from this part of the country or knows anything about the affairs here. Things will get ugly if I have to pick them all up."

At that moment both their phones buzzed. As they looked at their phones, the man said, "You are now receiving a text from Miss Smith. Please go find her and get her and her friends out of here as quickly as you can."

Agent Allen was indeed receiving a text from Camm and was irritated the man knew it. But she didn't want any harm to come to her young protégée. She stated flatly, "I'll take care of it. You just keep your part of the deal."

It settled back down into the slimy soil with a sense of satisfaction. Not the same satisfaction that came from killing and eating, but satisfaction nonetheless. It knew it could not be held forever. They didn't know everything. They didn't know the mansion itself, in time, would release it from its prison.

IX

Camm checked the time on her cell phone, and then gazed up at the sun as if to verify her phone's accuracy. Patience was not one of her virtues. Only minutes had passed since Agent Allen had texted she would meet them at Valley Wells, but Camm was still fidgety. While she did not know what they would do once they conferred with Agent Allen, Camm felt driven to start doing something, anything, before another child could disappear.

Besides, she was eager to see Agent Allen again.

Situated only a few miles north of town, Valley Wells was the now defunct community swimming pool. The whole complex was surrounded by a large fence strung with barbwire along the top. The fence was in turn surrounded by Trona's ever-present salt cedar trees. The trees provided a perfect hiding place for Cal's Camaro while they waited for Agent Allen to show up.

As kids, Camm and Cal had spent many hours splashing and swimming in the salty water. The plant had used Valley Wells as a large salt water reservoir and allowed the community to use it as a swimming pool. With summer temperatures regularly topping one hundred and ten degrees, and nightly lows staying above ninety-five, or even one hundred, Trona needed a community swimming pool, but as the cost of maintenance increased, the plant shut the pool down. It now sat unused.

The four college students wandered about near the car, stretching their legs and staying out of sight of passing cars. Camm kept edging out to look toward Trona Road, hoping to see Agent Allen's red Mustang speeding toward them.

Suddenly, Martha screamed, "A snake! A snake!" Running over to Camm, she grabbed Camm's arm and pushed up against her for protection, shivering as she looked back over her shoulder. "I hate snakes. I just hate them."

Camm gave Martha a hug, patting her on the back in a feeble attempt to provide some comfort. Camm had grown up with desert snakes. Her family often found them in the backyard or even in the garage. She was neither afraid of snakes nor particularly interested in them.

Cal and Lenny, on the other hand, ran over to where Martha had been standing to check out the offending reptile.

"Dude," Lenny remarked. "Look how it moves. That is so awesome."

The snake was slithering first one way, then another, obviously wanting to get away from them as badly as Martha had wanted to get away from it.

"That's a sidewinder," Cal explained. "It's a type of rattlesnake. See? It moves sideways, leaving parallel curved marks in the sand, instead of going straight ahead like a normal snake."

"But, dude," Lenny noted, "it doesn't have any rattles."

"Sidewinders don't have rattles, but they are still rattlesnakes and very poisonous."

Cal and Lenny followed at a safe distance, observing the snake closely.

Camm smiled. Cal was obviously enjoying this opportunity to show Lenny what he knew about desert wildlife.

The boys stopped, watching as the snake slithered off to lose itself in the sagebrush.

Sauntering back toward the car, Cal continued his lecture. "Basically, there are three types of rattlesnakes around Trona. The diamondback is the one you see the most. It's brown and has rattles. It has a pattern of diamond designs along its back.

"You just saw the sidewinder. You can always pick it out because of the funny way it moves. You can tell a snake is poisonous if it has an arrowhead-shaped head. The head is shaped that way because the sacks of poison sit at the base of the head.

"The most poisonous snake we have here, and the most poisonous of all rattlesnakes, is the Mojave Green. It has a diamond design like the diamondback, but it is green in color.

The Mojave Green is the most aggressive and by far most dangerous desert snake."

He glanced over at Lenny. "I've caught a lot of diamondbacks and even a few sidewinders. Not a lot scares me in the desert. Not scorpions, or coyotes, or even the occasional bobcat. But I stay away from Mojave Greens."

Lenny's face lit up, and he glanced over his shoulder. "Dude, can we go back and catch that sidewinder? We could scare the girls with it!"

Camm stiffened and glanced over at the two guys. As occupied as she was with reassuring Martha, Camm had still been following their conversation.

Cal shrugged. "We can catch it if you want, but Camm's not afraid of snakes and Martha's already had her scare. Camm used to help me catch snakes and lizards when we were kids growing up here."

Good answer, Camm thought.

Lenny looked disappointed.

Camm wondered if Lenny wanted revenge over the whole shower ordeal in Flagstaff. *You'll have to find something scarier than a snake,* she thought. *I know scary, and after what I've seen, some desert reptile is not going to bother me.*

Camm watched the two guys make their way back to the car. As Cal passed, she raised her eyebrows and shook her head with a look she hoped said there would be no catching of reptiles to scare anyone. Cal grinned and nodded.

Lenny, pacing excitedly in front of the car, suddenly burst

out, "Dude. This is so cool, catching stuff, wild stuff, like snakes and lizards. Just roaming out here free, living off the land. The only lizards I ever saw as a kid were in the zoo. What kind of lizards did you guys catch?"

"Oh, you know." Cal leaned back on the hood of his car. Facing the sun, he stretched his arms out in the warm spring desert air as if to catch more rays. "We'd catch iguanas, zebra tails, rainbow bellies, chuckwallas, and of course, horny toads. Whatever we could find. I'd keep them in an old aquarium and feed 'em bugs and lettuce, and then, you know, we'd let 'em go."

"Dude, let's find a lizard to catch." Lenny began hunting around in the nearby bushes.

Camm rolled her eyes. *Some boys never grow up.*

She had to admit, though, Lenny was never down for long, and he didn't seem to hold grudges. His childlike enthusiasm was always close to the surface. In spite of herself, Camm was beginning to, well, not like him, but maybe get used to his strange personality. While the constant use of the word "dude" was irritating, at least he was direct and to the point. He was obviously intelligent, and, like Martha, didn't make long speeches.

Camm heard the sound of an approaching car. Craning her neck, she saw Agent Allen's Mustang driving along the narrow oiled road leading in to Valley Wells from Trona Road.

She gave Martha a quick squeeze. "That snake is long gone. Come on. Help has finally arrived. I'll introduce you to Agent Allen."

Running out of the shielding trees, Camm waved her arms to show where they were. Too late, she saw that Agent Allen had a passenger. Panic rose in her throat before she decided Agent Allen must have been assigned a partner for this investigation.

The car pulled to a dusty stop. Agent Allen climbed out of the driver's side. Camm hurried over and gave Agent Allen a light hug before focusing on the tall good-looking man who was unfolding himself out of the other side of the car.

He wore a dark blue suit, a white shirt, and a nondescript tie. He stretched in the warm sunlight and looked expectantly at Agent Allen. His outfit was formal and very warm for Trona. Though it was still spring, temperatures were already pushing ninety. In a slow and leisurely manner, he removed his suit jacket, and after stretching again, tossed it into the back seat of the car. Camm could not help but notice the muscles bulging underneath the white shirt.

Nice partner, Camm thought, hiding a smile. The man had a firm jaw and a chiseled, manly face. He was not only tall, but also well proportioned. He clearly worked out. He was very good looking, but something about the way he was watching her was disturbing.

"Camm," Agent Allen began tentatively, "this is Mr. Roberts. He is with Swift Creek, the company overseeing the security of the mansion. You remember them, don't you?"

Camm gasped and drew away. She stared at Mr. Roberts in disbelief. Using Agent Allen as a barrier, she slowly backed away.

"Of course, I remember Swift Creek." Camm scowled at Agent Allen. "They threatened to put Cal and me in prison. Forever!"

Agent Allen's awkward pose showed she was uncomfortable about bringing the man from Swift Creek with her, but that did not take away Camm's feeling of betrayal.

Cal jogged up and stood next to her. Pointing at the suit, he asked, "Who's the new guy?"

Camm threw Cal a meaningful look. "Richards or something. He's from Swift Creek."

Cal's face immediately tightened. "Oh crap!"

"Roberts, my name is Roberts." The suit spoke up. "And I'm not here to throw you in prison—not yet anyway. Linda, uh, Agent Allen assures us she has the matter in hand."

Camm gave Agent Allen a pleading look. *How could you betray us?*

Agent Allen's shoulders slumped, but only for a moment. She took a breath. "Camm, I have never lied to you, and I would never betray you. They knew you were coming to Trona before I did. They knew you were sending me a text before I did. They came to me—I didn't turn you in to them. I promise. They've agreed to let me handle this my way."

Camm eyed the man narrowly. He flashed his white smile at her in spite of her obvious animosity toward him.

This guy is a charmer. He's well aware of how attractive he is. All the more reason not to let down my guard for even one second.

"You kids can't stay here." He directed his comments in a friendly way to both Camm and Cal, as if he already knew them. "You know that. It's for your own good. We will escort you through town and turn you loose on the other side, but you have to keep moving. You cannot stay. You cannot come back, or even Agent Allen won't be able to help you."

He hardened his face, trying to look like he meant business.

Camm resisted the temptation to ask questions. She was dying to know what was going on now in Trona, what the new developments were. She trusted Agent Allen, but was sure this Roberts guy would just lie—he would flash a big handsome smile, and then lie to her. She decided she didn't like him. She certainly didn't like being called a kid.

"Rick." Agent Allen laid her hand on his arm. "Just give me a minute to talk to them. These are intelligent adults. I just need a few minutes to converse with them in private."

He held up both hands as if in surrender. "Go ahead, Linda, but you know they'll be watching for us to drive through town and out the other side. We need to get these kids on their way to L.A. as soon as possible."

Camm thought, *So it's Rick and Linda, is it? They're on a first name basis. And how does he know we're going to L.A.?*

Looking behind Camm and Cal, Agent Allen called out, "Martha. Lenny. Would you two stay back by Cal's car, please? I need to talk to Camm and Cal alone."

Camm traded startled glances with Cal. Glancing back, Camm watched Martha and Lenny slow to a stop and turn back toward the Camaro.

"How do you know they're—" Camm began, but was cut off by Agent Allen.

"Swift Creek," she said, shrugging. "They know everything. Everything!"

With a wave, she directed Camm and Cal to walk with her out into the open desert, away from Agent Roberts. About fifteen yards out, Agent Allen turned to face them, but stood looking at her feet, rubbing her hands together. She was obviously not happy.

Camm stood tall, arms folded, watching her closely. *This better be good.*

Before Agent Allen could speak, Martha, who was standing back at the Camaro with Lenny, loudly exclaimed, "Ohhh! Ohhh!" Camm looked back just as Martha bent down and started vomiting violently onto the ground.

Suddenly, Camm felt uneasy herself, like she was carsick. Grabbing her stomach, she rocked backward, as if to catch her balance. The ground seemed to move under her feet, and she felt as though she were falling.

Camm steadied herself, slowly feeling normal again. She looked around, trying to figure out what was happening. Everything had a shimmery appearance, as if she were seeing through a special effects screen. The shimmering stopped. Then, she saw it. Something was coming toward her out of nowhere—something that definitely was not normal!

A fuzzy moving carpet emerged out of the desert sagebrush, scurrying along the sandy ground toward where Camm and Cal stood with Agent Allen. The carpet was bumpy and not of uniform consistency or color. It moved in an uneven pattern—some parts moving faster than other parts. It seemed to be traveling on thousands, no, millions of little legs.

Agent Allen took off sprinting toward her car, running at right angles to the direction the carpet was headed. "Run! Run!" she yelled. She had removed her pistol from its holster, but seemed not to know where to point it.

Cal ran a few steps away, following Agent Allen, but when Camm didn't follow, he ran back and grabbed her arm, trying to pull her with him. Camm stumbled a step or two in Cal's direction, but remained transfixed on whatever it was that was moving directly at her.

What is it? She realized it wasn't one thing, but many different things all moving in the same direction at different speeds. Some were larger. Some had fur, while others were shiny black. Some were brown or tan. She noticed all had their own legs. Many legs. Many, many legs.

Camm's heart stopped and an involuntary scream erupted from her mouth. They were spiders, huge spiders, the biggest spiders Camm had ever seen. There were thousands of them, a herd of spiders, a stampede of spiders, running on thin, wiry spider legs.

All of them running toward Camm.

She saw Daddy-Long-Legs the size of saucers, running with long, spindly legs rising two feet or more above the ground. Running underneath were brown, furry tarantulas that looked like deformed eight-legged schnauzers. Scattered throughout the stampede were shiny, glimmering black widows, their compound eyes and pinchers enormous! Camm could see the red hourglasses on their stomachs as they pushed up in the rush forward.

Enormous brown, black, and tan spiders zigzagged randomly through the herd, jumping over white spiders with black stripes and dark green spiders with brown dots. Evil-looking garden spiders scurried along the top of the others because they were faster. The smallest spiders were the size of rodents, and the largest were big enough to suck a rodent dry.

They were moving fast, and they were moving directly at Camm and Cal.

"Come on! Come on!" Cal was screaming. "Come on, Camm! Get out of the way!"

Cal still had a grip on Camm's arm and tried to pull her in the direction Agent Allen had run. Camm turned to run with him, but in turning, her feet tangled. She fell flat on her stomach. Cal lost his hold on her arm and stumbled away, trying to regain his own balance. Even as he turned to go back, it was too late.

Before Camm could get up, the spiders swarmed over her. While no one spider was very heavy, the swarm pushed her down, pressing her to the ground. She tried to protect her face by burying it in the sand and placing her hands over her ears.

The spider legs pumped up and down as they ran over her. She could feel them on her legs and rear, on her back, arms, and hands. They ran over her neck and onto the back of her head, snagging her hair and tangling it up in their feet. Like a hundred thousand tiny hammers, they pounded across her body, making her skin itch as if she had an open rash.

She sensed Cal thrashing nearby. He had come back, kicking his feet and flailing his arms, trying in vain to protect her. Sand, dirt, and spiders flew into the air. Brushing her with sagebrush boughs, he tried to get the spiders off her, to keep them away from her. But the swarm was too much.

The spiders ignored him, and her, too. None stopped to fight back. All were intent on running away from something else. In a panic, they continued their frantic rush over Camm's back and around Cal's flailing legs. It could only have been a few moments, but it seemed they were engulfed in a tsunami of hairy, ugly, nasty, enormous spiders forever.

The sensation of spine-like spider legs poking and prodding along her backside finally slowed, and then stopped. Camm rolled over and sat up in a slump, scrubbing her face with her hands. Her hair poked out in all directions. Her body tingled and itched as the sensation of prickly spiders legs lingered even after they were gone. She felt sick again, and thought she might heave at any moment as her mind kept replaying the helpless feeling of being buried alive in a living, squirming pile of giant spiders.

"Camm, look out! Look out!" Cal was screaming again, struggling to pull her to her feet.

Camm let go of Cal's hand so she could brush the hair out of her face, trying to see what Cal was screaming about. Then she saw it. One spider remained, moving slower than the others. The size of a footstool, it was brownish-gray in color and more furry than any of the others. But this fur was different. Each thick strand of fur seemed to move and wiggle independently of the rest. It was on her even as she saw it.

As it ran into her, it shattered into hundreds of pieces. Instantly, Camm realized this spider was not furry at all. It was a mother spider carrying hundreds of her babies all over her body. As the spider hit Camm, the babies came loose. Scurrying around, they completely enveloped Camm, trying to attach to Camm as if she were their mother. Each baby was the size of a quarter and, of course, had eight legs. Camm's body disappeared from sight as she was smothered by the infant spider hoard.

They trampled across her skin, on her legs and arms. She could feel them running through her clothes. They became entangled in her hair. She could feel their legs and squirming bodies as they ran under her collar, then along and around her neck. They covered her face, rushing over her closed eyes, sticking their legs between her lips, up her nose, in her ears. Her sitting form became an undulating spider heap. For long moments, they covered her entirely. She did not dare move, not even to open her mouth to scream.

Then, they left her and scurried off, following their lumbering mother, hurrying away after the rest of the spiders—all running, desperate to get away. All were fleeing in panic as fast as their spider legs could carry them.

As the last of the baby spiders left her, Camm rolled over

onto her hands and knees and violently spewed her breakfast into the hot desert sand. She tried to get up, but fell back down.

Cal reached down and pulled her to her feet. She brushed frantically at her torso and legs. "Are there any left? Get them off me! Are they all gone? I can't get them off!"

Cal was clearly shaken, too, but he looked her over carefully, his big hands brushing her back and shoulders and hair with a calming, steady motion. "I don't see any. They're all gone," he assured her. "Even the babies were big, too big to hide in your clothes. If there were any left on you, we would be able to see them for sure."

Camm felt as if they were still on her, moving across her body, in her blouse, down her pants. She could still feel those baby spider legs in her nose and mouth, across her eyes and ears. She rubbed her face vigorously and spit several times. Her body shivered violently as she spun around and around, brushing away what had already left.

Cal grabbed her by her forearms and tried to pull her to him. "Camm, they are gone. They are all gone." She fought against him, still trying to brush at her body, but he overcame her and pulled her to him, embracing her in his long, strong arms. She finally gave in, buried her face in his chest, and sobbed once, then twice.

That was all she needed. Her body relaxed, and her breathing slowed as her heart gradually caught its natural rhythm. As Cal held her, she seemed to absorb his strength, to assume his calm. When all else failed, Cal had always been there. She rested on him, letting him hold her as she centered herself on her own two feet.

Agent Allen appeared and patted her back. "They're gone, Camm, they're gone. You can still see them running away, but they have all left here."

Camm took a deep breath and gently pushed away from Cal. Dust covered her face except where tear tracks ran down her cheeks. She looked from Agent Allen to Cal, and then back to Agent Allen. Camm's eyes felt red and swollen. Anger and fear tinged her voice. "What in heaven's name was that?" She tried to sound firm, but her voice cracked.

Lenny called out an unhelpful answer. "Those were spiders, dude. Those were monster spiders." He turned to Martha, who was visibly shaken and crying, and said, in a lower voice, "Dude, there were times I couldn't even see her, there were so many spiders on her!"

Martha ignored him. She held her hands to her mouth, noticeably trembling.

Camm ignored Lenny, but continued to stare at Agent Allen, waiting for her reply. Agent Allen was shaken, too. She tossed her head toward Mr. Roberts. "Let's go get some answers."

Rick was just getting out of the Mustang when he saw Linda, Camm, and Cal walking toward him. As soon as he saw the stampede of giant spiders coming, he had hopped into the car and rolled up all the windows. Even after the stampede had passed, he was slow getting back out. He kept checking to be sure nothing else was coming. He had a spooky feeling those spiders were being chased by something, and he kept watching to see what it might be.

When he took the Trona assignment, he was warned to be ready for some pretty weird stuff. But that giant-spider stampede, coming out of nowhere, had totally caught him off guard. He wondered if he was being paid enough for this kind of duty.

Watching the FBI agent approach the car with Camm and Cal, he sighed, knowing they were coming for answers, real answers, and he had precious few. True, he worked for Swift Creek, but the top brass at Swift Creek didn't know everything, and they shared very little of what they did know with the lower ranks. He knew he was going to get the brunt of the blame for what just happened, but it was not his fault.

He had been sent with the FBI agent to see these kids removed from the valley so that something like this wouldn't happen to them. He hoped they had learned their lesson and would be a little more cooperative now about getting out of Trona and staying out.

As the three walked up to him, the girl, Camm, was still checking herself all over for left-behind spiders, patting her body and looking down her blouse. Cal kept assuring her he could not see any spiders anywhere.

Linda was giving him a narrow look that said, *What do you have to say for yourself?*

Why did he have to explain anything? He didn't cause the phenomenon, and no one knew how to stop it. They didn't even know how to predict when and where it would happen. Still, he knew what his employer required of him and the image he had to maintain, an image of complete and absolute control. He suddenly wished he had never taken this assignment and could go back to work for the CIA. Right now, the CIA seemed like the good old days.

The three came to a halt directly in front of him, but they were still focused on reassuring Camm, helping her calm down.

He decided to be proactive. Before any of them could speak, he said, "Ms. Smith come here. Let's check you over for bites."

He tried to sound calm and experienced in this type of thing—as if anyone could be experienced in what had just happened. At least, he would attempt to sound professional.

Camm did not move, but folded her arms over her chest, her face tight. "What in the world are you guys doing here? The last we heard, you had everything under control. Is this what you mean by control?"

He sighed inwardly. The implication was that Swift Creek was manipulating the situation, maybe had even caused the spider incident.

He responded, "Like the FBI, we're still investigating."

"Investigating what?" Cal demanded.

Rick looked around, searching for the right words, and then pointed at the retreating spiders. "Things like that, and like the disappearing kids. We are trying to keep all these things from happening, but we don't understand it, let alone know how to stop it."

Camm looked mulish. "You could have warned us."

"We did warn you. We warned you to stay away." He saw his response hit home. She couldn't deny she had been warned. It was obvious she didn't know how to reply.

He rubbed the back of his neck. "Look, there is stuff going on here related to what you two experienced last year in the mansion, except now it appears to be spreading. Some sort of crossover is happening randomly in many different places, but the phenomena do seem to be limited to Searles Valley. These events used to be contained within the mansion, but now they can happen any place in the valley. Sometimes things that cross over become agitated." He paused. "I believe that is what you just experienced with the spiders."

Agent Allen frowned at him. "You sound like Mr. What's-his-name, your boss, back at the mansion. Cross over from where? Where did those giant spiders come from? What is happening to the people who disappear? Do they also cross over?"

By this time, Martha and Lenny had walked over to join them. Rick knew these new kids had no idea what was occurring in the valley, and he was sure they weren't supposed to be hearing these questions, let alone the answers. But they also weren't supposed to have seen what they had just seen. He decided to buy himself some time to think.

"Can we get out of the sun, at least? It's hotter than blazes out here." He saw the two from Trona roll their eyes at each other. "Okay," he grumbled. "This is not hot to you, but it is to me." He led the way over to the shade of the trees, close to where the Camaro was parked.

Rick stood with his back to the trees, facing the other five. Expelling a large breath of air, he studied his shoes for a moment. He knew he didn't have to explain anything. He could, if he wanted, just haul them all out of Trona without another word.

But they had just seen something that needed explaining. Any answer would be better than letting them speculate wildly among themselves. Besides, he was becoming a little enamored with Linda Allen. He didn't want to look bad in her eyes.

Normally, he wasn't too hot on the FBI, but Linda was attractive, savvy, and physically fit, which was important to him. He also liked her spunky personality. She had stood up to him at the mansion, and he respected that. In her own way, she seemed partial toward him. He could see something happening between the two of them. He didn't want to antagonize her now.

He kicked the sand with his black Sketchers and looked up at his audience. What he saw alarmed him—they were all looking directly over his head with horrified expressions on their faces. Automatically going into combat mode, he whirled around, dropping down onto one knee as he removed his service revolver and pointed it directly above him in one smooth motion.

Glancing up, he hesitated only a fraction of a second. "What the . . ."

They were the last two words he ever spoke.

X

The gargantuan snake swayed above them, its round obsidian eyes fixated on Mr. Roberts. The others stood paralyzed behind him. With lightning speed, the head struck downward, its gaping mouth enveloping Mr. Roberts's head and right shoulder as it closed over him, lifting him high up in the air. His legs kicked wildly.

Almost simultaneously with the strike, Agent Allen began firing shots point blank into the side of the snake's head. The snake dropped Mr. Roberts and swung hurriedly back into the cover of the trees, where it had been hiding before the attack. Agent Allen followed, emptying her gun into the retreating snake. Cal and Lenny ran after her, keeping the snake at a safe distance. Agent Allen yelled, "Stay back! Stay back!"

"Don't shoot it! Don't shoot it!" Camm shouted.

Agent Allen wasn't listening. She was busy reloading her gun.

Camm was familiar with the results of shooting these creatures that had crossed over. It made them angry, without doing significant harm. At least that was the case with the green rat.

Agent Allen, Cal, and Lenny disappeared into the trees. Camm knelt next to Mr. Roberts's supine figure, and gently picked up his hand. He lay looking up into the sky. Martha came to kneel on his other side, her trembling hand pressed against her mouth. Tears dripped down her cheeks. Lifting her gaze from the injured man, she whispered, "What do we do?"

Mr. Roberts had two large puncture wounds, spaced more than a foot apart. The snake's bite ran diagonally from the upper wound in his chest to the lower wound in his abdomen.

Camm couldn't tell if his heart had been punctured, but he was bleeding profusely from both wounds. Along with the leaking blood, steamy green venom with a sulfuric smell drained from both puncture holes. The amount of venom injected into his system must have been enormous. Something about the venom seemed familiar.

Images of thick green fluid encased in crystal bullets rose in her mind. She saw again the green venom dripping from the rat's wounds, wounds inflicted by her own hand. Camm's stomach clenched with old feelings of panic. She trembled, not just from memories, but from the horror of what Mr. Roberts was going through. She gripped his hand tighter.

Mr. Roberts was gasping for breath, his pupils fixed and dilated. It was impossible to tell if he was conscious or not.

He was sweating profusely and had turned a white marble color, except for his veins, which protruded dark blue under his skin. Little tremors ran through him, though his body was rigid and stiff.

Camm gazed down at him helplessly, not knowing what to do. She could try stopping the bleeding by pushing against the wounds, or maybe, she should suck out the venom like she had seen on TV. The huge size of the puncture holes made the TV procedure impossible. Besides, the stinking, green venom sizzled in the man's blood like acid. She did not want that venom in her mouth, and she had no gloves to protect her hands if she pressed on the wounds. She felt absolutely useless, forced to watch Mr. Roberts suffer with no way to help.

Martha was looking at her with tear-soaked eyes, a look of confusion on her face. She apparently had no idea what to do either. After about thirty seconds, the trembling stopped. Mr. Roberts gasped twice, his eyes rolled back under his eyelids, and his swollen blue tongue lolled out of his mouth.

Camm's eyes stung with unshed tears. Slowly, she placed Mr. Robert's limp hand gently by his side. Looking over at Martha, she said, "I think he's dead."

Martha started to cry again. "But we didn't even do anything to try to help him."

Camm helped Martha up and they clung to each other for comfort. Camm shook her head, trying to convince herself. "What could we have done? It happened so quickly. How could anyone survive a bite like that? The venom is still bubbling like acid in his wounds."

They stood together, silently staring down at the dead man, soaked in blood and venom.

Martha was the first to speak. "Camm, what is going on here? What are we getting into? This whole thing is a horrible nightmare, and you know things you haven't bothered to share with me. I think I should have been warned about this place before you brought me here." As Martha spoke, she looked earnestly into Camm's eyes, searching for the truth.

Camm was wordless, finally realizing the terrible mistake she had made in bringing Martha and Lenny to Trona. *What was I thinking? What did I hope to do?*

She suddenly felt very vulnerable.

Before she could respond to Martha, Camm saw the other three heading back, running all-out toward them. Lenny was yelling something she couldn't understand, but she didn't stop to worry about it. The snake was following right behind them.

It was immense. Longer than a semi-truck and bigger around than a car tire, this creature would have no problem swallowing a person whole. The stone-like head, evil but expressionless, was raised five or six feet off the ground. The undulating body propelled it forward at an alarming speed. There was no doubt it intended to do more harm.

"To the car! Go to the car!" Agent Allen pointed as she yelled at the girls. Camm and Martha scrambled into Agent Allen's Mustang as fast as they could, Martha in the backseat. Just as Agent Allen slammed her car door shut, the snake struck her side of the vehicle.

The force of the strike heaved the car up onto two wheels

and pushed it sideways several feet. Martha screamed one short, loud blast, and then placed her hands over her mouth. Her eyes almost bulged out of her head, but she seemed to understand this was not the time to lose control and screaming did not help.

The car fell back on all four tires with a heavy thud. Camm felt the impact from her tailbone clear up her spine. She started to whisper, under her breath, "Let's go, let's go, let's go."

Agent Allen was digging in her pockets, trying to extract her keys. It seemed to take forever, each second dragging on and on.

Camm looked past Agent Allen to where the snake was bringing its long, cylindrical body into a striking coil. The coiling process brought the head higher and higher above them. The image was mesmerizing. Its smooth scales were covered by symmetrical diamond designs that shone with a delicate spring green color. It would have been beautiful had it not been a giant snake preparing to eat them.

Agent Allen finally discovered her keys still in the ignition, where she had left them. Then, in her haste to grab them, she knocked the keys to the floor. Snatching them up, she struggled to push the key back into the ignition.

Camm continued to whisper, "Let's go, let's go, let's go."

Camm felt Martha's light hand on her shoulder. "Camm, that's not helping," she said quietly. Camm nodded her head and closed her mouth. It was not that she was trying to hurry Agent Allen as much as she was voicing her anxiety.

The key finally slid into the key hole and the engine started up. The snake had now completely coiled itself and was rearing back, the head swaying from side to side, in preparation for another powerful strike.

Agent Allen slammed the car into gear and stomped on the gas. The back wheels spun furiously in the sand and gravel, but the car only inched forward, slowly fishtailing from side to side. Dust billowed up from the rear tires as they dug themselves deeper into the ground.

Camm took a breath. She knew how to drive on desert sand. Turning to Agent Allen, she said with more calmness than she felt, "Let up a little on the gas. You'll just get us stuck in the sand if the tires keep spinning."

Agent Allen nodded and released the gas pedal from the floorboards.

The snake stopped moving its head from side to side and pulled back further for its strike. At the same time, the tires quit spinning and finally caught hold. As the Mustang began moving, the rear tires popped up out of the holes they had dug, and the car jumped forward.

At that instant, the snake struck with blinding speed, hitting the moving target on its rear quarter-panel. The force of the strike spun the car two hundred and seventy degrees. Both Camm and Martha yelped. The speed of the strike was amazing. The head seemed to disappear from the snake's body and reappear, fangs and all, striking the car.

Agent Allen drove straight forward, a determined look fixed on her face. Her jaw was set so firmly that Camm could see the muscles bulging at the side of her head. A large, blue vein pulsed at her temple. The car lurched into the sagebrush with the snake in hot pursuit.

The snake was on their right side and only slightly behind, which prevented a turn to the right—that would have taken them back to the paved road and out to the Trona Road highway. Instead, Agent Allen was now forced to drive straight ahead into the open desert.

Still, Camm felt some relief. Even driving through the desert, the car should move faster than the snake. No one had thought to put on a seatbelt, and they all bounced around inside the car, slamming against the sides and roof as they slowly put a little distance between themselves and the pursuing snake. Camm finally got her seat belt on and saw Agent Allen doing the same, one-handed. There was no time to check on Martha.

Agent Allen desperately worked to steer the car around the larger bushes while going as fast as she dared across the desert terrain. The desert floor looked flat, but was filled with holes, gaps, rocks, and all sorts of obstacles not intended for automobile travel.

Agent Allen tried to serpentine her way through the brush, hopefully making it harder for the snake to follow. But it soon became clear, they couldn't out serpentine a serpent.

One large desert holly bush was impossible to avoid. As they crashed straight through, Camm felt the front right tire smash into a boulder hidden on the other side of the bush. The boulder did not give, so the tire did. The impact against the boulder was bone jarring. Camm's head crashed into the roof, making her bite her tongue. Feeling dizzy and seeing red stars, she pulled her seat belt tighter.

From the way the car was now handling, there was no doubt the right front tire was flat and the rim probably bent. It had been difficult enough driving through the desert brush on four good tires. Now, riding on a damaged wheel and rim, it was impossible to get up any real speed and keep the car under control at the same time.

Camm looked behind. Her stomach tightened. The snake was gaining again.

"Camm!" Martha hollered. "What happened to Cal and Lenny?"

Everything had happened so fast. This was the first chance Camm had had to wonder about the boys. Frantically twisting this way and that, she tried to see out of every window at the same time, hoping to catch sight of Cal's Camaro. As she turned to her left to look out the back window, her knee hit the stick shift, knocking the car out of gear. Slipping into neutral, the car slowed precipitously. The soft sand was sucking them to a stop, as if holding them in anticipation of the snake. The desert seemed to be working against them.

Agent Allen growled in a warning voice, "Camm!"

The snake approached the back window with amazing speed. Agent Allen thrust in the clutch and jammed the car back into gear. Carefully working the clutch, she got the car rolling again just as the snake struck.

Staring out the back, Camm was entranced by its dead black

eyes, gaping mouth, and long-dagger fangs. The car jumped forward and pulled to the right, moving out of the snake's range just as its maw reached them. It raised its venomous head and continued its mad pursuit.

At that moment, Cal's Camaro came bouncing through the sagebrush behind the snake. Camm felt relieved, then worried. Cal was putting himself in danger. What could he do? She knew Cal would never abandon her. There was no one in the world she depended on or trusted more than Cal. But, once Cal reached the snake, what help could he possibly offer?

Camm turned to face forward just as the Mustang bounded over a berm, and then sailed unimpeded down into a deep, dry wash that none of them had seen coming. They were all thrown upward as the car dropped down the almost vertical walls into the ravine. As the car hit the sandy bottom, the front bumper dug into the ground in front of them, sending sand flying over the hood and across the windshield. For a moment, Agent Allen drove blindly. Without thinking, she instinctively slammed on the brakes, locking up the tires.

As the little car tried to brake, it slid to the left. Sand grabbed the wheels and the car's momentum caused it to roll. This time all three occupants screamed. Camm couldn't tell how many times the car rolled, but it seemed as if the outside world was spinning around and around.

As the car rolled, Camm was spun, jerked, banged, and bruised. Trying to hold herself steady, she pushed against the roof, while her seat belt kept her in place. Agent Allen clung desperately to the steering wheel, her seat belt stretched across her lap. Sand and dirt washed over them as they rolled across the deep ravine, making them look like a horizontal whirlwind.

When the car came to rest, it lay on its right side, Camm's side. Camm was acutely aware she had no idea where the snake was, only that it now had time to catch up with them. Agent Allen must have been thinking the same thing because she immediately released her seat belt and promptly dropped on top of Camm, pinning her to the door. As Camm fought to release her own seat belt, they both struggled to get free of each other and see where they were.

Extricating themselves from the tangle of arms and legs, they stood crammed together in the front of the car, staring out the now vertical windshield. Martha was rolled up in an impossible position in the back. Wearing no seatbelt, she appeared to be unconscious. Glass fragments were scattered everywhere.

Through the windshield, Camm finally saw the snake. It seemed to be looking at her as it swayed back and forth. Its head rose higher as it coiled for a strike. Camm realized a direct hit on the windshield could pop out the glass, leaving them defenseless from the monster reptile.

Jammed together with Agent Allen, stuck between the passenger seat and roof of the car, neither of them had room to maneuver. There was no apparent way to escape the car, let alone the snake. The Mustang, which had been their means of escape, now became a small cage.

Agent Allen began to reload her gun, preparing for another assault on the snake.

Camm glanced at her and shook her head. "I don't think the gun will do much good. We let loose a whole arsenal on that rat, and it hardly phased it."

For the first time, she saw desperation in Agent Allen's face. "What do we do?"

Camm felt a strange calmness come over her. She shrugged and smiled. "I don't know, but we're not alone. Let's hope the cavalry gets here in time."

Just then, she heard the roar of the Camaro's engine. Cal and Lenny were still mobile. She didn't know what good Cal could do against that snake, but then, he liked to surprise her.

The snake had completely coiled itself and was ready to strike. Its tail stretched behind and to the right, shaking violently in warning of what it was about to do.

Cal's Camaro came into view behind the snake. He was heading straight for it. The snake sensed something coming and tried to rear away from the fast-moving, kamikaze car. At the last moment, the car swerved away from the snake, but not before banging into its rattles with the right front bumper and crunching some of the rattles under the right front tire.

The Camaro skidded sideways and even went up on two tires, as if it was going to roll. But it didn't. Cal knew how to handle his Camaro. The car plopped back down onto all four wheels and slid to a stop in billowing waves of dust.

The snake tilted its head to focus on the Camaro. At the

same time, the Camaro's engine roared back to life, fishtailing away, throwing sand and rocks up into the snake's face. The snake turned from the broken Mustang to pursue the fleeing Camaro.

A surge of relief flooded Camm's body. Cal had grown up here and had spent many hours driving off road, even before he had his license. She was sure he would be able to outrace the snake while leading it far away from the disabled Mustang.

As she watched the chase, the snake and car seemed to glimmer, and then fade. She had the same sensation of dizziness and nausea she had felt just before the spiders appeared. Suddenly, the roar of the Camaro's engine faded to nothing. The snake and the Camaro had all disappeared into the dry desert air.

Desperation and panic welled up inside Camm. She stretched out her hand as if reaching after Cal. "Noooo!" she wailed.

She turned to stare at Agent Allen. She wanted to scream. Instead, she frantically clambered over the top of the Agent and climbed out the driver's side window, which had been smashed out in the rollover. Agent Allen climbed out behind her.

Camm scanned the desert, searching for any sign of the Camaro. She took off running in the direction Cal had been headed, following the large path left by the snake. It looked as if a huge barrel had been dragged through the sand, uprooting bushes and turning over large rocks along the way. The trail suddenly faded into nothing as if the snake had been swallowed up into the empty desert sky.

"Camm! Camm!" Agent Allen called, coming after her. "Come back! They're gone, and where they've gone, we can't follow. We can't help them now. We've got to help ourselves."

Camm felt her throat closing up and her chest tightening. Her eyes burned as she fought back the tears. She couldn't lose Cal like this, not here, not now.

"Gone? Gone where? Where did they go? That snake thing is still after them!"

Agent Allen sighed, and then winced. Camm noticed she was holding her left wrist, and there was blood coming from one ear. She had been injured in the accident.

"I don't know where they went. What did Rick say? They 'crossed over.' I don't know where or how, but I promise we're going to find out. It's time to get some real answers."

Agent Allen turned back to the car.

Camm stared at the rocks and sand at her feet, overwhelmed with desperation. She needed to do something, anything. Cal had only come along on this trip to be with her. Somehow she had to get to Cal and bring him back. She fought the emotions flooding her, but it was no use. Her eyes filled with tears, which ran freely down her cheeks.

Peering into the back window of the car, Agent Allen called out, "Come on, Camm. We have to get this friend of yours to a hospital, stat!"

Wiping her cheeks, Camm hiked back to look inside the

car. Martha was still curled up on top of her head in a position that only a cat could sustain. She was unconscious.

It took them some time to carefully extricate Martha from the car, trying not to do her further damage. She was breathing, but she did not regain consciousness. Once they had her out, Agent Allen pulled her cell phone from her pocket. It had been hopelessly damaged in the wreck. Camm tried to find her phone and couldn't. It must have fallen out of her pocket. After a careful search around the car, her phone was finally given up for lost.

Agent Allen sighed. "Camm, I'm hurt, too. I will stay here and see to Martha, best that I can. You have to run up to the main road and flag down some help."

Heading out across the desert for Trona Road, Camm started at a run, then a fast limp, and finally a hurried shuffle. The main road was farther than it looked. She had been injured in the accident, too, but was only now starting to feel it. As she hobbled along, tears streamed unhindered down her face and sobs burst out from deep inside her chest.

Everything was wrong. It had all gone so wrong. Martha was seriously injured, and still unconscious. Agent Allen was hurt. Mr. Roberts was dead. And Cal and Lenny had disappeared, crossed over into who-knew-what.

Cal! Would she ever see Cal again?

Camm had never known this kind of pain. It was more than she could bear. The tears flowed freely.

XI

Cal swerved through the sagebrush. Working the brake and gas pedals, he twisted the steering wheel back and forth, spinning the Camaro around the bigger bushes and slamming through the smaller ones. He knew exactly where he was going. At least, he thought he did.

Squinting, he searched for the wide dirt road that ran past the south end of the small Trona airport and out around the east side of Searles Lake. He had driven that road many times and knew he could push his Camaro to maximum speed once he got on the hard, flat surface of the dry lake bed.

He did not find the dirt road. Nor did he pass the airport. He thought it odd that he had only been gone one year from town, but somehow had forgotten how to find that dirt road.

Lenny yelled in his ear, "Dude, here it comes again! Man,

it's movin'.'' Lenny was keeping track of the snake through the rear window.

Even though Lenny gave him constant updates, Cal kept an eye on the huge reptile through his rear view and side mirrors. That snake was huge, but also quick! Cal watched it grow larger in the mirror as it got closer and closer. He did not want to get too far ahead, not yet anyway. The Mustang had rolled with Camm, Martha, and the agent inside, and he was determined to lead the snake as far from the site of the accident as he could.

As the snake drew near, Cal saw its head rear back slightly. He recognized this as a clear sign it was going to strike. Lenny shouted, "Watch out, dude! It's comin' at ya!"

Stamping on the accelerator, Cal jumped the car forward, just as the gigantic head, fangs bared, struck out at them, barely missing the back of the car.

Lenny whooped. "Way to go, dude! You the man!"

Lenny is enjoying this way too much, considering that snake is trying to eat us for lunch. Cal smiled. Truthfully, with the all adrenalin coursing through his own veins, Cal was enjoying it too. It felt good to be on his home turf again.

They weaved and twisted through the desert sage, keeping just out of reach of the monster reptile. Every time it struck, barely missing them, Lenny would holler and Cal's heart would skip a beat. By maintaining a south by southeast direction, they eventually ran into the dry lake bed, never finding any kind of dirt road—which was strange.

As he drove out onto the lake bed, Cal glanced in his rear

view mirror and saw the snake was still following, but was way back in the sagebrush. It seemed to be slowing down. Cal guessed the long, hard chase had tired it, so he slowed, letting it get close, within striking distance again. When the head pulled back to strike, Cal hit the gas to jump out of the way.

The snake missed by a mile. It was definitely showing signs of fatigue. Cal led it onward at a leisurely pace. Finally, the snake seemed to stop, so Cal decided it was time to leave it in the dust.

Cal pushed the pedal to the metal. He had always taken good care of his car and knew the V8 engine had power to spare. This was just like driving on the Bonneville Speedway in Utah. The surface of the lake bed was hard and flat and went on for miles and miles. Leaving a large white plume behind them, they sped away at more than a hundred miles an hour with Lenny whooping at the top of his voice.

When Lenny checked back over his shoulder, the snake had disappeared in the cloud of white dust. "Yeah, dude! Go, go, go!" he yelled. "Eat our dust you limbless, venomous reptile! The mammals win this one."

Lenny flipped around in his seat. Holding onto the dash-board, he leaned forward so he could watch the surface of the lake bed fly by. He started laughing, almost hysterically. Cal couldn't help himself and laughed with him. It didn't get better than this!

When Cal deemed they were safe, having put several miles between them and the snake, he locked up the brakes and jammed the steering wheel to the right, causing the car to do several three-hundred-and-sixty-degree spins across the white alkaline lake bed. This was a totally unnecessary maneuver, but it was a good way to celebrate and flowed naturally from all the adrenaline pumping through his veins.

They finally came to a stop at the apex of a large, white, swirling cloud. As the cloud blew away, Cal looked over at Lenny. Lenny stared back, all the color drained from his face. Licking his lips and looking almost solemn, he whispered, "Dude, that was so, so . . ."

Lenny shook his head. ". . . that was so, like, on the Moon. No, man, wait. That was so like on Mars, dude. Yeah, that was totally way out there, you know, like on Mars."

They climbed out of the car. Cal jumped up on the rear bumper to get a better look around. There was no snake in sight. It must have given up the chase. He was so relieved to be rid of the snake, he didn't think about looking for anything else.

"Now that was one mean Mojave Green. Remember, Lenny, I told you to stay away from them. They all have real bad attitudes."

Lenny nodded. "Dude, I'm a believer."

"Let's go back and check on the girls." Cal wasn't sure how smart that snake might be. Though he had led it away from Camm and the others, it might try to double back on them. Also, as the adrenaline slowly eased out of his body, he began to worry about what had happened when Agent Allen's car flipped over. Someone might have been hurt. They might need his car to go to town for help.

Walking around to Lenny's still-open side door, Cal opened

the glove compartment and pulled out a Smith & Wesson .357 Magnum revolver.

"Whoa, dude, I didn't know that was in there. Where did that come from?" Lenny stared wide-eyed at the gun.

Cal shrugged his shoulders. "It's no big deal. It was a graduation gift from my dad. I think he got tired of me always borrowing his pistol, so he got me one of my own."

Cal pulled out a box of shells and loaded five bullets, leaving the chamber under the hammer empty, the way he'd been taught.

He looked up, trying to sound casual. "Never hurts to be prepared. Now, let's go back and make sure the girls are okay."

Before reaching the line where the desert sagebrush rimmed the edge of the dry lake, they saw the wide track left by the snake veer off to the east, toward the Slate Range Mountains. Either it gave up at that point, realizing it couldn't catch them, or it didn't like being out on the chemically saturated lake bed. It did not appear to be heading back to the Mustang.

At least that much is good news, Cal thought.

As they followed their tire tracks back through the desert, Lenny kept busy watching for the snake, just in case. Cal focused on driving, but a sinking feeling was growing in his gut, nagging at him. The euphoria from beating the snake disappeared. This was Cal's old stomping grounds. He knew it well, but something had changed. Something wasn't right. Not sure what it was, he decided it was his concern for Camm. He was really worried she'd been hurt.

Suddenly and unexpectedly, the tracks came to an end.

They just stopped. It was as if the Camaro had dropped out of the sky right where the tracks started.

They got out to look around. This time Cal climbed on top so he could see farther.

"Dude, what's up?" Lenny looked puzzled.

Cal turned, looking in all directions. He saw no signs of the Mustang or the salt cedars surrounding Valley Wells. He could not see Trona Road or the airport, both of which should have been clearly visible. He could not see Trona or Pioneer Point or any of the chemical plants in the valley. There was no sign of civilization anywhere. His entire hometown and all signs of humanity had just disappeared completely from off the face of the planet.

Watching Cal, Lenny began to look concerned. "Dude?" he asked.

Cal hopped off the car and looked over at Lenny. He inhaled the hot, dry air deeply, and then exhaled it through pursed lips. "Lenny, my man, I don't know how to tell you this, but we're not in Kansas anymore. As far as I can tell, we may in fact be on Mars!"

There was no doubt about it. It was totally grotesque—long, curved fangs, bulging eyes, a deformed nose, and a long hideous tongue pointing straight out of the mouth, like an accusing finger. But what really grabbed Camm's attention was that it was unique.

She had counted a total of 251 gargoyles in her third-floor room in the Searles Mansion. 250 were repeat carvings on the same five themes: two types of demons; a deformed jester; an evil angel with a flaming halo; and something with a troll or ogre face. Those same five gargoyles were carved over and over along the bed headboard, the wainscoting, and the chair rail, but there was only one hideous rat head.

What did that mean?

She had no one to ask.

Camm and Martha had been kept in isolation from the rest of the world ever since they'd been transported from the totaled Mustang directly to the mansion for medical aid and a series of debriefings. Those debriefings, conducted by the white-haired men, mainly involved Camm, since Martha was allowed to sleep most of the time per doctor's orders. Martha's room had been made into a makeshift hospital room, and she had been seen by a doctor twice.

Camm was in a room next to Martha's. Camm was allowed free access, if free access meant her room, Martha's room, and the bathroom at the end of the hallway.

Camm had tried asking for her one phone call, but was denied. Neither girl had been allowed any outside communications, even with parents or family. Agent Allen had come by occasionally, but Camm suspected that even her visits were being restricted. After failing in her task of getting Camm, Cal, and friends out of Trona without incident, Agent Allen was not on good terms with the folks from Swift Creek.

Men in dark suits and white shirts stood guard both inside and outside the mansion and watched Camm's every move. They did not talk to Camm, and she did not talk to them. By the cold expressions on their faces, she felt they blamed her for Mr. Roberts's death. She blamed herself a little. If she hadn't come here, he wouldn't be dead.

Even worse, for all she knew, Cal and Lenny could be dead, too. She hadn't heard from them or had any news about them since they had disappeared into the desert with the giant rattlesnake hot on their tails.

Just that morning, Camm had been taken down to the second floor for another interview with the white-haired men. They had started out by making it clear they were very unhappy about the way things were going. That made Camm mad.

"Cal and I are not responsible in any way for what happened! You need to send someone over there right now to find Cal and Lenny and bring them back."

The two men used high-sounding, technical terms in long, confusing explanations of why they couldn't do that, but to Camm it sounded like all they were saying was that no one knew how to do that. No one knew how to go wherever Cal and Lenny were. No one knew how to bring them back. Everyone, they said, was unhappy with the current situation, very unhappy.

Trudging back to her third-floor prison room, Camm did not know what Swift Creek was going to do with her, and she did not believe they knew either. The whole thing was a big mess. She was very sorry she had pulled Martha into the middle of it.

Since being brought to the mansion, Camm had occupied her time playing nurse to Martha and exploring their two rooms. Her nurse duties had been light. Now that Martha was conscious and more coherent, she worried constantly about getting to her internship in Los Angeles. Camm's biggest chore was convincing Martha she still needed sleep and was in no condition to be moved, let alone to start her internship.

As far as her exploring went, all Camm had discovered were some very old candles, some desiccated, stinky moth balls, and some old newspapers that had been used as drawer liners. Her room and Martha's room were almost identical, except for the intricate baroque carvings that decorated each room. Martha's room sported wild animals while Camm's had gargoyle heads. Boredom had driven Camm to count the gargoyle heads in her room and notice the recurring pattern.

Camm could not stop staring at the rat-head gargoyle, the one gargoyle not following the pattern. The gargoyles in the chair rail ran all around the four walls of the room. The rat-head gargoyle sat midway along the wall her room shared with Martha's. The walls were made of cross-cut oak paneling that was both beautiful and aged, trimmed with the gargoyle heads.

Camm knelt in front of the rat head and gently ran her fingers along the carvings. It was hideous, but intricately made. She could see where each individual strand of fur had been carved. She tested the teeth and found them pinpoint sharp.

As she touched the carving, a strange sensation came over

her. A soft, but frigid breeze brushed the back of her neck, causing the hairs there to stand on end. The sulfuric smell that she associated with the mansion wafted through the air. It was as if something was reaching out for her. She felt as if something was trying to touch her. After glancing around the room to confirm she was alone, Camm shook off the feeling and continued her examination of the rat's head.

She softly touched the extended tongue. To her surprise, it depressed slightly under gentle pressure, and then sprang back into place. She heard a clicking noise on the other side of the wall, and then one of the oak panels popped an inch out of place.

By hooking her fingernails on the panel's edge, Camm managed to swing the panel open on its hidden hinges. The chair rail split cleanly with the paneled edge. Once she got the panel door fully opened, she found a very narrow hallway hidden behind the walls.

Camm's heart started to thud. She had discovered another secret door and another secret passage. She was sure the Swift Creek people knew nothing of this passage because, if they did, they would not have put her in this room.

"Dude, that is one weird house! How we gonna get inside?"

Cal and Lenny were seated on the ground close to the Camaro, which was parked outside the Searles Mansion. As Cal thought about it, it wasn't 'the' mansion, but it was certainly identical to the mansion he had known in Trona. It was the same size, had the same number of floors, the same windows and doors, the same chimneys. In fact, it appeared to be identical in every way, except it was in another world. It was also locked up tighter than a drum.

To Cal's mind, it couldn't be the same mansion because they weren't in Trona. When he looked around, they were in what appeared to be Searles Valley, where Trona should be, but there was no Trona here. He had found some local landmarks like Turtle Rock, Circus Hill, and Tank Hill, except this Tank Hill had no water tank. Besides the mansion, there was nothing manufactured or man-made anywhere in sight. Only the mansion stood in its normal place, surrounded by a desolate desert landscape.

Cal shook his head. *It can't be the same mansion.*

In the evening sky, the sun was sinking behind the Argus Mountains. The slanted light gave a softer hue to the barren landscape. It was still warm, but Cal knew in high desert country the spring temperatures were going to drop rapidly with nightfall.

He sighed. Standing up to stretch, he gave Lenny a hand up. "We got no choice. It will be cold tonight. We're sleeping in the car."

The next morning was grim. They still couldn't find a way into the mansion, and nobody had come looking for them. Probably, no one knew where they were or even how to rescue them. They were on their own. They marshaled their resources: various snacks, juices, soda, and bottled water in the car, plus whatever was packed in all the luggage still loaded in Cal's trunk.

The biggest problem was water. Cal knew of only two places to get water. They could drive to Great Falls, where there was a trickle of water coming down the granite face of the rocks, or hike several miles up into the nearby hills to Indian Joe's natural springs. Or at least, that was where the water should be. Nothing was a sure thing in this alternate Searles Valley.

They decided on Great Falls, which was several miles north of the mansion. The driving had to be done through the desert, since all roads had disappeared.

Once they got there, Cal shook his head at his gas gauge. "The Camaro's getting low on gas. Maybe we should stay out here at Great Falls. That way we won't have to drive back and forth to get water."

"I don't know, dude." Lenny scratched his chin. "If people come lookin' for us, it'll be back at that mansion."

Cal glanced at the trickling water coming over the falls, then nodded reluctantly. "You're right, man. The mansion's our best bet if we're ever gonna get rescued."

Cal took a cold shower in the falls, and then they filled every container they could find with water. The drive back was delayed when they got stuck in the soft sand filling the deep wash at the upper end of Great Falls canyon. By the time they got back to the mansion, it was almost dark.

As the moon came out, they built a big fire with all the sagebrush they could gather and the matches in Cal's backpack.

The fire didn't burn long—it had been more for comfort than anything—but they did hope to do some cooking on the hot coals.

Cal had caught a large chuckwalla lizard, and Lenny was enthusiastic as they skinned and cooked it over the glowing coals from the fire.

"Hey, dude, this is so cool. We're living off the land for real." His enthusiasm died when he took his first bite. What little meat they got from the lizard was very nasty, as in Nasty with a capital "N." Neither of them could manage more than that first bite.

Finally getting his wish to live like a hunter-gatherer, Lenny did not seem very happy about it even though there was no one around complaining about his unwashed body—maybe because there was no one around to complain.

Fortunately, there had been no sign of the giant snake, though they figured it was somewhere in the valley with them. Most of the animals they saw around the mansion looked normal in every way, including size—normal-sized lizards, bugs, birds, and ground squirrels.

Most of the animals, but not all.

On the third day, Cal and Lenny were making another circuit around the mansion, searching for a way inside. Turning a corner, they came eye to eye with an immense, Harvey-sized jackrabbit. Literally, they were eye-level with its huge jackrabbit eyes. The top of its head was over six feet high, and its ears stretched another three feet heavenward. Smelly and mangy, with patches of missing fur, it didn't look too healthy.

All three were startled. Cal and Lenny froze, not sure what to do. After a long second and a half, the rabbit turned and bounded away like a gargantuan kangaroo.

"Wow, man, that was, like, one big bunny," Lenny said with a nervous laugh. "Good thing he wasn't the kind that bites."

"All bunnies bite," Cal said. "We better be more careful."

Cal was mad at himself for not remembering that oversized animals might be wandering about, and also for missing the chance to eat jackrabbit for dinner. That rabbit represented a lot of fresh meat, and Cal did, after all, have a .357 Magnum.

That day, Cal came to a critical decision. There was no Swift Creek secret organization here, nor any prison to be thrown into. Cal decided to break the agreement he had signed forbidding him to disclose anything about the green rat. He told Lenny everything.

Lenny stared, listening to every word Cal spoke. Occasionally, he interjected with a, "Wow, dude, that . . .", or "Dude, what about . . . "

Cal had a rapt audience. At times, Lenny's face would grow distant. Cal had a funny feeling Lenny was chalking up what Cal said against an internal checklist of some sort. What checklist that could be, Cal had no idea. But it was nice to finally have someone working with him who knew as much as he did about the Searles Mansion and the hideous green rat.

Wherever that giant green rat came from, there had to be other giant green rats just like it. If the green rat came from this world, the valley could be overrun with giant rats in certain seasons. Anyway, it was a possibility.

As the sun began to set, Cal and Lenny built a fire in front of the mansion, hoping to cheer themselves up. Going into their third night alone in the desert, they found themselves out of food and low on water. If they drove out to Great Falls again, they would have to walk back to the mansion. Their chances of survival looked grim. Hunched around the fire, they quietly contemplated their predicament.

Suddenly, Lenny looked up at Cal, the firelight reflected in his bright eyes. He thoughtfully rubbed the blond stubble on his chin with a nervous hand.

"Dude, I think I know what is going on and maybe how to get back to where we belong."

XII

"You can't leave me behind! I want to get out of here, too."

Martha's eyes welled with tears. Camm took her hand and squeezed it tightly, while bringing a finger to her lips, reminding her to talk quietly.

"I would take you if I could," Camm said softly, "but you are just not well enough. You still need to be under a doctor's care. Concussions are dangerous."

Camm was seated on the edge of Martha's bed, one leg dangling over the side.

Martha looked worried. "This place is like a prison. How long will they keep me here?"

Camm studied Martha with a critical eye and decided she looked pretty beat up as she lay there in bed. All the bandages, elastic braces, and other paraphernalia the doctor had insisted upon only added to the effect. "What do you remember about the accident?"

"I remember everything, the spiders, the snake, being chased. I remember that good-looking agent all puffy and swollen, and then dying. I remember it all."

Camm glanced toward the closed door. "I'll tell you how to get out of here. They will be up here soon to interview you now that the doctor says you're doing better. With the concussion, you can say you don't remember anything. Tell them the last thing you remember is driving into Valley Wells with Cal and me. Tell them you don't remember anything after that, until you woke up here. Trust me, they'll take one look at you and believe everything you say."

Martha chewed her bottom lip, her eyes fixed on the door.

Camm gave her hand a reassuring squeeze. "Listen. If you don't know the secrets they are trying to hide, I'm sure they will let you go home, maybe even to your summer internship. But wherever you go, don't tell anyone what you know about Trona. Believe me, those federal agents will find out if you do. They won't like it, and they will come after you.

"So, say you don't remember anything. And be sure to act all baffled by why the guys left you behind. I'm sure they'll cook up some story that explains everything. Just go along with whatever they say and keep insisting you don't remember anything. Okay?"

Martha nodded. "Okay. But where are you going? How are you getting out of the mansion? There are guards everywhere."

"If you don't know, you don't have to worry about telling them."

Martha sighed in agreement. "I wish I were half as brave as you."

Camm waved it off, still feeling ashamed for even bringing Martha to Trona. She wouldn't put her in danger again, and that meant not taking Martha with her into the passageway.

Camm had hoped to find matches to light one of the candles she had discovered so she would have light as she explored the secret passages. No such luck. Cal always had matches in his backpack in the car, but that did her no good now. However, a preliminary search of the passageways had shown that the large mirror in each room was actually a two-way mirror that allowed light into the passageway. As long as there was some light in the rooms she passed, whether natural or artificial, there was light in the secret passage.

The two-way mirrors not only allowed her to see into the rooms without being seen, but let her hear what was being said. Once, while exploring the secret passageways, she came upon the two white-haired men playing pool in a room at the far end of the second floor.

"Things are getting out of hand," the tall white-haired man said. "Those giant spiders have been seen in Trona by too many residents. The rumors are causing quite a ruckus. People are keeping their kids indoors, and many are carrying loaded firearms in their trucks and cars. The town is starting to look like a private militia."

"Bah! There are always rumors," the short man said as he studied his next shot. "It's good they keep the kids off the streets. Makes it easier for us."

"But what about those reports that giant spiders are crossing over the Slate Range and building nests high up in the Panamint Mountains? We may have to do something about that before we start losing tourists."

"Those are little concerns. The snake is our big problem now. With each appearance, it is getting closer to town and becoming more aggressive." The short man popped the number five ball neatly into the side pocket.

"If only we had some way to control when or where the snake appeared." The tall man shrugged. "But we don't. So unless we want to answer to irate parents about more missing children, we have to do something."

For the next hour, Camm eavesdropped as the two white-haired men discussed their options. In the end, the decision was made to evacuate the whole town, from Pioneer Point on the north to West End on the south. The plant would remain operational, and the workers would be bused in from Ridgecrest every day to work. A federal agency would assume responsibility for helping Trona residents find temporary housing in Ridgecrest.

"The costs and logistics of this evacuation are going to be tremendous. Thank goodness we have all those empty barracks on the Navy Base. That will take up some of the slack and make the whole process go faster." The short man picked up his cue stick to resume the pool game. "For now, it seems to be the only way to prevent further loss of life."

"What about the complaints that pets and small livestock are being stolen? Some blame the spiders, but we've had lots of reports of residents seeing two small, half-naked men running off with pet cats and dogs. Later, the remains are found, not far outside of town. Apparently, the animals are cooked over a campfire and eaten. That doesn't sound like spiders. The gnawed bones are just tossed into the campfire with no effort made to hide the crime."

The two men looked at each other, nodding.

"Certainly seems to corroborate Bob's story," the short man said, taking another shot.

What story that was, they didn't say. From their conversation, Camm recognized they were talking about Bob and his friends, Sean and Jim. The men seemed happy the rumor around town was that Sean and Jim had been flown out of Trona to parts unknown. They never said anything about Dave, but Cal had already told her he was missing, too.

Camm never heard what had happened to Bob, but in her travels through the passageways, she did discover Sean and Jim locked up together in a second-floor suite on the other side of the great hall. They appeared to be bored out of their minds. Nobody seemed to know what to do with them. Camm decided she could be of no help to Sean and Jim. She had enough problems of her own. She couldn't even help Martha.

The feeling Camm had had when inspecting the carved rat's head, the feeling that something was reaching out to her, became stronger when she was in the secret passageways. It was like feeling a breeze, except there was no breeze; like dampness, except there was no moisture; like coldness, except the temperature had not dropped. It felt like frigid, invisible fingers reaching out to touch her, feel her, and reach right through her.

Every time the feeling came, she smelled the strong, sulfur smell that emanated from the monster rat. Camm believed, desperately hoped, the rat was dead, so she did not know what to think of these new sensations.

Feeling anxious, like she was somehow running out of time, Camm decided to leave at dusk. There would be a little light in the passageways from the lighted rooms, and then very quickly, it would turn dark outside, so she could sneak away unseen by the exterior guards.

Though Camm had explored all of the passages on the higher levels, she had been reluctant to go down too deep and had not yet found a way out of the mansion. She felt confident, though, that the passages led to at least one outside exit. She knew the green rat had used a secret way to get in and out of the mansion unseen during all those years when everyone thought the mansion was locked up tight.

Camm did not say good-bye to Martha. For Martha's safety, she needed to be ignorant of when or how Camm left the mansion. Taking a deep breath, Camm gently pushed the rat's tongue to enter the passageway and search for the secret way out of the mansion. If she found it, she wasn't coming back.

As she made her way down dark, narrow stairs toward the quickly fading light in a passage below, the strange feeling came again, stronger than ever. Icy fingers wrapped around her heart, momentarily taking her breath away. Fighting panic, she recognized the feeling.

But that can't be, it's dead. I killed it. We watched it die.

Suddenly, the truth sank in, and horror paralyzed her with fear. *The green rat is alive!*

Lenny held up a spiral notebook that he had pulled out of the Camaro's trunk. "Do you see all these sheets of paper in the notebook? How they are all aligned with each other and parallel to each other?"

"Sure," Cal responded cautiously. He didn't know where Lenny was going with this. He knew Lenny was smart, but sometimes Lenny's explanations and reasonings left the realms of reality and entered into a wild, unsettled corner of the Twilight Zone.

"Well, assume that each piece of paper is a two-dimensional plane. Since each one has no depth, only length and width, they are not touching each other. Each dimension is its own

separate space, an independent plane of existence, unconnected with any of the other dimensions in the notebook.
Can you imagine that?"

"I think so." Cal nodded.

"Good. I'm simplifying, but in our three-dimensional universe, you can have literally an infinite number of parallel
two-dimensional planes, stacked up on top of each other. None
of them will actually be touching or intersecting with any of
the others. Someone in one of these planes of existence would
have no way of meeting or knowing about someone in any of
the other parallel planes. You still with me?"

"Uh, yeah. Of course. Standing in one two-dimensional
plane, there is no way to ever know anything about any of
the other parallel planes."

"So far, so good. Now, no one can actually visualize what
four-dimensional space would look like, but we can extrapolate
from the example of two-dimensional planes lined up within a
three-dimensional space. In a similar way, it should be possible
for unconnected three-dimensional planes to line up within a
four-dimensional space.

"In other words, a four-dimensional universe could hold
an infinite number of independent parallel three-dimensional
planes that do not touch."

Cal scowled. "I thought Einstein said the fourth dimension
was movement through time."

"Well, he did, kind of. But most of the string theories in
theoretical physics hold out the possibility of more than three

dimensions of space, actual additional dimensions in space, not just movement through time. In fact, there may be many more than just four dimensions, but four dimensions will work for what I'm trying to explain here." Lenny raised his eyebrows. "Okay?"

Cal shrugged and reached for another stick to put on the fire. "Okay. Go on."

"Remember the notebook." It was a directive, not a question. "You can have an infinite number of unconnected two-dimensional planes of existence in a space with just one extra dimension. Likewise, I'm saying you can have an infinite number of unconnected three-dimensional planes of existence, all parallel to each other, contained within a space with one extra dimension, which is what I'm calling four-dimensional space."

Cal scowled again. "I can't picture it in my mind. I can't picture all these three-dimensional planes all stacked on top of each other like the paper in your notebook."

"Neither can I. No one can. Our brains are programmed for three-dimensional space and that is what we picture in our heads. But, just assume that what happens between two and three dimensions also happens between three and four dimensions."

"Sooooo." Cal closed his eyes as he tried to put it together. "We have a four-dimensional notebook with three-dimensional pages all stacked on top of each other with none of the pages touching, and there is no way to get from one three-dimensional page to the next."

"Yes, yes, you got it! But what has happened in our case is that for some reason, two or more of those pages in the notebook have started touching. They touch at Searles Valley."

"Like parallel universes coming into contact?"

"No!" Lenny shook his head vehemently. "We are not talking about the multiverse. We are not talking about wormholes or alternate universes. Nothing like that.

"We're talking about just one universe, our universe, but it has more than three spatial dimensions in it. That allows for many, maybe an infinite number of three-dimensional realities all lined up parallel to each other in the same universe, none of them intersecting the others."

"But you're saying that at least one of the other dimensional realities has been touching or intersecting with ours here in Searles Valley. Right?"

Lenny sighed. "Right!"

Cal sighed, too. "But if the other world is that close to us, like paper in a notebook, shouldn't we see light from it shining into our world? Shouldn't we feel its gravity?"

As Cal waited for Lenny to answer these questions, it occurred to him that Lenny had been talking for several minutes and had not used the word "dude" once.

"Okay, that worried me, too, at first. Let's talk about gravity."

It *is still alive!*

She and Cal had killed it, or thought they had killed it. But Camm now knew, without a doubt, the green rat was still alive, reaching out to her, touching her.

Those men, how she despised them. Those men at Swift Creek had saved it, had somehow brought it back. Camm could feel it was still alive.

With a start, she realized it was still in the mansion. And it knew she was there, too. She recognized the feelings emanating from the rat. She had felt those same feelings when it came to her home in Pioneer Point, turning off the lights so it could kill her. She could sense it was again reaching out for her, still trying to kill her.

She shook her head violently, trying to keep it from taking hold of her mind. Icy tendrils snaked into her thoughts, trying to contact her, trying to communicate. All at once, she understood its message. It spoke to her not through words, but through cold, desperate feelings.

Know you, it said. *You came back. You not hurt me more.*

She fought the panic. The rat's thoughts burned like acid in her mind. It knew Camm and was connecting with her mind. It knew she was on its home ground.

Camm pushed at the air with her hands, as if she could push it away, push it out of her head. She hurried down the passageway, desperate to find the way out. Now that she knew it was still in the mansion, she had to get out more than ever.

The strong sulfur odor chased her down a hard stone tunnel. This was new. The walls of the secret passageways through the mansion were all hard wood panels. Now, the wood paneling had given way to stone walls.

In the dim light, she saw she had come to a set of stone steps leading downward. Again, this was new. These stairs reminded her of the stone steps leading down to the small stone room where she and Cal had first seen the painting of the green rat. But this stairway didn't spiral down. It plummeted downward at a straight, steep incline. She began to run. These stone steps seemed to be leaving the mansion, and she had to get away before that thing could come for her.

As the passageway got darker, she slowed to feel her way. Suddenly, the essence of the rat seemed to wash through her like a frozen wave, immersing her.

Know you. You made me hurt. Remember you.

The rat seemed to be following her. The sense of it was stronger now—its anger at the memory of what she did to it was palpable. In her mind, Camm saw herself from the rat's perspective, holding the little pistol and shooting it between the eyes. She saw the anger and intensity in her own face and could hear herself yelling at the rat. But the sounds she made were just noise and didn't mean anything. For a fraction of a second, she felt its intense pain.

Gasping for breath, Camm reached level ground again. The passageway forked out in two directions. When she faced one direction, the hate struck her like a freezing wind. She sensed the creature was down that passage, hating her, waiting for her.

She turned and hurried down the other passage, heading away from the source of the hate. She had to find a way out, a way that did not lead her back to the rat. Its thoughts followed her down the stone passage, pursuing her in the dimness.

You not hurt me more. Hurt you.

Its thoughts lashed out at her.

Kill you.

At the far end of the passageway, Camm found another stairway. She did not sense the rat down these stairs, so she hurtled down them. But the rat's feelings followed her down into the darkness. Not the physical rat, but its thoughts, its evil intents, scurried after her as she descended. Though they didn't speak the same language, Camm knew what it was thinking.

She reached the bottom of the stairs. The light was fading faster than she had expected. The sun was setting. Here, there were no more mirrors, but the walls glowed with their own iridescent sheen. It was almost pitch black. She had to slow down and feel her way.

Know you. Know you here. Know where you are.

Like rocks hurled at her, its feelings and emotions hit her mind.

Find you. Hurt you. Kill you. Eat you.

A vision came into her mind crystal clear. She was looking through the rat's eyes at her bloodied body lying mangled on a stone floor. Her eyes were wide open in terror. The monstrous rat was tearing at her flesh, devouring her while her blood ran hot. She shuddered. That thing was imagining what it would be like to eat her while she was still alive.

She could hear herself screaming in terror. Her muscles were ripped from her body. The taste of her own flesh was acrid and warm in her mouth as the rat shared its fantasy with her. Again and again, its dripping maw went at her, separating tissue from bone, dismembering her, devouring her. It ate her with relish and abandon, savoring each bite.

The image was so real that Camm, by reflex, pressed her hands to her body, protecting herself. She could tell the rat was not only pleased with its fantasy, but also by the horror the vision caused in Camm. The images became vivid, filling her whole mind. She heard her own screams losing intensity as she died. She was dying!

Camm collapsed to the floor of the passage. The sudden fall and cold stone against her skin broke the hold the rat had on her mind. She wasn't dead. As she sat up, the rat reached into her mind again, seeking to regain control.

"I am stronger than you!" she shouted.

Taking a deep, calming breath, she pushed the rat's thoughts away and stood, running her hand up the wall, not only to steady her balance, but also to keep her focus on reality. The rat kept saying, *Eat you! Eat you!* But its voice was losing strength. She was stronger!

She had to get away. She had to find her way out.

It was completely dark now, except for the iridescent sheen

of the rocks. She felt her way along the wall. The passageway had become narrow and seemed to go on and on. As fast as she could in the dark, she hurried down a roughhewn tunnel until she came to a dead end.

Desperately, she ran her hands over the stony surfaces in front of her and to each side.

No, no, she thought. *This has to lead somewhere. Where is the way out?*

She cowered against the wall that now blocked her escape, her eyes wide open in the blackness. Her heart pounded. She felt faint.

Camm closed her eyes, forcing herself to breathe slowly to keep from hyperventilating. With all her mental energy, she calmed her mind and again forced the rat out of her head, willing her heart to slow. She took a deep breath. She could do this. She could find her way out.

The passage ended at a rough stone wall. The way out had to be there. She felt up and down the wall with her fingers, touching and pushing each individual stone. As she searched, the rat was still there, its thoughts pushing at her, trying to get in, but she forced herself to focus.

Suddenly, there was a stone that felt different. It stuck out a little from the rest. Camm felt around it. The mortar was missing between this stone and those that surrounded it. She pushed on it, but it didn't budge. She pushed harder. Still no movement.

Camm spread her feet apart and braced herself. Leaning into the stone, she pushed with all her weight and might. It budged a fraction of an inch, and then a whole inch.

As it moved, so did the wall. A slight filament of moonlight sliced into the den. She could smell the dry desert air. Wedging her shoulder against the wall, she heaved against it for all she was worth. Slowly, silently, it slid open. Camm stepped out into the narrow canyon of a deep dry wash just as the last of the twilight disappeared behind the western mountains.

The rat made one last mental claw at her mind. *Find you. Kill you. Eat you.*

Camm pushed the stone door shut and ran through the night, running from the mansion, running from the rat. Running until its thoughts could no longer reach her.

Camm knew where she was going. The old men had said the evacuation would be from Pioneer Point on the north to the south end of the valley. She would have to go farther north, past Pioneer Point, past her old home and her old neighborhood, where she and Cal had lived and grown up as children. By foot, it would take her most of the night to get there. It was a long way to Homewood Canyon.

"Now then, gravity is a tricky thing." Lenny shifted to sit cross-legged in front of the fire. "We can measure gravity. We can predict what it will do, but we don't know why or how it works. Why do massive objects attract each other? Perhaps mass warps the space around it, like Einstein said. We have no idea. Are there 'gravitons' or 'gravity waves?' No one knows.

"Since we don't know what gravity is, we can't predict whether it will be felt from one plane to another even when both planes are in the same four-dimensional space. Maybe gravity is an independent phenomenon of each separate plane, even when touching. We don't know."

Cal brushed his hair back. "Okay, we don't know about gravity, but what about light?"

Lenny grinned. "Just before the spiders came through, I noticed a wavering-like visual abnormality. Did you see it, too?"

Cal nodded. "I did, like looking through heat waves rising from the ground."

Lenny leaned forward. "Also, I felt sick to my stomach at the same time."

"Yeah, me too. And, Martha threw up."

"I think the wavering images we saw were the result of light-wave interference patterns caused by light from two different dimensional planes crossing through each other. And the nausea we felt was a result of gravity-wave interference patterns caused by gravity from different dimensions tugging on us at the same time."

Cal considered all this. "So, why are the three-dimensional planes touching now and what do we do about it? I mean, I grew up my whole life in Trona. I have never had that sensation before, never saw giant spiders or giant snakes before. What's different now?"

"From what you have told me, the answer to your questions is right over there." Lenny tossed his head in the direction of the mansion. "There are two mansions, right?"

"Right. One here in this world and one back in Trona."

"Okay, when you were battling the giant green rat, and even before that, the intersection of the different dimensions always occurred at the mansions. That's why there are two of them, one in each world, somehow linked and somehow controlling the link."

The light came on in Cal's brain. "So that is why the first Mr. Samuels built the mansions? So he could travel between dimensions?"

"Exactly. The mansions are the door, the passageway between our three-dimensional plane, where Trona is, and this three-dimensional plane here, where Trona isn't."

"So, what happened? Why are the worlds intersecting at other locations now?"

"I don't know. My guess is those guys from the federal government, you know, uh . . ."

"Swift Creek."

"Yeah, from Swift Creek, must have turned the mansion off, so to speak, when they found out you guys had killed that big green rat."

"Yeah, what about that? Why the rat anyway?"

"Again, I'm just guessing, but snakes don't like rats, except to eat. Maybe this rat was kept at the mansion to keep the snake from coming through the passage to our world. Now that the mansion is turned off and the rat is dead, the worlds can intersect willy-nilly at other locations, and the snake can come through wherever it wants."

Cal tossed more wood into the fire as he considered everything Lenny had said. "Well, explain this: why does the intersection seem to occur wherever the snake is?"

"I don't know. I'm still working on that, but I don't think the snake controls the intersection. I bet the snake can sense a developing cross over between dimensions and is attracted to that location, wherever it might be."

Cal stopped poking the fire and turned to look directly at Lenny. "Well, if they turned the mansion off, can we turn it back on, so we can get back to Trona?"

"I think so."

"But it's just an old mansion. I mean, it didn't even have electricity or anything. I don't think I saw an on-off switch."

Lenny's eyes brightened. "Oh, I think you did."

Cal pondered the point, then his eyes widened as the realization hit him. He pointed at Lenny, exclaiming, "The grandfather clock!"

Lenny nodded his head. "That, my good man, is the ticket for our ride home!"

XIII

At first, it was just a steady breeze, blowing in Camm's face, keeping her cool. The moving air felt refreshingly clean after escaping from her terrifying encounter with the rat's telepathic threats. The perspiration soaking her shirt was quickly drying out.

As she jogged through the night, the breeze intensified into a gusting hot wind, and then magnified into a steady, howling gale. Camm hated to admit it to herself, but she now faced a stiff northeastern desert wind, a direct headwind, pushing against her, slowing her down as she made her way toward Homewood Canyon.

Trona was a long, thin town, and one could never stray very far to the east or west from Trona Road, the main north-south artery. Nevertheless, Camm tried to stay on the west edge of town, hoping to avoid most of the traffic. By the time she reached the high school, the wind had whipped up into a full-scale desert sandstorm.

Camm was very familiar with these winds, and stayed out of them whenever she could. They usually came in the fall or spring and could be very fierce, sometimes lasting for days. The school in Trona never had to worry about snow days or extremely cold weather. But accommodations had to be made for the howling desert winds, when they came. Children would be hustled directly from the buses to their classrooms. Recess, P.E., and lunchtime would all be altered to keep everyone out of the gale-force winds.

The problem wasn't just the force of the wind, which was considerable, but also the sand carried by the winds. Sometimes, these winds blew enough sand to cover the whole town with inches of new sand. The high drifts that built up against walls and around corners took weeks to clean up.

Camm felt like she was standing in front of a commercial-grade sandblaster. The sand stung her arms and legs like hundreds of pointy needles. The wind blew sand into her face and eyes, up her nose and into her mouth. Camm's only defense was to cover her face with her shirt and turn her back to the relentless stabbing pain.

Since the direction she wanted to go was directly into the oncoming gale, it made her progress extraordinarily difficult. She couldn't face directly into the wind when it was at its worst, and she couldn't jog backward all the way to Homewood Canyon either. Her progress slowed almost to a standstill.

To make matters worse, Camm was now convinced her

escape had been discovered. As she hid in the dark corners of deserted buildings and houses, more to get out of the wind than anything else, she saw black SUVs patrolling the streets along with Sheriff vehicles. Once, she thought she recognized Agent Allen riding in one of the SUVs. At least the wind and blowing sand helped conceal her, but it also made progress excruciatingly slow.

When she reached the north end of the high school campus, near the football field, she found shelter from the wind, where she could see down to the old tennis courts and past them to the traffic on Trona Road. Because of the wind storm, traffic was light and seemed to be mostly government vehicles, probably out looking for her. She knew the hard-blowing sand was not doing the paint on their cars any good. The searchers were probably cursing her right now.

Looking at the football field, Camm smiled, remembering Cal playing on that field. Cal had a talent for football, and the other teams had had a hard time stopping him, especially on Trona's home field. Like the rest of Trona, the field had no grass, only hard-packed sand and gravel. Other schools hated the Trona football field, which gave the Trona Tornados a real hometown advantage. The passing sand storm, like so many before, would do no harm to the field. It would only add another layer of sand to Trona's field and strengthen its advantage.

Glancing back at Trona Road, Camm decided that wind or no wind, she could not afford to stay in town with so many searchers on the roads. To avoid detection, she would need to head west to the foothills on the edge of town. Of course, from where she was, that would take her directly through the Trona graveyard.

Agent Allen glanced to her left. The Swift Creek agent driving the SUV clearly was not happy to have her along. He had been guarding the mansion with Agent Roberts a few days earlier when she had served court papers on them. All she knew about him was that he went by J.R. From his attitude toward her, she was sure he held her responsible for Roberts's death.

They crept through the streets of Trona in the black vehicle, squinting through the blowing dust and sand for any sign of the renegade young woman who had escaped the mansion. Occasionally, J.R. would shine a bright spotlight into unlit corners, searching for her. So far, they'd had no luck. Instead of conferring with Agent Allen, pooling their knowledge about the young woman, J.R. constantly cursed under his breath.

Agent Allen volunteered, "I don't think we are going to have much luck in this windstorm. Have you ever seen anything like it? Besides, she must have dozens of friends all over town where she can seek refuge."

The Swift Creek man continued to stare straight ahead, not even glancing her way. His aspect was overly formal and severe. "Our instructions are to find her and bring her back to the mansion. You *can* follow instructions, can't you?" He placed heavy emphasis on "can."

Agent Allen scowled. "I know what our instructions are. You don't have to be a putz."

"I don't have to be, but . . ." He smiled slightly, and didn't finish the sentence. The implication was obvious.

Agent Allen gritted her teeth and decided against the two-word reply that first came to mind. She had no idea how long she would have to work with these Swift Creek guys, but she didn't want to make that time any more miserable than it already was.

She had learned a few things about this secretive agency during the last few days. For one, it wasn't exactly the model of affirmative action. Every employee and agent, as far as she had been able to see, was male.

To be fair, they weren't all white. There was one African American agent who stood about six foot eight and had biceps like oak tree trunks and a chest like a locomotive engine. But they were all men, and seemed to be especially adept at producing testosterone.

Agent Allen decided to try for peace. "Look J.R., I'm sorry about Roberts, but it wasn't my fault. After all, he was killed by that giant rattlesnake."

He gave her a look that bordered between incredulous and mocking. "A giant snake?"

Agent Allen wondered if she had said something she shouldn't have. "You don't know about the giant snake?"

He snorted in derision and rolled his eyes.

"Do you know about the giant spiders?"

He rolled his eyes again.

She continued, "Do you know about the giant green rat?"

He barked out a scornful laugh, but continued to stare straight ahead as they drove along a road bordering the back of the high school.

Agent Allen wasn't intimidated, but she was annoyed. She turned her head to look out the front, too. "Well, J.R., someone doesn't think enough of you to keep you in the loop."

He slammed on the brakes, stopping the SUV in the middle of the road. He turned to look at her, a scowl etched across his face. "What does that mean?"

"How do you think Roberts died?" In a situation of high animosity, Agent Allen always answered a question with a question, pressing the onus back on the other person.

"We all know how he died. You were chasing those brats across the desert in your car when you rolled it, killing Rick."

Agent Allen gritted her teeth. *So that's the story they're putting out there.*

She forcibly relaxed her posture and face. She would not let him know he had agitated her. "Obviously, you do not have the clearance necessary to be brought into what is really going on here. It's not my job to bring you up to date. Please, drive on."

J.R. made no effort to hide his agitation. "Like we need the FBI here getting in the way. You can't even drive your car without causing an accident and killing another agent. Why don't you go back to L.A. and let competent agents handle this matter?"

Now, it was Agent Allen's turn to snort in derision. "You have no idea what is actually going on here. You don't even know what this 'matter' is all about."

Truthfully, Agent Allen would have been glad to leave this all behind and go back to Los Angeles to do normal FBI work. But after making her last report about the snake and the death of Roberts, she had been instructed to stay in Trona, assigned as part of the Swift Creek task force. She suspected the assignment had been made not because she was needed, but because she knew too much, and Swift Creek wanted to keep an eye on her.

She added, "Just keep driving."

J.R. sneered at her. "I don't take orders from the FBI." Nevertheless, he drove to the north edge of town and turned the SUV west, toward the foothills.

Agent Allen muttered under her breath, but loud enough to be heard, "Putz."

As Camm jogged by the small Trona graveyard, she thought about the time she had driven her VW out on this road to pick up Cal. It had only been a year or so ago, but it seemed like ages. Cal had been made up to look like some kind of zombie and had scared a number of the football players' girlfriends.

Camm had thought the joke so juvenile at the time. Now, she recalled seeing glowing red eyes in the bushes near where she found Cal and also smelling an overwhelming sulfur odor at the same time. The same thing had happened the night Hughie disappeared. She shuddered to think she might have had close encounters with the green rat without even realizing it.

The thought of Cal and his zombie face and goofy smile made her sad. She missed him.

The graveyard, *per se*, did not bother her. She had seen a lot of scary things in the last year—a monstrous green rat, an enormous man-eating snake, and a hoard of giant swarming spiders. But those things were all real. She didn't believe in ghosts, vampires, or zombies. Ghosts and zombies were just silly, and vampires were, well, for silly girls who wanted to be scared.

Camm still found the going difficult in the desert gale, but now that she was heading west to the foothills, she could turn her head to the left when the sand blew and keep jogging. The wind was now pushing her along at a faster pace.

As she neared the hills, she suddenly noticed her shadow jogging directly in front of her. She turned to look behind her and caught a face full of sand from a particularly mean gust of wind. Spitting out the sand, she shielded her face with her hand and saw two bright headlights several hundred yards behind her. At that very moment, a spotlight on the driver's side of the vehicle lit up and fixed a cold, white beam of light on her.

Camm sprinted up the dirt road at her top speed, gaining altitude on the hill before leaving the road and running across some open desert to the foothills below the Trona "T." Then she started up the hillside, going north through the bushes and rocks. The brilliant spotlight beam tried to follow her, but she was running erratically from side to side, trying to lose it. She reached a large group of boulders and scrambled among them, hiding from the light.

Once she had lost the spotlight, she continued to scramble uphill, staying behind rocks and bushes that would block the line of sight from the vehicle to her. In spite of the wind, she now traveled directly north, putting distance between herself and the road she had been running on. She was climbing through rough country, very steep and rocky. There was no way they could follow her in a car.

Glancing over her shoulder, Camm saw the vehicle was one of the big black SUVs. The spotlight crisscrossed the face of the hill below her, searching. The light slowly moved up the hillside. They would eventually spot her again. She had to find a place to hide.

Agent Allen jumped out of the SUV before it came to a complete stop. They had lost Camm among the rocks in the foothills to the north. In spite of herself, Agent Allen felt a little proud of Camm. By moving off the road and upwind, Camm had forced them to stare directly into the blowing sand and dust, which made finding her in the dark very difficult.

J.R. shined the spotlight across the area where they had last seen their fugitive in a fruitless effort to catch sight of her again. He shouted at Agent Allen, trying to be heard above the howling wind. "I'm calling for backup. I'm going to have them bring dogs to track her."

Agent Allen walked over to where J.R. stood so they could hear each other. She glared at him in exasperation. "Dogs won't accomplish a thing in this sandstorm. Don't waste your time. Call in the other vehicles and have them park at the bottom of the hill, shining their headlights and spotlights up in the area where we last saw her. I'll bet she is hiding somewhere up there in the rocks or behind a bush."

Agent Allen shielded her face from the blowing sand and pointed up to where Camm had last been seen. Squinting at the terrain, she noted countless places where Camm could be hiding.

J.R.'s expression hardened as if he were going to refuse, but then his shoulders jerked, and he stalked back to the SUV. He radioed for the other SUVs and sheriffs' cars to join them, parking according to Agent Allen's plan.

She smiled. Her instructions made too much sense for him to ignore.

A part of Agent Allen was rooting for Camm to get away. She admired Camm's courage, her intelligence, and her sheer hutzpah. She had little respect for the Swift Creek agents. The agents at the mansion had been in total disarray when Camm was discovered missing. It should have been impossible for her to sneak out. Nobody could explain it.

But Agent Allen also understood how dangerous the situation had become. Her affection for Camm, and her best judgment, told her the safest place for the teenager was with them, not running around in a desert where evidently anything could and did happen.

The other vehicles started to show up and J.R. tried to give them instructions about where to park and where to shine their lights. There seemed to be quite a bit of confusion at the bottom of the hill as if no one knew what to do.

Agent Allen strode over to J.R. Gently, but firmly, she took the radio mike out of his hand and began giving instructions. The confusion quickly changed to action as the vehicles lined up, saturating the hillside with electric light. J.R.'s mouth worked silently for a moment, but instead of saying anything, he simply turned his back on her and walked away.

Agent Allen had no sympathy for him. He shouldn't have been such a putz.

It was obvious what they were doing. They were painting the entire hillside with light from their headlights and spotlights. A chill ran down Camm's back in spite of the ferocious, hot desert wind attacking her. Soon there would be agents crawling all over the hillside, tracking her down. She couldn't move to another location without crossing one of those beams of light. Once they caught sight of her again, it would all be over. They would easily run her down.

The chill hit her back again, and Camm shivered. She was crouching amongst a number of very large boulders that were part of a bigger jumble of car-size rocks. Though safely hidden in the deepest shadows for now, someone need only walk by her position and shine a flashlight down into her hiding place to discover her. She wanted to sprint farther up the hill, but knew she would be seen. She didn't think she could out run them all.

The cold hit her in the back again and, with irritation, she looked behind her. *What is that back there? Where is that cold air coming from?*

She reached back into the inky darkness and felt a cool breeze lightly streaming up from behind the largest boulder in her hiding place. She had missed the gentle breeze earlier because it could hardly compete with the fierce, hot desert wind that had been buffeting her. But now it was unmistakable. Camm was feeling the draft from a hidden mine shaft, apparently a deep one.

In this part of the Mojave Desert, there were hundreds of old gold mines that had been dug and abandoned more than a century earlier. Camm knew that the temperature never changed in the deeper mines. It was always an average of the hottest days of summer and coldest days of winter. It could be a hundred and ten degrees outside, but an old gold mine would maintain a temperature of around sixty-five degrees year around.

This one had a slight breeze blowing out of it, which meant it must be quite deep or long, or both. Hundreds of these mines had been discovered and sealed over the years, but there were hundreds more that had not yet been officially rediscovered.

During their high school years, she and Cal had discovered and explored many of these old mines. She couldn't help thinking how excited Cal would be to know she had discovered another one so close to town. For Camm's sake, it was just in the nick of time.

Climbing deeper into the pile of huge rocks, she found a small vertical opening that was just big enough for her to squeeze down through. Probably partially collapsed with time, the opening had been invisible until she was right on top of it. Once inside, she slid down a small pile of rubble to where the tunnel opened up enough for her to stand, though the top of her head brushed the ceiling. The air inside was stale, smelling dusty with a tinge of musky.

Camm had found the perfect hiding place. Even if someone directed a light into the rock pile, it might cut across the mouth of the mine, but would not shine directly down into the mine where she was standing. They would never find her. She could now wait out her pursuers.

She stood below the opening, with her back against a slab of rock, facing into the mine. She knew enough not to go exploring without a flashlight. Who knew how far the tunnel went or if there were vertical shafts? For now, she was safe where she was and had no need to move.

Looking up diagonally through the opening above her, she saw lights darting across the dark night sky from both directions. Her pursuers were still hunting her. Directly in front of her, she could see nothing. The mine was pitch black.

Wondering which direction the mine went, she stretched

her hand out in front of her as far as she could reach. She felt nothing. Swinging her hand to the side, trying to feel the mine wall, her hand touched something that wasn't rock or dirt. It felt like a heavy cloth, maybe wool.

As Camm patted it with her fingers, she thought she could feel buttons. Underneath the material was something dry and dusty. As she raised her fingers, sliding along the object, she felt a leather-like substance, and then an opening with hard pointed objects much like teeth.

At that moment, a light from outside cut across the opening of the mine. While it did not shine directly into the opening, it did, ever so slightly, illuminate the object Camm was touching.

A zombie! was her first thought.

She snatched away her fingers, which had been inside the gaping mouth. The desiccated corpse was standing only inches away from her. Its vacant eye holes stared straight through her. More to reassure herself than anything else, she whispered, "You're not a zombie!"

It wasn't a zombie. It was a body, long dead, but preserved in the dry desert air. The corpse stood near the mouth of the mine, as if keeping guard. The desert air over the years had completely mummified it. By the way it looked, it had been there for many decades.

Only inches away, Camm saw it clearly in the searchers' light. A few pathetic strands of red hair hung off the top of its head. The skin was stretched tight across the skull. It had an open mouth, no nose, and black, empty eye sockets. Wearing an old flannel shirt, its leathery hands with long yellow nails extended beyond the sleeves. A rusty iron spike through the middle of its chest appeared to be holding the body up straight against the wall.

How did this man come to be here? Why has no one ever found him?

As quickly as the light appeared, it disappeared, moving farther up the hillside. Camm was again in total darkness, except now she knew she was standing inches away from a mummified corpse. She had been touching it. As much as she wanted to, she dared not move, for fear of being discovered by the searchers clambering by her rock pile.

She wanted to scream. She wanted to squirm out of the mine and run away. Her skin now itched as if little bugs were crawling all over her. She had an almost overpowering urge to take an extremely hot shower, to wash the corruption from this corpse off her body, but she could do nothing, except stand perfectly still and try not to hyperventilate.

With the wind still howling outside, it was difficult for her to hear what was happening out there. Occasionally, she caught a snippet of a voice, someone shouting instructions or calling a name. Looking diagonally, she saw blades of light, from large flashlights, slicing through the sky. They were still searching for her. She dared not move forward for fear of bumping into the dead body or move back up into the mouth of the mine for fear of being seen.

At least, she comforted herself, it wasn't a zombie, or it would have sucked her brains out by now. Her sick sense of humor almost made her smile. Almost. It took ages for the searchers to move away. Her legs ached and her knees grew weak. It made her sick to think the air she was breathing came out of the bowels of the mine and slithered across the shriveled corpse in front of her before arriving at her nostrils.

Standing there was pure torture, and she did not know how much longer she could bear it. Eventually, if nothing else, she knew she would need to go to the bathroom.

When she thought she could hold out no longer, a light suddenly flashed across the mouth of the mine again. From what she could hear, Camm decided two people were out there, standing by her rock pile while they caught their breaths after hiking back down from the top of the hill. She caught a few incredulous comments about the girl who had somehow escaped from the mansion and gotten over the hill so quickly. She had outrun even the fastest agents.

They weren't looking for her in the jumble of giant rocks, but stood talking just outside the pile, with one flashlight carelessly shining through the gaps among the rocks. From where they were standing, they could not see down into the mine, but the light was again illuminating the dead body in front of Camm.

Once more, she could see it clearly. She didn't want to look at it, but she couldn't peel her eyes away. She was close enough that if she leaned forward just a little, she could kiss it.

The shrunken skin pulled the face back into a look of perpetual horror, the mouth gaping in an endless, silent scream. The terrified look frozen on its face, along with the wide open mouth, set in an anguished, but mute shriek, made her think of a painting she had studied in a humanities class in college, but now the effect had lost all artistic appeal.

It took all her willpower to keep from retching. She closed her eyes, but that did little to relieve her anxiety. Opening one eye, she thought again of the silent scream frozen on the shriveled face.

Letting her sick humor take control again, Camm brought her forefinger to her lips and quietly shushed the body. "Don't make a sound," she whispered, nodding her head toward the people standing outside. "We don't want them to catch us."

Her newfound friend quietly obeyed.

Somehow, talking to the dead body made it seem less terrifying. Camm relaxed a little, but did not move. The people talking outside moved farther down the hill, taking their light with them, casting Camm and her friend back into utter darkness.

She—or they, if you included her buddy—had no choice but to wait out the search. Cramping began to grip her calves and buttocks. That, at least, was a problem her lifeless buddy no longer had to deal with. He could just rest on the spike through his chest.

Finally, after an eternity, the lights all moved away and the voices disappeared. With trepidation, she climbed up to peer out the mouth of the mine. The searchers, with all their search lights and cars, had moved north, correctly thinking that was the direction she wanted to go.

Camm expelled a sigh of relief. She turned toward the dead body, now hidden in the inky darkness. More to comfort herself than anything else, she said out loud to her deceased mine companion, "You scared the living daylights out of me."

From somewhere in the blackness of the mine, not too far from where she was standing, came an agitated reply. "You rather frightened me, too."

XIV

C al and Lenny stood side by side, staring at the ginormous grandfather clock in front of them. The glass front had been shattered, the face of the clock peppered with shotgun pellets, and the hands and pendulum were missing.

Lenny picked up a large piece of broken glass, still showing small etchings that were both intricate and hand-made, and slowly shook his head. "Dude, tell me again why Camm shot the clock. It's, like, all ruined and broken and everything."

Once the boys realized there really were two mansions, one back home and one in their present dimension, a lot of things finally made sense to Cal. The one in Trona that he and Camm always saw during the day was the clean and tidy version. The untidy mansion that Cal and Lenny were in now was the one that appeared at the striking of midnight and apparently only stayed until morning, when the tidy version came back again with the sunrise. The nighttime version carried all the signs of their struggles—the bullet holes, broken doors and chairs, the dried blood, dead bugs, dust, dirt, and green slime. It was also the one with the broken grandfather clock that Camm had accidently shot with the shotgun when fighting the green rat.

Feeling exasperated, Cal explained again, "She was trying to shoot the rat, man. The rat was in front of the clock, and she was just freaked out. She hit the rat, but she also hit the clock. You had to be there to understand. You would have freaked out, too. Anyone would have."

The boys stared at each other for a moment, then Lenny glanced back at the ruined clock, thoughtfully rubbing the fast-growing stubble on his chin.

Finally, Cal asked, "Do you think we can fix it?"

Lenny shrugged. "We don't even know how it works."

"But you figured out the clock was what turned the mansion on and off, causing it to move between the different dimensions. I mean, if you figured that much out, surely you got an idea of how it works."

"Dude, when I was little, I didn't know about how electricity and stuff worked, but I knew a light switch turned a light on and off."

The boys stared at the ruined clock in silence. Finally, Cal straightened his shoulders. It was time to make decisions and do something. He was used to having Camm around to take control and decide what should be done, but Camm wasn't here. They needed to do something, so Cal took charge.

"Okay," Cal started, "let's first canvass the mansion, and see what we can find. Maybe there is water or food. There could be tools or something else we can use. After that, we'll take a closer look at the clock. It might just be damaged on the outside. Maybe the inner workings are okay, and all we have to do is rehang the pendulum and put the hands back on. It might work."

"Dude." Lenny shrugged his shoulders, implying he had no better idea.

Getting inside the mansion in the first place had not been easy. Ever since they had arrived, Cal and Lenny had circled the mansion several times each day, inspecting every outside surface, looking for some chink in the armor. Cal had never noticed before, but all the windows on the ground level were protected with metal bars. Every outside door was thick, iron-hard oak and double or triple locked.

In the end, the compelling need to inspect the grandfather clock had made them daring. Lenny boosted Cal up to a narrow window ledge on the second level where Cal tried to jimmy the latch with his pocket knife. The ledge was only slightly wider than Cal's feet. When Cal started to lose his balance, he leaned in to keep from falling off the ledge and crashed through the window instead. Not very neat, but it did finally get them in.

Putting aside their worries about the grandfather clock, Cal and Lenny started on the first part of Cal's plan with enthusiasm. Because food had been constantly on their minds lately, they decided to begin their search in the kitchen.

The first bright note was the discovery that the faucets in the kitchen produced water. Where the water came from, they didn't know. It tasted a little stale with a slight sulfur odor, but was water just the same.

However, they did not find a single morsel of food anywhere in the cavernous kitchen. That disappointment was hard to bear because, when the rubber met the road, the prospect of hunting a live animal, and then killing, cleaning, cooking and eating it did not strike either Cal or Lenny as too appetizing. Especially after their lizard snack. Cal would have given anything for a bowl of his favorite baked beans. Both Cal and Lenny were very hungry.

They split up, hoping to explore the entire structure before nightfall. Cal knew he should examine the small stone room at the bottom of the spiral stairs. That was where the picture of the green rat was kept, and where he and Camm had seen the rat draw its last breath. But he didn't feel ready to go down there yet, not even with his .357 Magnum in hand. Lenny was interested in seeing the stone room, but did not push the issue.

Cal started on the third floor, going room to room, looking under, over, and in everything. He found little that would be helpful, just a lot of old furniture, dust, and dirt. He did find a few old candles, which would help when it got dark. He also discovered a number of bullet holes and spent shell casings from firefights he remembered and ones he knew nothing about.

After a while, Lenny yelled for him. "Dude! Come down here. Check this out!"

Cal hurried downstairs and found Lenny in a small closet-size room on the main floor, not far from the huge fireplace. Inside the room were three large utilitarian backpacks. They looked like military issue with printed names and ranks, but Cal didn't recognize the colors or insignia on them. They did not appear to be of US origin.

Lenny raised an eyebrow. "What do you think, man?"

Cal studied them closely for a few seconds. "Mr. Samuels told Camm and me that he sent mercenaries in to kill the rat, and they never came back. This could be their gear. Let's check 'em out. We may find weapons or tools or something."

Cal started in one backpack and immediately gave an excited whoop as he pulled out extra rounds of .38 Special ammo and a long, elegantly formed hunting knife.

Lenny opened another backpack and began digging inside. He licked his lips. "Dude, there may be food here!"

The white-haired man sat in a comfortable chair against the back wall. His tall companion was in an identical chair in the opposite corner. An elegant pool table sat in the middle of the room. A true slate table made of black walnut and dark oak, beautifully carved in every respect, it was part of the original mansion furnishings. The two men had enjoyed many hours playing pool. It was the only positive thing about the mission so far.

Agent Allen had been sent for, and she was taking her time in coming. The short man supposed it was fair retaliation for keeping her waiting in Washington D.C. When the door opened and she strode in, he could tell she was annoyed that the only two chairs in the room were taken. Making your victim stand was a well-known, yet simple, technique for asserting dominance.

Agent Allen placed her hands on her hips and with some impatience said, "Well?"

He had to admit to himself that she cut quite a striking figure. She was tall, lean, and athletically built. Her hair was pulled back into a businesslike ponytail. She wore practical, but masculine, clothes. The clothes, however, emphasized the female aspects of her physique and made her more attractive.

In his younger days, he could have been interested in a woman like her. Not just because of her physical appearance. In fact, not primarily because of it. She was more attractive because she was intelligent and assertive. She was attractive because of her natural leadership abilities and her creative methods in attacking problems. But the days of romantic interest in a woman were gone to him. That didn't mean he wouldn't mind making her a permanent member of his team. She was tough and had a lot to offer. He had been annoyed with her in Washington D.C., but he had come to respect her here in the field.

He began, "We would like your assessment of Miss Smith's situation and any thoughts you may have as to how we can locate her."

Agent Allen shifted her weight from one foot to the other and studied his face closely. "Before we go any further, I would like to know what to call you. I mean, I can keep referring to you as 'old man number one' and 'old man number two' if you don't mind sharing references with kindergarten bathroom terminology."

The man smiled in spite of himself. He nodded his head toward his taller companion. "You can refer to him as 'Mr. S' and to me as 'Mr. C.'"

Agent Allen rolled her eyes. "Mr. S and Mr. C, huh? S and C, as in Swift Creek?"

Mr. C continued, "Please, your assessment of Miss Smith?"

She rolled her eyes again. "My assessment is that you screwed up by keeping Camm here in the mansion, and then screwed up again by letting her escape."

The man refused to be offended. He and his companion were well aware of the mistakes that had been made. They would not make the same mistake twice.

Mr. S spoke. "Do you have a theory as to where she might be now?"

"She is a smart girl and adept at thinking on her feet. As you know, she is the only person we know of who has been able to kill the green rat. She won't make any foolish or careless mistakes. I don't think she would go to the home of any of her friends here in Trona. She would know that is where we would start looking. She wouldn't hide out in any of the abandoned houses either. They are too easy to search. She might be up in the hills hiding. She might not. She does know the surrounding landscape better than all the rest of us put together."

Mr. C stated flatly, "You really don't know."

"I really don't."

Mr. S continued. "How would you suggest, then, that we go about finding her?"

"I would keep your boys busy by checking with her friends, just in case, but basically, I don't think you need to do anything. You will find her soon enough."

Mr. C leaned forward. "What do you mean?"

"She's not going anywhere. I mean, she's not leaving Trona. She will not be content until Cal Jones returns. She will come back on her own, when she has developed a plan to help her best friend and to mess up whatever it is you two are doing."

The two men looked at each other. What she suggested seemed very reasonable.

Mr. S asked, "What do you suggest we do about her friend, Martha Bussey? She has recuperated enough—we don't need to keep her here. Besides, as you implied, this place is not as secure as we thought."

Agent Allen nodded. "She says she doesn't remember what happened. That is certainly plausible, given her injury. But I would keep her close. See if you can get her a clerkship with the court in Ridgecrest, or maybe a legal position on the base, you know, China Lake Naval Weapons Station. We may be able to use her as bait to bring Camm in."

The men had not considered that option. This Agent Allen was impressive. Mr. C got up from his chair, walked over to the pool table, and started racking up the balls. He glanced up at Agent Allen. "We are going to assign you to work with Agent Williams, since Agent Roberts is dead. You two will continue to search for Miss Smith."

"You mean with J.R.? That will not work. I don't want to be paired with him."

Mr. S stated firmly, "Nevertheless, that is what we have decided. He will be the senior agent and direct the search, with your input, of course."

Agent Allen stepped forward and leaned on the pool table. "Listen to me! I'm not working with J.R. He's dangerous and he's a putz."

Mr. C removed the rack and limped to the wall where he hung it on a hook. He calmly placed the cue ball on the table. Raising an eyebrow, he cautioned, "Don't get hysterical."

Agent Allen removed a cue stick from the wall and unexpectedly slammed it down on the pool table. The hard wood against the slate top made a loud smack. Both men jumped.

Having gotten their full attention, Agent Allen replaced her hands on her hips and calmly lectured, "Hysterical means 'excessive or uncontrolled emotion, without an organic cause.' It comes from the Greek term for womb, and therefore refers to women who can't control themselves. The term is sexist, and I won't allow its use in reference to myself, especially when I have not demonstrated excessive or uncontrolled emotion.

"I won't work with J.R. He's a putz." She hesitated, trying to think of the black agent's name. "I will work with Agent Kline."

Mr. C stood up straight and stared at her for several seconds, sorting his options. A show-down on this matter would be pointless. He could reassert his dominance when it mattered. Finally, he bent over the table and picked up the cue stick left there by Agent Allen. Taking aim, he hit the white ball with a thud. It spun toward the triangle of colored balls, knocking them in all directions. Five balls went into pockets—all of them solid colors.

Mr. C glanced up at her briefly. "Very well. Go find Agent Kline and have him come here. You and he can go search for the young girl until we think of something better for you to do. You are probably right. She will eventually come back to the mansion on her own."

Mr. S stood up, took a cue stick and started to chalk it. Without looking at Agent Allen, he calmly dismissed her. "You may go."

Without another word, she turned and walked briskly from the room.

As Mr. C prepared to take his next shot, he commented, "I like her. I think she may be very useful to us." He smacked the cue ball again sending a ball into the side pocket.

"I like her, too. We may want to make her permanent."

"Agreed." A double bank shot went in the corner.

Cal and Lenny sat on the front steps of their mansion, each of them eating an MRE, which was military jargon for "Meals Ready to Eat." They hadn't found many packets, so they had to make them last. The sun was setting, and all was perfectly calm around them. Nothing stirred as they voraciously consumed the old, dry contents of the packages. The evening's meal was gone all too soon. Both of them were still hungry.

The sun cast an amber glow on the sparse clouds. Daytime temperatures had been very hot, and it hadn't rained since the boys arrived.

Lenny spoke. "Have you noticed that backward S emblem in the carvings inside? You see it all over the place. You know, the backward S with kind of a teardrop on the end."

Cal rubbed his still empty stomach. "Yea, we saw it when we first came to the mansion. And it was on the Japanese puzzle box, too."

"Dude, I've seen that before, in an anthropology class. That is a Native American pictograph for a snake."

Cal leaned back. "Whoa. All of a sudden that makes sense."

Lenny leaned back with him, gazing up at the sky. Suddenly, he pointed to the northern horizon. "Dude. Look at those clouds over there."

Cal saw two thin clouds that were long and parallel, very high in the sky, fading off behind the mountains. "Yeah? What about them?"

Lenny chewed his lip, a serious expression on his face. "That looks exactly like a contrail."

"A what?" Cal was rummaging through the MRE packaging to make sure he hadn't missed any crumbs of food.

Lenny shot Cal a look of exasperation. "The evaporation cloud, or trail, caused by high altitude jet aircraft!"

Cal shrugged his shoulders and gave Lenny a blank look. "You think so? In this world? That's not possible, is it?"

All Lenny said was, "Dude." This time it meant, *Anything is possible.*

XV

Agent Allen liked working with Agent Kline. For one thing, everyone told him the truth. Everyone was totally intimidated by him. He was big. He was beyond big. The other agents called him Shaq, after the famous basketball player. In truth, he was shorter than the real Shaq, but had a larger chest and biceps the size of Roman columns. His skin was black black, very dark and very African. Everyone was afraid to lie to him, so conducting interviews was easy.

When he talked, he had a slight eastern accent, maybe Bostonian, very upper crust, very educated. And educated he was, with a master's degree from MIT in electrical engineering and a PhD from Boston College in applied physics. Agent Allen didn't know if people were more intimidated by his size or his remarkable intelligence. No, that wasn't true; she knew.

People were more intimidated by his size. But his intelligence certainly helped.

Interviews around town with Camm's friends had yielded nothing. No one had even known she was back in the valley. Some knew she was coming, but she hadn't contacted anyone since her arrival. Obviously, she hadn't had time to.

It wouldn't have mattered much if she had. The whole town was being packed up and moved out. Swift Creek had put out some story about a chemical leak at the plant and hinted at possible radiation poisoning. Everyone was being moved to unused military housing on the Navy Base, near Ridgecrest, about twenty-five miles away.

Agents Allen and Kline were taking a break, sitting in a black SUV and having a burger in the parking lot outside of Trail's End. A sign on Trona's only fast food joint said it was closing the next day as a result of the evacuation.

To make conversation, Agent Allen asked, "So, what brings you to this party anyway?"

Agent Kline eyed her carefully. "I'm at a disadvantage. I don't know how much you know, nor how much you are supposed to know."

Agent Allen smiled ruefully. "That's the way those old guys work, isn't it? Keep everyone in the dark. Don't share information, unless you have to, and never give anyone the whole picture." She raised an eyebrow at Agent Kline. "You realize, don't you, that is one way they keep control? That is how they manipulate.

"Unfortunately, it works against them, too. By keeping everyone from sharing what they know, we can't help each other. We all have different pieces of the puzzle, but only they are allowed to know what pieces each of us has. The problem is, we might be better at putting the pieces together than they are."

Agent Kline considered what she said as he finished his burger. He volunteered, "They haven't actually told me I can't tell you anything. It's just that we all are used to keeping secrets, especially about the mansion."

Lowering his voice, he said, "I was brought into this mission to fix the grandfather clock. Someone worked on the clock before me, but he did something wrong, so they decided to disable it. They won't tell me what went wrong. I'm just supposed to make the clock work, so it will be ready when they decide to turn it back on.

"Problem is, as far as I can tell, there is nothing wrong with the clock. Certainly, it's not like any grandfather clock I have ever seen. I mean, besides its bizarre and ghoulish design, the interior working mechanism is completely different from anything I have ever encountered. It's obviously more than a clock, and its intended function is clearly something other than keeping time. If they would let me start it up again, I could figure out what it does, but they won't let me. They are waiting for something."

He hesitated and ate a couple fries. Clearing his throat, he said, "I've told them it works, but they won't tell me what it's supposed to do. They keep telling me it is classified information. How can I make it do what it is supposed to do when I don't know what that is?"

Agent Allen remembered the last time she had seen the clock, just about a year ago. She looked intently at Agent Kline. "When I was here before, the clock had been damaged. Camm and Cal had used guns in the mansion, and it looked like someone had shot the clock with a shotgun."

Agent Kline looked perplexed. "Why would they shoot the grandfather clock?"

"I think they were shooting at that green rat, and the clock was just collateral damage."

Now Agent Kline looked really perplexed. "The what rat?"

Those dirt bags, Agent Allen thought, *they make all our jobs so unnecessarily complicated by compartmentalizing the information they give out.*

"You don't know about the green rat, huh?" She then asked carefully, "Do you know about the giant snake or the giant spiders?"

Agent Kline looked at her as if she were from outer space. "I have no idea what you are talking about. Though, I am aware of the rumors floating around town about numerous giant spider sightings. I guess until now, I hadn't given them much credence.

"But I can tell you this clock in the mansion is a massive mechanism. Not just in size, but in actual mass. I haven't been able to identify all the metals used in its composition, but it weighs tons. And while it functions, it seems to me there is more to this clock than is actually located there in the great hall. Our clock is designed to work with another piece, to interact with something else. Our clock in the mansion is working, but the other piece . . ."

He raised an eyebrow and shrugged. "Well, that is the missing piece of the puzzle. Something, whatever it is, wherever it is, is not interacting with our clock. I'm guessing that the other piece isn't working. I just don't know what the other piece is or how to get it to interact with our clock."

They continued to eat in silence for a few minutes. Finally, Agent Kline cleared his throat and swiveled in his seat to look directly into Agent Allen's eyes. "Maybe, if you told me what happened in the mansion last year, when you were here with those kids, Camm and Cal . . . and, maybe, if you told me everything you know about giant discolored rodents and insects . . . then, maybe, just maybe, you and I could put together a few more pieces of the puzzle."

Agent Allen considered his proposition in silence. For all the complaining she did about Misters S and C, she too was hesitant to share all she knew. How much did she trust Agent Kline? Knowledge was power, and power had to be shared carefully.

XVI

The boys were hungry, very hungry.

Neither showed much interest in the grandfather clock. They didn't know if it would work and didn't know how long they could go without getting something substantial to eat. The MREs were about gone, and those skimpy, dry meals had not cured their hunger anyway.

They decided to come back to the clock later, when they weren't starving to death. Though it wasn't their first choice, they both agreed they would have to actually kill something, cook it, and eat it, in order to have the strength to keep working on the clock.

Cal had hunted, but that had been with his dad, who always gutted and skinned the deer. A butcher in Ridgecrest always cured and cut up the meat. Cal's mom always prepared and cooked the meat for dinner. Other than shooting the deer and eating it, Cal hadn't really done much of the work. Besides the eating part, Lenny had even less experience, but he was complaining the loudest about the fast-approaching prospects of starvation.

While that big jackrabbit had never come back to the mansion, they had occasionally seen it in the distance, eating whatever rabbits eat. Cal had seen it again that very morning, not too far away, so both Cal and Lenny went hunting.

Getting close to where the rabbit was feeding, they split up. Cal hid behind some large mesquite bushes with his .357 ready. Lenny circled their prey, intending to scare it toward Cal, who would try to get close enough to kill it with the pistol. A .357 revolver was a powerful weapon, but Cal knew it was not accurate at long distances. If he could get close enough, he could just point and fire, killing their prey.

A hot sun was out in a clear sky and hardly a breeze stirred. The temperature was already hovering in the nineties. A shadow crossed over Cal and moved on, but he hardly noticed it. All his concentration was on the giant jackrabbit. He hoped that Lenny would not spook it too soon and end up chasing it in the wrong direction.

Cal figured they could eat for days off this one kill. He had heard that jackrabbits were not good eating, but he was hungry enough now that he didn't care. He crouched on one knee, leaning forward on the other foot. His left hand was knuckles down on the ground. He held the gun in his right hand, cocked and ready to fire. The idea was that as the rabbit ran by him, he would sprint from behind the bushes and get off at least one good shot as close as possible.

It was a bit like waiting for the ball to be hiked, and then blitzing the quarterback. He smiled at the thought of using a .357 Magnum as a linebacker in a football game. That would be a game changer for sure.

Lenny had circled around the rabbit and was coming up on it from the other side. By being exactly opposite the rabbit from where Cal was hiding, they hoped that when Lenny jumped out, the rabbit would run directly toward Cal. At least, that was the plan.

Cal could see Lenny staring at him, trying to see if he was ready. Cal gave him a little salute, indicating all was set. Lenny jumped up, waving his arms, and started shouting and running toward the rabbit, which had been grazing quietly.

The six-foot rabbit startled to attention, glanced at the running, yelling Lenny, and bounded toward the stealthily waiting Cal. Cal rose up in the starters' position and checked the revolver, making sure the safety was off. The rabbit was only about twenty yards away and coming fast. Cal tensed, ready to charge out of hiding and make the kill.

Before he could move, Cal heard a terrible noise above him. It felt like someone sticking needles in his eardrums. It sounded like a thousand fingernails being scratched across an enormous chalkboard. Lenny had stopped running and was holding his hands over his ears, looking up in disbelief at the sky over Cal's head.

A giant shadow flashed by. Sensing that something was

descending down on top of him from behind, Cal dropped flat onto his stomach. As he flopped to the ground, he accidentally fired the .357, sending a bullet bouncing off the dirt only feet from Lenny. The flying dirt from the bullet caused Lenny to jump, then dance to the side in a comical way.

It would have looked comical, except Cal was fixated on what was happening to the rabbit. A giant hawk reached down with colossal talons and snatched the oversized jackrabbit up into the air. A hawk? No, it had to be an eagle, or condor, or . . . what?

At that size, it could have been a Cessna. It was the size of a four passenger Cessna airplane, and it was flapping away with the squirming rabbit held firmly in its claws.

Lenny jogged over to Cal, who was picking himself up off the ground. The two stood and watched together as their intended dinner was carried through the sky into the nearby mountains. The boys, their stomachs still rumbling, looked at each other with wide eyes.

Simultaneously, they both said, "Dude!" That pretty much said it all.

XVII

Camm woke up, but didn't open her eyes. Her head hurt, and she felt totally disoriented. She couldn't remember whether it was day or night, or even where she was. So much had happened in so little time. She was afraid to look and see where she had ended up. Was she in the mountains? Had she been discovered and taken back to the mansion? She didn't know. If she opened her eyes, would Cal be there? The thought made her heart ache. Had she lost Cal forever?

Cal's disappearance had been the most difficult thing she had ever had to deal with. Even when they were separated by hundreds of miles, when she was in Connecticut and he in Florida, they could still communicate with each other whenever they wanted. Only now that he was gone from this world, possibly never to come back, did she realize what a large part of her life he filled. It was a part of her life that could no longer be explained away with simple phrases, like a lifelong friend or her best friend.

Camm finally admitted to herself that Cal was much more than a friend. Their relationship had become deeper than she ever thought it would. How sad, she thought, that it took his unexpected disappearance to make her come to this realization.

Now, she regretted the way she often treated him. She was often exasperated with him, talking down to him like he was a child. Too easily, she took him for granted, not appreciating the little things he did for her. When she bossed him around, he rarely pushed back, but in his good-natured way, he supported her in whatever she wanted to do. He happily called her the boss.

What she had taken for immaturity now seemed like the unbridled love of the moment. What she thought was silly now seemed to be the natural outgrowth of a good sense of humor. Once, she had thought him disorganized and impetuous; now she missed his enthusiasm for life and willingness to take risks.

She wished she had been less impatient with Cal and instead had been able to adopt his passion for whatever he was doing in the moment. Never had she met someone who was as naturally excited about life's simple pleasures and constantly as happy as he was—not even Sally. With a pain in her heart, she felt she had been trying to dampen that happiness, as if somehow that would make him more responsible, more like her. She realized she didn't want him to be like her—she wanted him to be like Cal. She needed him to be like Cal.

Tears welled into her tightly shut eyes as she allowed herself to feel the extent of his loss. She covered her face with both hands. Her body spasmed as involuntary sobs quaked through her frame. Then, she made herself stop. Only for a moment would she allow herself the comfort of emotion. What she really wanted was action.

He isn't dead. He has just gone away for a while, she told herself.

From what she understood, that stupid snake had come and gone several times. Cal had simply gone with it this last time. He would come back. She would help him come back. It was time to get to work. She promised herself she would find a way to bring Cal back. Her jaw clenched. When Camm made herself a promise, she always kept it.

Through brute strength of will, she forced the heavy emotions away from her. Still keeping her eyes closed, she slowly began to sense her surroundings. She was lying on her back on an uneven, hard surface. Touching it with her fingers, she determined she was lying on a flat, but chiseled, rock. Reaching up to her forehead, she felt a painful knot. The air felt cool, almost uncomfortably cold, and was full of a familiar, earthy, musty smell.

Listening, she heard nothing. Nothing stirred. There were

no birds chirping, no breeze blowing. Everything was deathly quiet, absolutely still. Her only sensations were the cool air, a headache, and a slight ringing in her ears.

Finally opening her eyes, she saw . . . nothing. It was completely and entirely black. She moved her hand inches in front of her face and saw nothing. It was darker than the darkest night. There was nothing to see, not even a single photon of light.

So, where was she? Was she underground? Was she back in the mansion, down in a deep dungeon? Was she sealed in a vault or casket? Was she totally crazy?

Taking a deep breath, Camm collected her thoughts. In spite of the pain in her head and in her heart, it was time to start thinking logically. She wasn't crazy.

What was the last thing she remembered? She clearly recalled discovering the secret passage in the mansion and running away into the windy desert night. She had been discovered, and had run up into the foothills west of the high school, below the Trona "T."

The mine! She had found a mine and hidden inside.

The body! There had been a dead body, standing like a sentry at the mouth of the mine. She recalled shushing it, talking to it. She remembered the Swift Creek agents had moved on without discovering her hiding place. They did not find her. No, but something else did.

Her head ached. *Did I imagine that?*

Feeling around her, she decided she was lying on a rock ledge, near its edge. She sat up and swung her feet over the edge. Her feet touched a dirt floor. Was she still in the mine?

The voice! The voice was the last thing she remembered. Did that dead body talk to her?

Gripping the edge of the ledge, she assured herself, *Zombies don't talk.*

She had not been alone in the mine. Someone else, someone alive, had been inside with her and had talked to her.

At that moment, Camm saw a dim light approaching. Slowly it brightened. She realized she was in a small rock alcove off a main tunnel. So, she was still in the mine. The light was approaching the room through the tunnel.

The low doorway lit up as a very ancient man hobbled up, stopping just outside. He was small, so hunched over that he seemed almost bent in half. Wisps of white hair floated off the top of his head and around his chin. His skin was shriveled and deathly pale. Round, homemade frames held thick lenses in front of bright gray eyes. In his right hand was a thick candle. His left sleeve was empty, folded and pinned to the shoulder of his shirt.

"Oh ho!" he chortled. "At last, sleeping beauty has awoken!" He smiled an almost toothless smile at her. "You had quite a case of syncope, fell and banged your head, you did. Though, I don't think you hurt yourself too bad."

As he entered the little room with the fat, flickering candle, Camm finally got a clear view of all her surroundings.

She gasped. *OH NO! Not more dead bodies!*

XVIII

"Holy . . ." Agent Kline hesitated, his eyes wide in disbelief. "Mary, Joseph, and the twelve apostles." Without even realizing what he was doing, he solemnly genuflected.

Agent Allen couldn't help smiling, but she knew exactly how he felt. The first sight of the green rat was always shocking. She had brought her partner down the narrow stone stairway to the rat's prison—without permission from Swift Creek. Agent Kline's immense frame barely squeezed into the available space.

The rat stood on all four feet, glaring hate at them. Its pointed fangs were bared with mossy-colored saliva dripping into puddles. Sharp claws gripped the dirt floor as the rat crouched backward, as if it would spring through the Plexiglas and eat them.

"Is it secured in there?" Agent Kline asked, concern painted on his face.

Agent Allen jabbed a finger at the ceiling. "Ask your buddies upstairs." As she spoke, the hanging lights dimmed. "Let's go before that thing plunges us into the dark. It hates light."

Agent Kline had a difficult time pulling his eyes off the beast. "It can control the electrical circuitry to the lights?"

"According to Mr. S, it doesn't turn off the power—it suppresses the radiation of light."

"How does it . . . I mean, what is it anyway?" They both started up the stairs.

Agent Allen commented over her shoulder as she climbed upward, "Like I've been trying to tell you, it is one freaking nasty, giant, green rat, but you have to see it to believe it."

Agent Kline shook his head in disbelief and followed her up.

"I think we should try fixing the grandfather clock first." Cal studied the military backpacks, camping gear, food packets, guns, and ammunition that were scattered in untidy piles by the fireplace. The food pile was pitifully small. His stomach growled noisily.

Lenny also studied the disorderly piles. Then, holding up the long, hunting knife, he said, "This is, like, dude, big time hunter-gatherer stuff."

Cal and Lenny had pulled everything out of the backpacks that might be of use on a big-game-hunting expedition. After losing the giant jackrabbit, Lenny had pointed out that overly large animals needed more fauna and flora than grew in the desert. That kind of abundant greenery needed more water than was found anywhere near the mansion.

Lenny argued there had to be forests not too far away to sustain the big animals. His plan was to hike west over the foothills in the direction the giant hawk had flown with their dinner. There they would find greener lands with big game for Cal to shoot with his .357 pistol.

Lenny was optimistic. Cal knew it was a risky venture. Who knew how far away those greener lands might be. Cal knew they couldn't travel far without food, and their travels would be over even quicker if they ran out of water along the way. If they went on a long expedition and found nothing, they probably wouldn't make it back to the mansion.

Cal tossed down the box of matches he was holding. "If the clock works and gets us back to our own world, then, man, we've got no problems. We won't need to go hunting. If we can't get the clock to work, then we'll have no choice. We can pack up what we've got here and go hunting." Cal's stomach rumbled again. "If we haven't already died of starvation."

Lenny reluctantly conceded the point, and they went to work on the gigantic clock. First, they made a careful search around the clock, gathering up all the parts and pieces they could find. Most of what they found was glass fragments.

Lenny called out, "Hey, dude, come over here. What's this? It can't be clock stuff."

Cal hurried to see what he had found.

Lenny pointed at a huge picture frame, lying face up on the floor. All the broken glass from the clock had already been cleared away around it. "Dude, have you ever seen this before?"

Cal squatted down to get a better look. "It's definitely not part of the clock, but it does look familiar." He paused, then shook his head. "Man, I think I've seen it before, but maybe just 'cause the frame looks the same as those on the freaky paintings upstairs and on that rat picture down in the stone room, except this one's empty. There's no picture in it."

He shrugged. "Let's set it over by the wall and get it out of the way."

It took both of them pulling together to drag the frame across the slate floor.

"Dude, what's this thing made of? It weighs a ton," Lenny complained.

Most of the clock pieces were inside the clock's giant housing. Though the parts had been peppered with shotgun pellets, nothing appeared to be seriously damaged, except of course, the front panel of glass had been blown to pieces. Lenny cleaned and sorted the parts, then removed all the shattered glass from the casing. He examined the clock mechanisms, dusting as he went.

Doing the intricate repairs was a one-man job. Cal had taken to pacing back and forth, but stopped to peer over Lenny's shoulder. "How does it look?"

"It's going to be way easier to put together than I thought."

Lenny glanced up. "Hey, dude, how about making yourself useful, like, a little further away from me? You make me nervous, man, and I can't afford nervous. How 'bout figuring out a way to climb up high enough to put these hands back on that clock face way up there?"

Cal left, returning several times with loads of chairs and other furniture to build a precarious stack for Lenny to climb on.

Carefully, Lenny replaced the hanged-man pendulum and wound the weights to the top.

Cal paced nervously in front of the giant grandfather clock while Lenny made final adjustments and brushed away more dust. Stepping back, Lenny admired his handiwork.

"Do you think this will work?" Cal looked anxiously at Lenny even though he already knew the answer.

Lenny returned his look and sentiment. "Dude?" The translation was, *Who knows?*

Climbing to perch on the precarious stack of furniture, Lenny returned the hands to the face of the clock. He scratched his head. "Dude, what time is it? What time do we set it to?"

Cal glanced at his watch. It was 2:35 pm. "I don't know, man. It always went off exactly at midnight. I never saw the hands set in any other position, except straight up. Maybe we are supposed to set it for straight up twelve o'clock."

Lenny pushed both hands until they pointed straight up. He climbed down from the improvised scaffolding. "I don't know what else to do, dude. I don't even know how this thing works, but the innards don't seem damaged or anything."

He shrugged. "Here goes nothin'."

With that he reached through the open front of the clock, the broken glass having been completely removed, and pushed the pendulum to start it swinging.

Cal held his hands over his empty, shrunken stomach. Closing his eyes, he said a silent prayer. This had to work. It just had to.

Agents Allen and Kline had just returned to the main hall when, without warning, the pendulum in the large grandfather clock started swinging and the clock began to chime. The first dong startled them both. The clock said it was twelve o'clock, but it was actually early afternoon.

The clock donged again as Misters S and C hurried out of their upstairs study.

"Kline, what are you doing with that clock?" Mr. C shouted down at them from the second floor balcony. "I thought you said there was nothing more you could do. In any case, we told you not to start the clock again without clearance from us. We don't know what it will do."

Anger etched across their faces, Misters S and C tried to hurry downstairs. Clutching the handrail, both old men hobbled and limped as quickly as they could down the stairs. The clock continued donging its midnight chime.

Agent Kline held his hands up defensively. "We did not touch the clock, sir. I swear. We were just passing through the hall when it started chiming on its own. We don't have any idea what's going on now."

Agent Allen put her hands on her hips. "Look," she started, "we haven't messed . . ."

Before she could finish, even though she hadn't been moving, she lost her balance and started to stagger. It felt as if the floor beneath her feet was moving, sliding back and forth.

At the same time, the great hall, which had been warm with the heat of the day, suddenly became cold, icy cold. It felt as if all heat had been instantly sucked out of the room and was now being sucked out of their bodies.

Agent Kline widened the distance between his feet, securing his balance. He then reached over and placed a hand on Agent Allen's shoulder, steadying her. The clock continued to chime as if it were twelve midnight. The temperature continued to drop.

Mr. S neared the bottom of the stairs, holding tightly onto the railing. "How did it . . ."

He stopped mid-sentence, staring in the vicinity of the clock. Agent Kline furrowed his brow and slowly brought an arm up, pointing in the same direction. "There is something there."

Appearing in front of the clock were two ephemeral figures. Not quite coming into focus at first, the figures seemed to grow solid with each dong of the clock, but in between dongs, they would evaporate, becoming transparent again. With the next dong, the figures became more substantial again, only to lose substance until the next donging of the clock.

"What is that!?" Agent Kline demanded.

Agent Allen shook her head. Could it be? She squinted, trying to bring the ghostly forms into focus. It suddenly hit her. Her mouth opened in disbelief. "That's, that's Jones, uh, Cal, and . . ." she stammered, trying to remember his friend's name. "That's Cal and that other kid!"

The room was spinning, without spinning. Everything moved in and out of focus. It was like looking at a double exposure of the same photograph, moving back and forth on itself.

"NO, NO, NO!" Mr. C was shouting at the figures. "It only works at midnight. Only at midnight! It won't work now."

Mr. S put his hand on Mr. C's shoulder. "They can't hear you."

Mr. C had a panicked look on his face. "If they move wrong, they will end up being torn apart." The clock continued to dong.

Mr. S hurried over to the figures. Withdrawing a notepad from his pocket, he started to write. Agent Allen had not been counting the number of times the clock had chimed, but it must be close to twelve. Ripping the paper from the notebook, Mr. S hesitantly held it toward the wavering images of the two boys, who didn't seem to see him.

He reached out as if sticking his hand into a burning fire. With the last dong of the clock, the two images disappeared for good. Mr. S snatched his hand back to his chest as if it had been burned. Blood dripped copiously from his hand as he wrapped it in a handkerchief.

Cal would have thrown up, had there been anything in his stomach. It was unclear what, but something had happened. The clock had started donging. The room had gotten suddenly ice cold and had seemed to move, or jump, or something. And, it seemed as if other people, ghostly people, who faded in and out with each gong, had appeared in the main hall with them.

For a few seconds, he thought it had actually worked, and they would be back in their old world, the world where Trona was. But things from the Trona world never got substantial, never got completely solid. They saw a little of where they wanted to go, but didn't get there.

At the last dong of the clock, what they could see of the other world disappeared. Just before it did, though, an apparition had hurried toward them and held something out. As the figure disappeared, it left something behind. A piece of paper floated toward them. Cal snatched it out of the air.

The following note had been hastily written on the paper. *"Only works at midnight. Try again in 57 hours."*

The boys read the paper together. Cal sighed and rubbed his empty belly. They had a few food packets left, but not enough to last them for fifty-seven hours. They were going to have to find something else to eat while they waited.

"It almost worked," he said with obvious regret in his voice.

"We're on the right track. Now we just have to do it at the right time." Lenny smiled. "There is reason to be optimistic."

"What fell on the floor?" Cal pointed down at a pink object, the size of a thimble.

Lenny bent over and squinted at it. "Dude, it's the bloody end of someone's finger!"

XIX

"Come this way."

Martha followed the Navy ensign, the heels of the young officer's shoes clicking on the worn linoleum as she led the way down a long dingy hall. Once the doctor had declared Martha fit to leave, the old men had informed her they had arranged for her to do her clerkship with the Judge Advocate General's office at the nearby China Lake Naval Weapons Station.

"A very prestigious clerkship and well paid," the tall white-haired man had declared. "It is much to your advantage, and we would like you close this summer to be sure you have no residual ill effects from the accident. You were, after all, injured in the company of a federal agent. Let us know if you remember anything more about what happened. It could be important."

Martha's requests to talk to the Los Angeles law firm that had hired her for the summer were brushed off.

"Everything is taken care of," she was told. "It was the least we could do."

"I can only work a few months before I must be back to law school," she had pointed out.

"No problem," the old man said. "We expect a full recovery by the end of the summer. This fall you will be back in school, continuing your legal studies right on schedule."

That promise went a long way in putting Martha's mind at ease. She could tolerate a lot if she wasn't going to lose her place at the Yale school of law.

"Can I call my parents to tell them about my new clerkship?" Martha was excited when she was taken to a phone and given at least a show of privacy.

"Martha, are you sure you're all right?" Her mom had been horrified to hear she had been in a car accident. "I can fly out tomorrow. I hate having you there all by yourself."

"I'm fine, Mom, really. The doctor told me to just take it easy for a while and not do any sports or activities where I might hit my head again."

Martha did her best to reassure her parents, not mentioning her painful, deep bruises. As Camm had cautioned, she was cooperating with the NSA, or more accurately, playing the thing out. She would wait to see what developed and formulate a better plan when she knew more.

In the meantime, she was hoping to hear from Camm, or

at least discover what had really happened to her. She knew everything the NSA told her was nonsense.

Staring at the ensign's back, Martha thought, *At least they seem to be buying my story that because of my concussion, I can't remember anything after we pulled into Valley Wells.*

The young ensign, looking sharp in her navy blue skirt and white blouse, led Martha to the end of the hall where two small offices faced each other across the hallway. The hall ended in the open door of a small, bleak break room.

The offices were contained in a temporary structure, old and plain. Everything at this end of the long, narrow building had recently been covered with a thick coat of paint. There were no windows. A loud evaporation cooler blew moist air through a hole in the center of the break room ceiling. The rest of the old building was warm and smelled moldy, in spite of the paint job.

The ensign ushered her into the right-hand office and indicated her work station, which consisted of a simple square cubicle containing a small desk, an old computer, and a rickety secretary's chair. A thin folder, a notepad, and a couple pens lay next to the computer. The color scheme was military blah. There were no pictures, no plants, nothing to brighten the atmosphere. It seemed very sterile, very isolated.

Martha glanced around for signs of any coworkers. There were none.

She had expected to be working near the Judge Advocate General's office, but it seemed she was to be kept away from everybody. Even her living quarters were single-occupant military housing. All units around her were vacant.

Pointing at the bulky computer, the ensign said, "You will receive all your legal research assignments by email. You will find sign-in, email, and any contact information contained in that folder. Your computer is connected to all pertinent government and Internet sites so you can complete all your research online. Prepare and send all your reports in electronic format. Hard copies will not be necessary. After you have returned each report by email, you will be given another task. Any deadlines will be explained in the task summary. Any questions?"

"So," Martha asked hopefully, "will you be working here with me?"

The ensign looked startled. Her eyes darted quickly around the barren room. "Oh no, I have other duties, and I appear regularly in military court."

Martha sighed. "Will I be working all alone?" She felt as if she had leprosy.

"Oh no," the navy officer responded curtly.

Striding across the hall, she opened the door to the other small office. Inside were two teenage boys hardly old enough to be out of high school.

Each sat at his own small desk, the top covered by an ancient desktop computer. The back corners of the room were stuffed with what looked like abandoned office equipment.

The boys did not seem to be doing anything. Both wore dull expressions and appeared to be shell shocked. Neither boy looked up.

"These two young men will be assisting you. Let me introduce you. Boys, this is Martha. She will be your supervisor.
Martha, this is Jim and Sean. They will be your assistants."

XX

Cal leaned back against a large smooth rock that served as a chair back. Smiling with contentment, he patted his bulging stomach. For the first time in several days, he wasn't hungry.

Above him, the sun was setting behind a bank of thick black clouds. Visibility immediately around him was not good because of the tall savannah grasses surrounding the little campfire he and Lenny had made in a small clearing. But Cal's attention was on the sky, which was changing colors minute by minute as the sun went down.

Somewhere behind him, hidden in the lush vegetation, was a rustling noise. Cal knew he should be cautious about such noises, but in the mellow aftermath of his meal, he didn't want to bother. Besides, the area was inhabited by large birds. He guessed he was hearing bird noises.

He glanced over at Lenny, sitting across the fire from him. "Do you want more?"

Sucking the meat off a leg bone, Lenny held up his hand. "Dude," which meant, *I'm full.*

A rustling noise came from behind Lenny as a wave-like motion moved through the tall grass. "Man, the birds are getting restless," Cal said as he continued watching the spectacular show in the sky. "Looks like that big thunderstorm is coming our way."

Large cumulonimbus clouds were rolling into the valley, the underbelly of the clouds turning dark. Further up the valley, Cal saw it was raining, a summer thunderstorm. He could smell rain on the wind, but it was dry where they were.

The setting sun turned the clouds crimson. Cal loved a desert sunset. A cool breeze blew, bringing the promise of stronger winds. Somewhere in the distance, a faint clap of thunder sounded. Cal guessed the storm was moving in their direction.

He thought he probably should stand up and look for high ground away from the stream bed, but the storm didn't seem to be moving very fast. Right now, it felt good to simply lean back and not be hungry. Putting his hands behind his head, he stretched his feet out toward the fire.

The grasses rustled again, like a fire hose being dragged along the ground. Cal thought, *That doesn't sound like birds.* He had been assuming all the local wildlife was birds.

The boys had followed a game trail up through the Argus

Mountains in the general direction they had seen the hawk flying with the jackrabbit. On the west side of the mountains, they entered into what would have been the China Lake Naval Bombing Range, back on their world. In this world, they discovered a long green valley with a small, but active, stream of water. The stream had cut a deep ravine through the bottom of the valley. Inside the valley were all kinds of large trees and bushes, flowering plants, and other lush vegetation. It was paradise.

While exploring the area, they had run across a large bird, similar to a wild grouse hen, but the size of a tom turkey. Fortunately for them, it was flightless. A little chasing and running around had confused all three of them. Eventually, the bird ran directly at Cal while trying to get away from Lenny. With one shot, which Cal admitted to himself was more luck than skill, he had dropped the bird dead in its tracks.

A quick fire and a makeshift rotisserie had given the boys their first real meal since they had crossed over to this strange alien world. With a full belly, Cal stopped to consider his life in the long run. For the first time, he decided it would be possible to survive in this world if they couldn't find a way back. He also realized that while he could live very comfortably in this world without K'tlynn, he would be just surviving without Camm.

With plenty of food and water in the valley, he thought they should camp there until it was time to try the crossover again back at the mansion. The valley was certainly more pleasant than the bleak mansion, but without Camm, there would be nothing in this world for Cal no matter where he might choose to camp.

If . . . when he got back home, Cal was going to make some changes in his life.

Lost in his own thoughts, Lenny hadn't said anything, but suddenly, he raised himself up on one elbow and peered behind him into the obscure windblown grasses. After a moment, he shrugged his shoulders and resettled closer to the fire.

Twilight was upon them and night was close behind. Cal threw more wood on the fire. They planned to spend at least one night here, so they would have time to do more hunting. When they did travel back to the mansion, they wanted to take a large supply of meat with them. Cal's dad had taught him about preserving meat with salt. Searles Valley had plenty of salt. In addition, Cal thought he might be able to collect some edible vegetation. At least, they would not have to starve to death.

What is that noise?

The mysterious noise started to bother Cal. He picked up a big rock and tossed it at the rustling sounds in the grass. It hit something with a heavy thud. A loud hiss came in reply, like air leaking from a punctured tire. Lenny's head jerked up, and Cal's blood froze.

"It's a good thing you had them wait, though I think fifty-seven hours is a bit excessive."

Agent Allen rubbed the back of her neck. She hated being cramped together in the narrow space at the bottom of the circular stone stairs. Agent Kline took up most of the space because of his size. Mr. C stood directly behind her. All were staring at the monstrous green rat.

The giant rat, its filthy green fur matted and wet, paced restlessly back and forth in its little cell. The Plexiglas shield, by itself, no longer seemed adequate.

The manacle that had been chained to the rat's rear leg had come off.

"The rat is phased with the mansion," Mr. C explained. "When the mansion moves back and forth between our dimensional plane and the other plane, the rat moves with the phasing. When the boys started their clock mechanism, they triggered a phase cycle. Even though the mansion didn't complete the pass-through, it phased enough to allow the rat to move outside the grip of that manacle. This happened once before, when we were experimenting with the clock on our side, but at that time, the rat was too weak to be a threat. That's no longer true.

"We are fortunate the rat didn't make it to the other side of this Plexiglas. You see, there is no Plexiglas protector in the other dimensional plane."

Mr. C patted the Plexiglas with his hand. "If the rat had caught the phase at just the right moment, it could have moved out of its cell while in the other dimensional plane. Then when it came back to our plane with the end of the phase shift, it would be on this side of the Plexiglas."

Agent Allen shook her head. If only she had studied harder in her college physics class, she might understand better what Mr. C was talking about. She looked at Agent Kline, who had a look of disbelief painted on his face. She hoped it was because he was amazed at what they were learning, and not because he didn't understand. She had come to trust him more than any of the other agents. She really hoped he understood what was going on.

"We cannot try bringing those boys back until we have secured the rat," Mr. C explained. "We will need something more than just that chain." Agent Allen understood why the rat had to be secured—anyone could see why just by looking at it. She sighed.

"Why not kill it?" That clearly seemed the best answer to her.

Agent Kline added, "Or at least tranquilize it?"

Now it was Mr. C's turn to sigh. "It is not that easy. It's not a life-form like here on earth. Come upstairs where we can breathe more freely. I will try to explain."

As they trudged up the stairs, the creature shut down all the lights again. Feeling her way along the wall in the dark, Agent Allen called out, "Will those boys be safe over there, wherever they are, until we can bring them back to this world."

"It is not safe over there," Mr. C replied matter-of-factly. "With the few records we do have, we know of some who went over and never came back. They were heavily armed, highly trained soldiers. We're not sure what happened to them. The record doesn't say.

"Let's hope the boys stay in that mansion on their side, with the doors all locked. The farther from the mansion they stray, the more dangerous it will be for them in that other world."

Cal grabbed a burning branch, long and thick, from the fire and wound his shirt around the end that was burning. With this improvised torch, he and Lenny took off down the narrow game trail, heading out of the small canyon valley, back toward that world's version of Searles Valley. The sun had set; the moon was blocked by growing cloud cover; and the going was dark and difficult. True, they had found flashlights in the paramilitary backpacks, but the batteries were old and corroded. They did not work.

As the trail grew steeper, small rocks from behind came bouncing past them. Cal glanced over his shoulder. No doubt about it, they were being pursued. He could not see their pursuers yet, but he had a good idea what was making the loud hissing noises.

Lightning lit the night sky behind them, and a cold rush of wind caught them from the same direction. The smell of ozone and moisture was thick. It was raining somewhere, not far away. The trail steepened even more. They slipped and slid, sometimes on their feet, sometimes on their butts. The torch did not provide enough illumination to light their way clearly. A constant wind twisted and turned the flames, never allowing the conflagration to burn brightly.

They reached a small, but relatively flat spot in the trail. Lenny reached over and grabbed Cal by the arm, stopping him. With a hand on his side, Lenny bent down and gasped, "Just a second, dude. I have to rest a minute or I will puke."

As he spoke, the night lit up blue-white bright. The lightning was so close, Cal heard it sizzle. Its shock wave hit him in the chest. The crack of thunder startled them both. The lightning had been so bright, he was blind in the returning darkness. It took a second for his eyes to readjust to the dim light of the torch.

Regaining his equilibrium, Cal cast a wary eye up the trail. "I don't think we have a minute." From beyond the shallow reach of their torchlight, more rocks rolled down the hill toward them. "Something big is following us."

They turned their attention from uphill to continue down the path, only to stop dead in their tracks. Something was now in front of them. Their pursuer was a snake. Not the giant Mojave Green that had chased them across the desert. Not that big, but large enough.

The snake faced them with its ever-probing tongue sampling the air. The length of the coiled snake was hard to guess, but the diameter was eight to ten inches. There were no rattles on its flickering tail. Cal knew what it was—a sidewinder. The biggest sidewinder he had ever seen.

More rocks, a lot more rocks, came bouncing down the hill from above. There must be more snakes up there. Too late, Cal realized they were surrounded. Considering how big the

Mojave Green was, these sidewinders could just be babies. Cal knew if they were truly baby snakes, there might be dozens of them, hunting together.

As Agent Allen climbed the stairs in the dark, she could hear Agent Kline and Mr. C ahead of her, shuffling up the stairs like blind men. She was starting to get tired of always climbing back up the narrow stone passageway in the pitch black.

"Hey, Mr. C, or whatever your name is, why can't you do something about these lights?"

She was annoyed at the incompetence of Swift Creek. Surely, they could do something about that rat's creepy ability to suppress light.

Before Mr. C could answer, there came a loud thud, like a side of beef being dropped from several stories high. Agent Allen knew immediately what was happening. Ice water seemed to run down her spine and into her legs. All she could say was, "C, what the . . ."

Before she could finish, there was another booming thud.

Mr. C produced a small flashlight from his pocket. "Hurry!" he exclaimed. "It's trying to escape! Without the chain on its leg, I don't know if the shield will hold."

Mr. C led the way up the narrow spiraling stairs, the light from his flashlight barely visible to Agent Allen. For an old white-haired man, he was moving fairly quickly, but not nearly fast enough for Agent Allen. Between her and Mr. C was Agent

Kline, his enormous frame filling the circumference of the stairway. Agent Allen could not see around him.

Another crashing thud boomed up the stairway. Agent Allen imagined the nauseous-colored rat throwing its huge bulk against the Plexiglas, trying to break free. She tried to hurry Agent Kline, pushing against his posterior with both hands.

"Hey, hey," he protested. "Watch the hands. Mr. C, sir, let's speed it up!"

Before Mr. C could respond, there was another thud and a cracking, scraping noise along with it. The Plexiglas was breaking free of its mooring and coming loose.

Mr. C hurried his pace to a fast hobble. Another thud, more scraping, and the squeaky sound of claws against the hard plastic-like surface came from below. The rat was squeezing past its prison door.

Agent Allen pulled out her Glock. "I'll hold it off," she said louder than she intended to Agent Kline. "You get Mr. C upstairs."

"No! No!" Mr. C protested. He was huffing and out of breath. "Your gun won't stop it. We have to beat it to the top and secure the stone door behind us."

Agent Kline was right on top of Mr. C, but there was no room to move past him. Agent Kline bellowed, "You have to move faster. We have to go faster."

"I'm trying, I'm trying. . . ."

Before Mr. C could say anything else, Agent Kline grabbed him with both hands from the back. One hand held the collars of his shirt and coat. The other gripped the waistband and belt of his pants. Picking him bodily off the stairs, holding him out in front, Agent Kline ran up the stairs with Agent Allen running directly behind.

Held like a marionette, Mr. C tried to scramble the best he could, his feet barely touching the stone steps. His flashlight provided only minimal light, but enough for Agent Kline to avoid banging Mr. C into the stone walls.

Even though they were running, the stairs seemed to go on and on, twisting and turning. Agent Allen expected to see the doorway leading into the cellar at each turn, but it never came.

The scratching, scraping noise had stopped. Agent Allen imagined the rat must be beyond the Plexiglas and was now bounding up the stairs. In her mind's eye, she could see it leaping up the steps, taking a half-dozen stairs in a single jump. It was not lost on her that she would be the first person the rat came to. The first one it would kill and eat.

She would not go without a fight. Glancing over her shoulder, she thought that even if she couldn't kill it, she would fill it with lead. She decided to shoot for its face and eyes.

Still no doorway, no end to the stairs. With that thought, the flashlight Mr. C was holding went black, and the sulfuric, stinking smell of rotting road kill became overpowering. They were in total darkness, and the rat was catching up.

XXI

C al heard movement through the rocks and brush on both his left and right. It was hard to guess how many snakes were gathering. He and Lenny had to get down the trail, and they had to do it in a hurry, a freaking big hurry. That meant getting past the sidewinder coiled in the middle of the trail, threatening to strike at any second.

At that instant, another lightning bolt flashed with blinding, searing light. In that flash, the entire area around them became visible. The intensity of the flash washed the color out of everything, like an overexposed black-and-white photograph. It was only an instant of light, but long enough for Cal to make out at least four other snakes around them. All were about the same size as the one curled in front of them. All were sidewinders.

As a last-ditch defense, he would use his .357, but he didn't have a lot of confidence in the stopping power of his pistol. Neither the giant rat nor the Mojave Green had been slowed by firearms. To the contrary, the bullet wounds had made them more angry and aggressive.

The last thing Cal wanted to do was to waste all of his ammo making a whole family of sidewinders more aggressive. He wanted to save as much ammo as possible for future hunting expeditions, if necessary.

Plan A was to slip away without inciting a bunch of angry sidewinders to chase after them. If that failed, Plan B was to shoot as many as possible. He didn't know how many of the giant sidewinders he could actually kill before one filled him full of venom. Hopefully, he could slow them down enough to give Lenny a chance to escape while the snakes were swarming Cal.

"We have to move, man. Stay with me. Get ready to run!"

Lenny nodded his head and moved closer to Cal.

Cal stepped forward and jammed the makeshift torch at the coiled snake's head. It pulled back and hissed loudly. Stretching out his arm, Cal kept the smoldering torch directly in front of the snake's eyes, while he moved to the left, pulling Lenny along with him.

With a movement too quick to see, the snake struck at the torch's flame, hitting the torch, but missing Cal. Holding the torch tightly, Cal pushed it closer to the snake's head. As the snake's beady eyes followed the torch, it drew back, sliding out of its coiled formation.

Without hesitation, Cal and Lenny raced around the snake and galloped down the rocky hillside. Soon, another flash of lightning showed snakes on both sides, moving with them down the game trail. In spite of the momentary blindness caused by the flashing lightning strikes, they ran headlong downward. Thunder boomed like deep detonations directly overhead.

Cal's foot caught on a stone. As he fell straight forward, he tucked his naked torso with his head curled down. Without losing grip of the torch, he rolled once and popped back up onto his feet, hardly missing a step. Lenny was still right behind him.

The clouds opened a hole, releasing a shaft of moonlight on the panicked race. In the dim light, it was easier to see their way and easier to see their predators. There were at least a half dozen moving with them down the hill, matching their pace. The snakes moved in that queer sideways motion unique to their species. With heads about four feet off the ground and tongues slipping in and out, their dead, unblinking eyes seemed to follow their intended prey.

With snakes on both sides, Cal felt they were being herded down the hill, but down to what? A trap? Just as quickly as the moonlight had appeared, it disappeared. Now the only illumination was the almost nonexistent torch light.

The hair on the back of Cal's neck stood straight up while a tingling sensation coursed down his arms and legs. He had a premonition that something was about to happen.

Another ferocious strike of lightning exploded into the ground just yards to his left. It was an electric explosion. Bushes burst into flames. Searing hot sparks of red, white, and green erupted into the air, showering down on both Cal and Lenny.

Lenny yelled, "Dude!" and jumped aside, away from the sparks, but directly into Cal. Both tumbled to the ground, rolling and sliding over rocks and bushes.

They stopped, sprawled along the trail. Cal still held his torch, but it was extinguished. Gasping for breath, neither moved. They heard hissing on all sides. They were surrounded.

Agent Allen could not stand the thought of the rat taking her by surprise from behind. She let Agent Kline continue ahead, carrying Mr. C, while she twisted to point her gun down the stairs. She ran sideways as fast as she could without losing her balance. As she made her way, she listened for any sound of the approaching rat. The stairway was dark. Nothing was visible. All she could hear was Agent Kline moving farther and farther ahead of her up the stairs.

It wasn't with her ears that she first detected the rat. It was with her nose. A tidal wave of horrible, rotten-egg smell burst up the stairwell and enveloped her. It smelled so bad, so overpowering, she felt sure that if there had been light she would see a green gaseous cloud attacking her. The rat must be almost on her. She gagged and fired a single shot down the stairwell into the blackness.

"Allen! Where are you?" Agent Kline called. "We're at the top! Hurry!"

Agent Allen continued running sideways up the stairs. "I'm coming."

"We have to close the door. We can't wait." That was Mr. C.

Was he going to shut her in with the rat?

"I'm coming!" Panic tinged her voice.

She quickened her pace, but continued pointing her gun down the stairs. The smell was so overpowering it was difficult to breathe. Whatever happened, she did not want to be caught unaware and taken in the dark. It occurred to her that a bullet fired at the correct angle might ricochet down the spiral staircase.

Pointing the gun at an angle roughly equal to the descending stairs, she let a bullet fly. The muzzle flash briefly lit the passage way. It was less than a second, but in that small fraction of time she saw it. She saw the rat. Its nose and front paws were just visible around the interior wall. She had fired above it.

Quickening her pace, she fired another shot where she thought it should be. The light of the muzzle flash showed the rat had disappeared. She continued firing every few seconds, hoping to hold it at bay. Before she knew it, her weapon clicked, signaling an empty magazine. Now, however, she was close enough to the top that light penetrated down to her level.

Without slowing her pace, she ejected the empty magazine and pulled another magazine from her coat pocket, jamming it smoothly into her weapon. With no wasted motion, she cocked the gun, placing a live round into its firing chamber, and then released the safety.

The rat's nose appeared around the inner wall, so she fired again. She thought she hit it, but the shot did not intimidate the beast. Instead of backing off, it jumped forward. As it drew closer, its stink increased sharply, making breathing impossible.

Agent Allen now stared down its long brackish nose and directly into its furious red eyes. Below the nose, its elongated, pointed fangs dripped green foam. Its lip curled to one side as if it were snarling. It matched her pace up the stairs, so she fired again and again, directly into its face, even into its eyes. The shots seemed to irritate it, but not slow it down. Suddenly, her gun clicked again. It was empty. She had no more magazines, no more bullets.

Running faster, she knew with certainty, *Now it will pounce on me.*

Cal jumped to his feet, swinging the extinguished torch this way and that with his left hand. He now held the .357 in his right hand, pointing it into the darkness. The snakes did not advance. In fact, Cal could no longer see or hear them. With another flash of lightning, Cal saw the sidewinders had all continued down the ravine. They were all heading away from Cal and Lenny as fast as they could go.

"Dude, where are the snakes?" Lenny's comment startled Cal. Lenny had gotten up off the ground and was now standing close by.

Cal pointed his charred branch down the trail. "They kept going. I guess they weren't chasing us after all."

Lenny's eyes widened. "Dude, what were they chasing?"

Cal rubbed his chin. "I don't know, man."

He looked up the hill from where they had run. A strong wind was blowing down on them, carrying the heavy scent of rain. At this lower altitude, the narrow valley had been swallowed up into a very steep and deep ravine. Cal looked at the nearby stream. It was running more forcefully now. He knew this ravine carried on for several hundred yards and ended in a large sandy basin, where the water from the stream disappeared into the ground.

"Maybe," Cal speculated. "Maybe, they weren't running after anything. Maybe they were running from something."

Lenny gave him a perplexed look. "Dude?"

At that moment, another bolt of lightning struck across the sky. With the loud clap of thunder came an instant downpour. It didn't start with a drop or two. It just poured hard with rain drops so large and cold, they felt like liquid marbles pelting Cal's naked torso. In seconds, they were both totally soaked.

More flashes followed in quick succession. The storm had overtaken them in its full force. Almost hidden by the thunder, Cal heard another noise. It was a rumbling, like a distant stampede. Muted at first, the volume of the rumbling quickly increased.

As the realization of what was happening hit Cal, Lenny

grabbed him, looking at him with surprise and consternation written all over his face. "Dude!"

There was no mistaking his meaning this time. The snakes hadn't been chasing them. The coiled one had probably thought they were chasing it. Its actions had been defensive. No, the snakes hadn't been chasing anything. They had been running from the coming flash flood, which was now almost on top of Cal and Lenny.

As one flash of lightning quickly followed the next, the roiling, tumbling wall of water approached as if in a stop action film. It was a bubbling, boiling wave of white and black, sticks and debris, eating up everything in its path. The rumble was so loud now, they could feel it. There was no time for even another "Dude" comment.

Shoving the .357 into his pocket, Cal dropped the branch with his burned-up shirt still tied to the end. Both he and Lenny began a frantic scramble up the side of the ravine. The ravine walls were steep and unstable, making any ascent difficult. In the dark, it was almost impossible. Hand and footholds were sparse. Any rock they grabbed came loose from the sandy sides. For all their desperate efforts, their progress was excruciatingly slow.

They were just over half way up when the first wave of the flood hit their feet. A couple steps took them higher, but the next wave came to their waists. Now, they were frantically grabbing for handholds not just to pull themselves up higher, but to cling to anything that would keep them from being swept away in the muddy, gurgling water.

As Lenny's footing washed out from underneath him, he cried, "Dude!"

At the same time, Cal managed to thrust himself up far enough to grab a tangle of sagebrush roots hanging from the side of the ravine. Sliding down into the water, Lenny managed to grab hold of Cal's leg.

The flood rose higher, and Lenny's head went under water. Straining every muscle, Cal struggled to hang on. Branches and debris struck his body as the black water swirled around him. Lenny's head bobbed above the waves, and he managed to catch a few gasping breaths before he went back under. The water pulled and sucked at Lenny, who was pulling Cal down with him.

Cal refused to let go of the roots, but the rushing current was washing the dirt out from under his feet. Before he knew it, Cal lost his footing. The only thing keeping them both from joining the jetsam downstream was Cal's grip on the scrawny sagebrush roots.

The water level was now up to Cal's chest, and Lenny was completely submerged. With everything he had, Cal pulled himself higher, reaching up hand over hand for more roots, bringing Lenny's head just above water.

Cal's biceps strained against the skin as he held his position. Lenny, gasping for breath, held onto Cal with one hand as he grasped above him with the other, searching for a handhold. Both were battered and bashed by the water and everything the flood carried down the hill with it. They were weakening quickly.

With his last ounce of strength, Cal found the muscle to pull them both up another six inches out of the flood. One foot found a rocky ledge that seemed to hold, so he pushed up even more. Lenny grabbed a handful of roots with his free hand. For the moment, both rested, feeling they had finally reached a solid position.

They didn't rest long. Before either could move another inch, the sagebrush roots Cal had been holding came out of the hillside in a tangle. Cal lost his footing, and the water slammed him into Lenny. The roots Lenny was holding broke loose under their combined weight. The swirling flood grabbed them both. Down with the rest of the debris they went, completely at the mercy of the frenzied deluge.

Slowly stepping backward, Agent Allen stared into the rat's furious red eyes, daring it to move. She expected it to pounce any second now. While she stared, the rat crouched back on its haunches. Dropping lower to the ground, it prepared to spring. Agent Allen's eyes felt hot as they continued to bore into the rat's eyes, challenging the rat, defying the rat. Her eyes felt as bloodshot as the rat's eyes looked. Their gazes locked, she continued to step backward.

Without realizing it, her hand touched the broad stone doorway into the cellar, and she stepped back onto the top stair. Though every muscle had tightened, like a deadly spring, still the rat had not pounced. Agent Allen did not dare look away. Both remained locked in a deadly stare-down, waiting to see who would blink first.

Mesmerized by the deadly red eyes, Agent Allen tried to take another step up, but her foot hovered in the air. Agent Kline grabbed her with one hand and lifted her bodily through the doorway. With his other hand, he helped Mr. C pull the stone door closed.

The rat saw the door closing, and finally pounced, trying to reach the doorway while it was still open. Just in time, the door closed with a loud bang as the full weight of the rat hit hard against the other side. Agent Allen heard a click as a locking mechanism secured it closed.

On the other side of the door, they could hear the rasping of the rat's foul breath. Before anyone had a chance to relax, there was another click and the door started to creep open.

Agent Allen rolled her eyes. *Of course, it knows how to open the stone door.*

All three pulled on the door to close it. Rough stone edges provided makeshift handles. With their combined strength, the three barely managed to close the door. It clicked shut again.

The rat had not given up. Again, the door mechanism clicked and the door started to open. The tug-of-war started all over again.

"How is it doing that?" Agent Allen growled through gritted teeth.

Mr. C replied between gasps. "It has hold of something on the other side with its mouth."

While Agents Allen and Kline strained to hold the stone door closed, Mr. C made a quick survey of the cellar. Suddenly, he picked up a wooden barrel, covered with a dirty sheet, and threw the barrel against the wall, shattering it.

"What is he doing?" Agent Allen gasped in Agent Kline's ear as they struggled to keep the door from opening.

Mr. C gathered up handfuls of the pieces of broken barrel slats and hurried over to the door. He jammed the slats into the crevices between the edge of the stone door and its stone jam. He then stepped back and, with the sole of his shoe, crammed the slats deep into every crevice.

Surprisingly, at least to Agent Allen, the maneuver worked. The broken slats jammed the door so that it could no longer be unlatched from the inside. Suddenly, they heard a series of loud crashes, which seemed to shake the cellar wall. Repeatedly, the rat threw itself against the other side of the thick stone door. The heavy door remained solid and unmovable.

A loud screeching wail came from the other side of the door, getting louder, more shrill, until it was a piercing squeal. The sound was hideous, angry, and plaintive, all at the same time.

Agent Allen backed away from the door. *It knows it's trapped behind a solid stone wall.*

Breathing hard, the three of them sat down on the stone floor. Mr. C's face was blotchy red as he wheezed and struggled for air. When he could finally gasp out a few words between breaths, he said, "Thank you both."

Agent Allen ignored Mr. C. "So, what do we do with it now?"

Agent Kline looked at her with a sober expression. His huge frame heaved in and out with each breath. "I think we have no choice. We have to kill it."

Mr. C was too out of breath to join the conversation. Wheezing, he lay back on the stones in a prone position and worked at catching his breath.

For some time, they could hear the rat scuffling and scratching on the other side of the stone door. Eventually, everything went quiet.

XXII

It listened at the stone door and traced their scents. They had all gone upstairs. It had no doubt they were planning to hurt it. They had hurt it already. Not seriously, but with everything they did, pain was inflicted. It hated them. It hated all humans. It had always hated humans!

It knew the mansion better than they did. They had carelessly removed the frame. And now, the chain was gone as well. It was almost free!

It knew how to get out of the mansion. It knew another way. It had only to wait for the darkness of night. It loved the night.

XXIII

Camm sat on the edge of the rock ledge that served as her bed in her little rock alcove, nibbling on the last of the meager meal the old man had brought her. He had stayed to watch her eat, his gray eyes following her hand each time she brought a morsel to her lips. His scrutiny made her nervous, but she had been hungry enough to keep eating.

This guy needs to get out more if watching me eat is so fascinating.

Once she had been able to explore her surroundings, Camm realized she was not in a mine, but in a natural cave that seemed to extend far back under the mountains. Since she was not in a mine, she did not need to worry about vertical shafts or mine dust, but she still wondered about the old man and why he was living in the cave. Growing up in Trona, she had never heard anything about an old hermit living this close to town. She wondered how he had managed to stay hidden for so long.

She cleared her throat. "Thanks for the food."

He bobbed his head, but remained silent.

"I'm Camm. What's your name."

His face crinkled in amusement. "J.R." He giggled, as if it were some inside joke. Then he went back to staring at her with a straight face.

She tried again. "What is this cave we're in? Do you live here?"

"Before my patriarch, it was the switching point, but not always, for at times the V. ready seer pans was the switching point, but roaming. And then the switching point changed by design, and 'it' was there. These came to assist, but not knowing, they were mortified."

He swept out his only hand, indicating the three dead bodies that were Camm's roommates in her stone alcove. All stood solemnly against one wall of her little room, secured with spikes like the one at the cave opening.

"But now, we are at the switching point, but not always."

Giving her a vague smile, he reached for her empty plate and water cup and ambled out of the room, leaving behind the short stubby candle he had placed on a narrow ledge for light.

Camm leaned back against the rock wall and took a deep breath. "Whoa! I think we speak the same language, but I didn't understand a thing he just said."

For the next couple days, Camm stayed in the cave mainly because she was afraid of getting caught if she left. But she also had a nagging sense that somehow all this weirdness was connected with the mansion and the rat, maybe even the snake.

The old man gave her food and water, and he seemed to like having her around. He didn't ask her to leave. But he talked in riddles and circles, which made getting information out of him difficult. And some things, like the mansion, he just wouldn't talk about at all.

Needing someone to think things through with, Camm began conversing with her three dead roommates. Unfortunately, they weren't very talkative, and no matter how she twisted what she knew in her head with what the old man was saying, only vague connections emerged.

"Curly, you are no help at all," Camm said matter-of-factly. She cocked her head at the dead body in the middle as if waiting for a reply.

She knew giving the bodies names was stupid, and it made her feel a little foolish, but it also made her feel more at ease with them. Curly was completely bald and had a frozen expression on his face that made him look like he died in the act of laughing.

The body on Curly's right wore an angry expression on his face with a few long strands of black hair hanging off his head. He was Moe. By default, the third body, with blonde hair, closed eyes, and wearing a calm expression, was Larry.

To keep with her theme, Camm had considered calling the body by the entrance Shemp, but at that point it all became too ridiculous. She settled for calling him the sentry.

J.R. came twice a day to bring Camm food. On one of those visits, she asked about the mummified dead bodies.

"They came from here, and went over there to help, but they didn't know how, so they were mortified." Pointing at Larry, Moe, and Curly Joe, he said, "These three were of a legionnaire type, but not aware of the power and the scope, nor did they understand the dimensional switching, and ultimately 'it' did them in. How mortifying! I brought them here so that when switching switched they could come here, and not be there, although if switching switches again, they could be back there."

"What about the guy standing guard in the cave opening," Camm asked, hoping to keep the old man talking long enough to actually say something she understood.

J. R. shook his head. "He came not by agreement, but by coincident, and though he needed assistance, he would not be persuaded. Panic and foolishness caused his undoing, and I brought him here, like the others, to watch and keep them of the tribe away."

Staring at J.R. in confusion, Camm asked him to be more clear. He just repeated what he had already told her. Little of it made sense.

J.R. smiled gently and left.

Camm pushed off her ledge seat to pace around the space she had come to think of as her own—the cave opening and her little sleeping alcove. She needed to put together what J.R. had been telling her with what she already knew. She knew J.R. must be connected somehow with the mansion and the green rat. She wasn't sure how, but she knew it was important.

She was sure the "switching point" had something to do with what had happened to Cal and Lenny, and that when J. R. referred to "it," he was talking about the rat. She was still confused, though, by the "V. ready seer pans" and most of the rest as well.

The identity of the corpses was still a mystery, but they had to be connected with the mansion. The Three Stooges had serious gashes and body wounds that must have caused their deaths. Camm had no doubt they were killed by the green rat.

Marching up to the cave opening, Camm stood in front of the sentry to examine him in the sunlight. She saw no signs of the cause of his death. Maybe it was the rat, maybe the snake, or maybe something else altogether. Or maybe it wasn't important.

Camm was running out of clues. She couldn't stay in this cave forever, and J.R. wasn't saying anything new. It was time to move on, but she wanted to stay in J.R's good graces. She might need to talk with him again, and in any case, she might need a place to hide again.

She saluted the sentry. "Carry on."

Camm turned on her heel and went in search of J. R.

When she left the mansion, she had been heading north toward Homewood Canyon. That still seemed like a good idea. Maybe she should talk to Sarah again. Of course, Sarah talked in circles, too. Maybe she should bring J.R. with her. Perhaps, by joining J.R.'s circles with Sarah's circles, the answers she needed could be put together.

XXIV

"You guys keep working. I won't be gone long. You should be able to get that brief ready before I get back."

Sean and Jim startled at the interruption and stared back at her, nervous as always when she spoke to them. Papers were slowly chugging out of the ancient printer Martha had found in the small office used by the boys. Another find had been a collating machine, antiquated, but still usable. Although she did all her basic work online, she had started printing and collating the briefs she wrote for the Judge Advocate General's office as a backup record of her work and as a mild form of rebellion.

Besides, she needed something to keep Sean and Jim busy. Both boys wore permanent GPS wrist monitors. They were prohibited from leaving the Navy Base at any time and were not allowed any outside communications. Their office barracks contained no phones. Martha believed this was to discourage the boys from trying to make phone calls.

It had been easy to deduce that the two boys had been through a traumatic experience, probably similar to her own. But they weren't talking. Only their pale, strained faces and the way they jumped at sudden or strange sounds gave them away.

Martha's mouth twisted wryly. *Those Swift Creek bullies have scared them into silence.*

She wished she could help them, but she could not admit she had met up with a swarm of giant spiders and had been chased by a monstrous snake without revealing that she had not forgotten everything. She was sure she was being monitored most, if not all the time.

She called to the boys, "If you get done before I get back, do something fun. I found an old Pac-Man program on my computer. Believe it or not, Pong was there, too. Those games were before your time, but you might want to try them out for their historical value."

Leaving the sterilized offices to Sean and Jim, Martha drove her government-issue jeep to a natural history museum in Ridgecrest called the Maturango Museum. Its grounds were studded with Native American artifacts and art work.

Martha had figured out that "Maturango" was a local Indian word, and Maturango Peak was the name of the highest point along the Argus Mountain range. The peak was located within the boundary of the China Lake Naval Weapons Station in an area closed to the general public.

Though the museum was small and under-funded, she

soon found what she was looking for. Thumbing through a large locally published picture book, she studied page after page of ancient pictographs that had been discovered on the rocks in the area around China Lake and Searles Valley. Martha carefully thumbed through the photographs, looking for symbols similar to those she had seen in the old Searles Mansion. Several of the pictographs consisted of a backward 'S' figure with a tear drop at the top end.

Is that a snake? Martha decided to seek help.

Back behind some bookshelves in the library portion of the museum, Martha found a schoolmarm-type woman with pince-nez reading glasses, her hair pulled back into a bun.

"Excuse me," Martha asked. "Do you work here?"

The woman gave Martha a friendly smile. "I volunteer here one day a week. Can I help you with something?"

"Yes, uh." Martha stumbled a little. Something about this woman made Martha uncomfortable. She pointed at the backward "S" pictograph. "I see this symbol a lot in these pictures. Do you know what it means?"

"Why, of course dear. That is the local Native American symbol for snake."

"I see. Did they worship the snake or something? Because you see it a lot."

The woman smiled again. "We don't know what they worshiped for sure, but I don't think that putting the symbol on the rocks around where they hunted meant they worshiped snakes. It may very well mean they were afraid of them."

"They were afraid of snakes?"

"Yes, of course, dear. Lots of people are afraid of snakes. Just because the snakes were indigenous to this area doesn't mean those early people weren't afraid of them."

"I see," Martha repeated. She hesitated, then asked, "The symbol is large in comparison with the pictographs of people, but I guess that relative size in these Native American drawings doesn't necessarily mean anything."

"Maybe it does, maybe it doesn't. Maybe that is a pictograph of a very large snake—maybe even a giant snake." The woman gave Martha a matronly smile, but behind her glasses, she stared at her intensely, as if looking for her reaction.

While her insides went cold at the mention of a giant snake, Martha didn't react. She returned the smile. "Thank you! That is very interesting."

She tried to say interesting in such a way that made it sound as if it was not interesting. She turned and started to walk away from the woman, but then turned back. "Excuse me, but I didn't get your name."

The woman gave Martha another one of her smiles. "Of course, dear. Everyone just calls me Miss Cathleen."

XXV

Mr. C sat upright in his chair, a look of annoyance written across his face. His fingers nervously drummed on the armrest. Agent Allen smiled at his irritation. She had hauled two more chairs into the pool room so she and Agent Kline could also be seated. She would not be left standing while she argued with these two old men. Not again. Mr. S was also present, his hand bandaged where he had lost his finger tip.

Mr. C swept them all with an especially stern look. "We are not killing the rat. I believe that course of action would be extraordinarily unwise."

Agent Allen heaved a heavy sigh. They had been at this argument for some time. Mr. S and Agent Kline had been largely silent, but Agent Allen had insisted on killing the green rat before midnight. At midnight they were going to start the clock and try to bring Cal and Lenny back. Mr. C remained vehemently opposed to the idea of killing the rat.

Agent Allen decided to try a different tactic. "Then, you come up with a better idea. Once we start the clock, that rat can transition into the mansion on the other side, where the boys are now. On our side, that thing is trapped in the secret stairway. If it transitions into the other mansion's stairway, it can get out into the cellar by opening the door. It will be free to move between that world and this one, and go wherever it wants. And we know what it likes to eat!"

Mr. C drummed his fingers, staring hard at Agent Allen. "Then we have no choice. We will delay the transition until a later time, until after we get the rat under control."

"NO!" Agent Allen bolted straight up in her chair. "Those boys are expecting us to bring them back tonight. Who knows what will happen to them if they stay any longer? We don't even know if they have anything to eat. We told them—no— you told them," Agent Allen pointed at Mr. S, "that we would try again tonight at midnight. We can't let them down now."

Mr. C slapped the arm of his chair for emphasis. "We can't risk the rat getting loose. We all agree on that. We cannot—we should not kill it. It is essential to the science we are doing here. I believe we will need it as the guardian once we get both clocks working in sync and get the dimensional frame back on this side again."

"We cannot let those boys down." Agent Allen leaned forward and spoke slowly and sternly. "We must make every effort to bring them back tonight."

Finally, Mr. S spoke up. "I agree with Agent Allen. Those boys must be brought back if at all possible. True, they are in danger there, and as dangerous as the rat is here, the boys could be upsetting the system of things over there. We've got loose cannons on both sides."

Mr. C sat back in his chair. "It seems we are at an impasse."

"Maybe," Agent Kline put in, "we could tranquilize it. You know, with powerful tranquilizer guns. Shoot it and knock it out."

"With what?" Mr. C sounded annoyed again. "Things from this world don't always work on things from the other world. And, I think, vice versa. What are we going to shoot it with?"

Agent Kline furrowed his brow. "I suggest a cocktail of ketamine with some kind of strong sedative. Ketamine works on horses. It might work on the rat, especially in large doses."

Mr. C shook his head. "Not good enough. Might is just not good enough. Besides, where do we get ketamine by tonight? I doubt there is any in Trona."

"No, but there will be in Ridgecrest," Mr. S pointed out. "A number of people in Ridgecrest and Trona have horses. I'm sure a veterinarian in Ridgecrest will have some."

Agent Allen was relieved to hear Mr. S had come over to her side, at least on the issue of trying to bring the two boys back.

"But, what if it is not enough? What if it doesn't work?" Mr. C persisted.

Agent Kline glanced around. "We could add lysergic acid diethylamide to the cocktail."

"LSD?" Agent Allen was incredulous. "You want to shoot

that crazy rat full of LSD? Like it's not crazy enough already? Who knows what it will do if it is tripping out on LSD?"

Agent Kline shrugged. "I just know at one time it was used quite effectively as a tranquilizer for horses."

Agent Allen sat back in her chair to think. "What did Camm and Cal use when they almost killed it? Why can't we use what they used?"

"We're not sure how they got it," Mr. S explained, "but we believe they shot it with snake venom. Not from local snakes, but venom from a snake on the other side. Probably from that giant Mojave Green snake that chased you."

Mr. C snorted. "You're welcome to try and milk that thing if you want to."

"Now, now." Mr. S momentarily raised an eyebrow at Mr. C.

Then he suggested, "Let's not mix the two. Let's shoot the rat with two different darts. One dart will have the ketamine cocktail and the other will have LSD. Perhaps one or the other will work, or perhaps they will work in concert. I think that is our best option."

Agent Allen shook her head. "I can't believe you want to shoot that thing up with LSD. Anyway, we might be able to get ketamine, but where do we find LSD in time for tonight?"

Misters S and C exchanged glances.

Mr. S responded, "We already have some."

XXVI

Dusk was falling as Camm made her way down the hillside toward the outlying homes in Trona. J.R. stumbled next to her. She steadied the old man, holding onto his arm, the one he still had. Neither Camm nor J.R. noticed they were being stealthily followed. Two sets of eyes kept them in sight at all times.

Camm had determined she needed to get J.R. together with Sarah. Maybe they could understand each other. She knew she couldn't bring Sarah to the cave and had concluded there was no way J.R. could walk all the way to Homewood Canyon. The solution to her problem had come to her while sitting outside the cave, looking down on her tiny desert hometown.

Her friend, Becky Jimenez, lived with her parents on the edge of town in a weather-beaten, sun-blanched house. Becky had been in Camm's high school graduating class, one of thirty-three graduates. Becky had not left town. Instead, she now worked at the plant.

During high school, Becky's parents had bought her an old Dodge Dart. It was a beat-up old car, sand blasted and sun baked to the point its original color could not be determined. The ignition had malfunctioned, so Becky's dad had hard wired it so it could be started without a key. One had only to turn the ignition to engage the starter.

The car was parked behind the house most of the time. Camm knew Becky hated taking it anywhere, even to work, because it was so worn and ugly. Her plan was to walk J.R. down to the Jimenez house and borrow the car to drive out to see Sarah. Afterward, Camm would see that the car was returned.

She was sure Becky would gladly give her permission if asked, but knowing what Camm did about Swift Creek, Camm figured it was better for Becky if she just took the car.

As Camm approached the edge of town, she suddenly noticed J.R. was not with her. Anxiously glancing around, she saw him hiding behind a large bush they had just passed.

"J.R., what are you doing?" she whispered loudly. He didn't answer, but pointed toward a nearby street. A dark colored SUV was headed up the road. Camm ducked behind the bush with J.R. just before the headlights struck her. Once the car had rolled slowly past, Camm helped J.R. up, and they continued toward the Dodge.

Camm studied the old man hobbling beside her. Constantly vigilant, J.R. seemed to notice everything going on around him. He must have been hiding in that cave, keeping out of sight, for years and years. No wonder she had never heard anything about him. Sadly, she decided, avoiding cars and strangers must be second nature to him now. *What a lonely life.*

When they got to the car, Camm was perturbed to find it locked. *Why would anyone want to steal this car?* Which was ironic because that was exactly what she planned to do. Though the car was locked, the windows were down a little. In Trona, no one ever parked a car in direct sunlight with all the windows closed. The inside of the car would literally turn into a hot oven. Fortunately, Camm was able to squeeze her arm into the car and pull up the latch.

Opening the car door, she turned to help J.R. into the front seat. He was missing again.

"J.R., J.R., where did you go?" Camm scanned the nearby bushes for him.

"I'm right here!" The loud voice startled her. It certainly did not belong to the old man from the cave. Around the corner of the house came a short, thick man in a dark suit and white shirt, obviously an agent of Swift Creek. He approached, looking at her suspiciously. "What do you want? Why are you calling my name?"

Her blood ran cold. She recognized him as one of the agents from the mansion. He hadn't said two words to her the whole time she was imprisoned there and had even avoided looking at her.

All I need, she thought. *An agent who has a grudge against me for killing Roberts.*

"Well, what do you want? Why are you calling my name? Who are you anyway?"

He spouted off questions in an abrupt official manner, like a police officer might question a suspect. Camm's initial thought was to run, but she couldn't leave J.R.—her J.R., that is.

As the short agent scowled at her, it finally occurred to her, he didn't recognize her as the escapee from the mansion. He made no effort to go for his gun, to detain her, or to call for back-up. He just wanted to know why she was calling his name.

Looking especially annoyed, he leaned forward and asked loudly, "You called me. What do you want?" Each word was pronounced slowly and precisely, as if he were talking to an idiot.

Camm's mind raced for a response.

"I wasn't calling you," was all she could think to say.

The agent put his hands on his hips as his scowl deepened. "I heard you call my name. You were calling for J.R. I am J.R."

"Oh," she said faintly. *What are the odds of finding another J.R.?*

Scrambling for a reply, she mumbled, "I, uh, I wasn't calling you. I don't know your name. I was, um, calling for my dog."

The agent peered at her over the top of his sunglasses. "Your dog's name is J.R.?"

Camm tried not to glare at him. *So what if it is?*

Deciding not to be a smart aleck, her mind calmed. She was in control of the situation. This agent didn't remember her. She need only play along, and she wouldn't get caught.

"My dog's name is Jeter, you know, after the Yankee baseball player. I was calling for Jeter." She flashed a big, harmless smile at the agent.

Agent J.R. continued to scowl at her. He seemed to sense something was wrong, but couldn't put his finger on it. "Who are you anyway? Identify yourself."

"My name is Becky Jimenez. I live here." Camm pointed at the house. "You questioned us a few nights ago. Remember?"

The agent's brow furrowed. "Oh, yeah, that's right. Okay. I thought you were calling J.R." He shifted nervously. "Did you get your evacuation orders? Only workers are allowed in town."

"Yes, I know. I was working today. I just came by the house for a few things."

"Okay. Carry on, Miss, uh . . ."

"Miss Jimenez."

"Yea, I remember. Miss Jimenez. Carry on." He turned and strode away.

What a dufus!

After the agent had rounded the corner and disappeared, Camm hurriedly searched for her J.R. She found him crouched behind the garbage cans next door. He certainly was good at

277

hiding. She sighed. She wished he would give her some warning when he saw someone coming.

Camm took hold of his arm and helped him up.

He smiled at her and quietly exclaimed, *"Mentirosa!"*

Camm didn't know what that meant, but it sounded like something from her high school Spanish class. She eased him into the front seat of the car. No one seemed to be home at the Jimenez house, so they drove away to see Sarah without further incident.

Camm never saw the two nearly naked men with a small dog, watching her drive away.

XXVII

Lenny shoveled another load of sand onto the stairs leading up to the front door of the mansion. It was a hot, hot, dry day—still hot, even though it was evening. It was too hot for manual labor. Lenny did not like manual labor on any day, not even on the best of days.

He dropped the compact folding shovel, which they had found in one of the military style backpacks, and squinted against the light from the setting sun. "Dude, I'm not sure this is wise. I mean, we're lucky just to be alive. You know what I mean?"

Lucky was not a word Lenny was comfortable using. Not for this situation. The natural laws of the universe were at play, of that Lenny had no doubt. But exactly how they were playing out, Lenny did not know. That he and Cal should be dead, he was certain. He felt the universe had somehow been cheated. He was having trouble deciding how to deal with it.

Cal put down the hubcap he had been using as a shovel and returned Lenny's squint. "So, we're alive. We survived the flashflood. Quit beating a dead horse. By one power or another, you choose which one, the ravine suddenly opened up onto the flat desert floor so the water could quickly spread out and lose its force. Obviously, we're just fated to die some other way besides drowning in a flashflood. Big deal! What's that got to do with my car?"

Cal and Lenny had been shoveling sand for much of the day onto the stairs leading up to the oversized front doors of the mansion. They were building a ramp to drive Cal's Camaro up into the mansion's main hall. At midnight, an attempt would be made to bring them home. Cal was determined not to leave his car behind. He wanted it in the mansion so it could make the transition back with them. Lenny was not so sentimental.

"Look. We know some things, but I'm not sure how this whole transition thing works. It's like, dude, moving two people back and forth from one dimension to another is one thing. Moving two tons of lifeless steel, well, dude, that's something else. I don't know if we should try it. Let's just try to get back ourselves. I mean, really, dude!"

Cal hung his head and took a deep breath. Lenny knew he was working on a response.

Cal looked up. "From what you told me, the two different mansions actually change places. That makes sense, from what Camm and I saw last year when the grandfather clock was working. This beat-up one goes over to the other side at midnight, and the clean one over there comes here until they change back sometime before morning."

Lenny scratched his head. "I guess. I mean, I think. I don't know, dude, that's my best estimate of what happens."

"So, the entire mass of this huge, stone mansion goes through the transition. My Camaro weighs only a little fraction of what the mansion does. Right? It doesn't seem like such a big stretch to bring this little bit of extra weight along. Right?"

"Yeah, but dude, we just don't know. It's all guesswork and stuff. We just don't know."

Cal sighed and rubbed his sore hands together. "I just don't want to leave my car behind. Not here, not in this weird world of giant snakes and hawks and stuff. This is my first car. I know it's not alive and doesn't have feelings and crap, but it's my first car. I don't feel right leaving it behind. At the very least, I'm going to park it in the main hall and shut the front doors. There's plenty of room. The mansion won't mind. My car is smaller than some of the furniture."

Now it was Lenny's turn to sigh. "I know. Or maybe I don't know 'cause I've never owned my own car. But dude, it's like, we should be dead, you know, drowned and dead. Somehow the weird rules between this world and our world have kept us alive. I wonder if now we're pushing things a little, like stepping on the rules too much, you know, like bad dimensional karma, you know, like that."

Lenny smiled to himself. He knew no one could mix eastern religion with theoretical physics like he could.

The truth was, and Lenny knew it, they should be dead. The flashflood had carried them several hundred yards before spreading out across the sandy desert floor.

Lenny was a surfer, a strong swimmer. Cal was no slouch himself. On the football team, Cal lifted weights and kept in shape. But swimming in a pool or even surfing in the ocean did not compare to riding a flashflood down a narrow canyon amid heavy limbs and debris.

Both Cal and Lenny had been held under water for much of the ride, being battered and banged by all the debris in the flood waters. But the ride had been mercifully short. Both had been washed up on a sandbar as the flood waters quickly spread out. Waterlogged and bruised, gasping for breath while puking up nasty, dirty water, they were nevertheless alive. Both believed that something besides dumb luck had kept them alive.

Cal's theory was more simple. After all those years of going to Sunday School with Camm, he believed there was a higher intelligence at work in the universe, and his desperate prayers for help had been answered.

But this was too simple for Lenny. He didn't know what had happened, but he was sure inter-dimensional forces were at work. He wanted to know what laws of physics had saved them, what it was about being from one dimension and living in another that had kept them alive.

Something had, but what? It was the not knowing that worried Lenny. He was scientific in a superstitious kind of way. Since there was so much he didn't understand, it seemed foolish to press their so-called luck any more than they had to.

Cal had resumed shoveling sand onto the stairs. A person's attachment to his or her car was something Lenny had never understood, but he knew that such attachments existed. He figured he had no choice but to accept it, especially in this case. In the end, he didn't want to disappoint Cal.

Lenny squinted at the last rays of sunlight as they disappeared behind the Argus Mountains. He picked up the shovel again and started shoveling sand onto the stairs leading up to the mansion. Midnight could not come fast enough for him.

XXVIII

Agent Kline directed the thermal imaging camera at the stone door that opened onto the spiral staircase. Squinting at the readouts, he shook his head. "I am detecting no heat signature at all on the other side of this door."

All of the surveillance cameras down in the little stone room seemed to be working just fine, but no one on the team of observers had seen any sign of the giant alien rat all day. Everyone assumed it was hiding out somewhere along the deep spiral staircase, and, if not perched directly behind the stone door, it would be hiding somewhere near the top of the stairs where it could reach the stone door within seconds after it was opened.

Agent Kline looked over at Mr. S. "Do you hear anything?

Mr. S wore a distant look. His hand pressed the listening device against the closed edge of the stone door as he listened through his earphones. "I cannot detect any sounds at all on the other side of the door. The rat should at least be breathing, if not moving otherwise. In any case, we should have been able to detect its heat."

"Good." Mr. C had been hunched by the door with the two men. "Then the rat must be farther down the stairway." Straightening, he said, "Okay, everyone, it's time to open the door and get this done. From here on out, we move fast. Agent Allen, you're in charge."

Mr. C had been heading up the venture to this point, but only three agents were going down the stairs to tranquilize the rat. Misters S and C had reluctantly admitted they were too old and too slow to be a part of any assault team. Agent Allen would head up the team and also be the point person. Everyone was beginning to trust her instincts. Her team would consist of herself, and Agents Kline and J.R. While there were other agents on site, the narrow stairway was too small to accommodate a bigger team, so the others were being used at critical sentry points both inside and outside of the mansion.

J.R. had been brought up to speed on the snake, the rat, and the mansion, and was still blown away by what had really happened to Rick. As J.R. and Agent Allen stood waiting for the results from the listening and heat sensing devices, she noticed a confused look on his face.

"Are you okay?" Agent Allen was always wary where J.R. was concerned.

"Tell me, uh, what did that girl, Camm Smith, look like?"

The question confused Agent Allen. "What?"

"Never mind." After that, J.R. seemed to concentrate more on the task at hand.

They had thought through this mission carefully. Agent Allen would take the lead with a pistol containing darts full of ketamine and a heavy sedative. She also had her Glock loaded and ready. J.R. was to be right behind her with darts full of LSD. He had a twelve gage, sawed-off shotgun attached to his thigh. Agent Kline brought up the rear because he could see over the other two, and he carried the high-power weaponry.

Agent Kline had made a quick call and received a special delivery just for the occasion. He was carrying a Smith and Wesson 500 Magnum revolver. Its five chambers were loaded with .50 caliber shells. Each shell was over a half inch in diameter and almost two inches long. The loaded pistol weighed over five pounds. It was the most powerful double-action revolver in the world, perhaps the most powerful handgun of any type. It was almost three times as powerful as a regular .44 Magnum and could stop a running grizzly bear dead in its tracks. They all prayed that it could also slow down a giant green rat.

All three agents wore ear pieces that not only allowed them to communicate, but also prevented deafness should the Smith and Wesson be fired in the confined space of the stairwell. They each wore a headband with an attached light. Specially made for the military, the lights were extraordinarily bright. The headlights were to be held in reserve and used only when the rat started extinguishing the ceiling lights.

Agent Allen glanced round at her team. "Four hours to midnight. Let's go put that obscene rodent to sleep." She nodded to Mr. C, who opened the door to the stairwell. The broken barrel slats had been pulled out earlier, allowing the door to swing open.

Mr. S turned on the lights. As agreed, the team waited thirty seconds. When the lights didn't go out and the rat didn't charge through the open door, the three agents began their descent.

Cautiously, Agent Allen started down the steps, holding her dart gun in front of her with both hands. She would have felt more secure holding her Glock, but she remembered what effect it had had on the rat before—almost none.

The two other agents followed close behind. She sensed J.R.'s dart gun just over her right shoulder. "Don't you shoot me with that LSD dart," she said. In her mind, she added, *you putz.*

"Don't worry," his voice came through her ear piece, "I know what I'm doing." He sounded offended she would even suggest he might accidently shoot her. That was okay. As far as Agent Allen was concerned, he could be offended as long as he was careful.

Slowly, they made their way down. The ceiling lights above their heads stayed on. Agent Allen sniffed the air. *That horrible smell isn't here.* When the rat had chased them up these same steps, that awful, stinking, sulfur-like smell had almost suffocated her.

She knew the old men wanted to keep that ugly, mangy thing alive, but if it so happened that she filled it with enough tranquilizer to slow it down, and then shot it until it was dead with her Glock, well, too bad. She would not be sorry.

It still made her angry that Swift Creek had brought it back to life with the anti-venom serum they had come up with from somewhere. She thought of what a frightening experience it must have been for Camm and Cal to face the rat when they tried to kill it. They had risked their lives and had almost succeeded. A huge sacrifice for nothing. These Swift Creek guys had their priorities all wrong. This rat deserved to die.

Slowly, they inched their way down the steep spiraling stairway, never able to see more than a few feet in front of them. The rat could be around any turn, waiting, crouching, ready to spring. It would reach Agent Allen first. One crushing bite would snap her neck.

Although it was not especially warm this far underground, Agent Allen could feel the perspiration run down her back and drip from her forehead. This was the most nerve-wracking, the most fearsome, and without a doubt, the scariest thing she had ever experienced in her life.

Another step, and then another, and then one more step, and still the stairs continued as if there were no end. Each step down revealed only a little more around the unending curve.

With each step down and each little extra view, Agent Allen expected to see that black nose, the matted green fur, and the evil red eyes. She felt in her bones it was waiting, right around the corner, ready to pounce. She kept thinking, *Just one more step.*

Down, down they went. All the way down. When they arrived at the bottom, at the little stone room where the rat had been imprisoned, they saw nothing. The room was there. The Plexiglas leaned to one side where it had been knocked off its mooring. The chain with the empty shackle snaked across the dirt floor. But there was no rat.

Agent Allen reported through her mouth piece to the old men waiting upstairs. "We've reached the bottom. There is no rat in sight. I repeat, there is no rat. It is gone."

Mr. C responded, "Are you sure? Did you miss it somehow?"

Agent Allen rolled her eyes. "Sir, there is hardly enough room for us to come down these stairs. There is no possible way we could have missed it."

She climbed over the Plexiglas and searched the little room that had been the rat's prison cell. Just to be sure, she pushed against all the walls and the ceiling. She could not find a secret door. There was no rat. It was not there.

She turned to face her two colleagues, and held her hands up in defeat. "We might as well go back upstairs."

J.R. looked confused. "So, where is this big green rat?"

"I don't know." Agent Allen glanced about, worried.

Agent Kline scratched his head. "It was on the stairs the last we saw it. We locked it in. I don't see where it could have gone."

J.R. turned to face Agent Kline, and as he did, his gun bumped against the wall, causing it to fire a dart. The dart shot down, straight into Agent Kline's foot. The needle penetrated his shoe, and before he could pull it out, the contents emptied into his body.

"You shot me!" Agent Kline was incredulous. "You shot me full of LSD!"

Agent Allen fought her way past the Plexiglas to where the

other two agents were standing. J.R. had a look of horror on his face as if he couldn't believe what he had just done. Agent Kline, who at first looked shocked, now seemed to be relaxing, even smiling. Agent Allen was sure that was not a good thing.

"You putz!" Agent Allen pushed J.R. out of the way. Carefully, she helped Agent Kline sit down on the steps.

"I . . . I didn't try to. It was an accident." J.R.'s mouth hung slack.

Mr. C's voice came through each ear piece. "What's going on down there?"

Agent Allen held Agent Kline's face in her hands, trying to get a fix on his condition. He was a very big man, but he had been shot with a lot of LSD. Carefully, she removed the Smith and Wesson from his giant hand. He gazed up at her, his eyes slowly becoming unfocused.

"Holy . . . !" he whispered in an amazed voice as he reclined all the way back on the steps. His eyes rolled back up into his head.

Fury flared up inside Agent Allen. She turned to face J.R. who still had an idiotic expression on his face. "You dumb, stupid putz," she shouted at him.

Without warning, she slugged him in the mouth. Stunned, he backed away, blood running down from multiple breaks in his lip.

Mr. C spoke up again. "I say. What's going on down there?"

With a sigh, Agent Allen responded, "Sir, we've got injured agents down here. We will need help getting the wounded back up top."

XXIX

By the time they arrived at Homewood Canyon, it was
nearly dark. Only a sliver of sunlight hung over the
western hills, and the moon had not yet risen in the
east. A glow over the Slate Range suggested the moon might
soon peak out from behind those eastern mountains. Camm
knew the glow did not come from the moon, but was from
the casinos and street lights of Las Vegas shining all the way
to Trona.

So much for what happens in Vegas stays in Vegas, Camm thought.

She parked the decrepit Dodge in front of the old, battered
house where Sarah lived. J.R. had been enthralled with the
car ride, but now sat silently next to Camm. For a moment,
Camm surveyed the homes and yards around her. Nothing
moved. Even in the dusk, everything looked beaten, weathered,
bleached, and shabby. The combination of the unrelenting

desert sun and the fierce sandblasting winds had sucked the life and color out of everything.

Growing up, Camm had thought Trona the ideal place to live. The edge of town was never far if she wanted to go exploring. Finding her friends at their favorite haunts was so simple. And she had liked knowing everyone in her high school. Not just everyone in her own class, but everyone in the whole school, teachers, administration, and janitors included.

The town was so small, if you were rude to someone, you were sure to see them the next day delivering your paper or ringing up your purchase at the grocery store. When Agent Allen had visited a year ago and been so condescending toward Trona, Camm had fiercely defended her beloved hometown. Now she could see what Agent Allen had seen.

Attending college in Connecticut for the past year had changed her perspective. Sure, she had been outside of Searles Valley before. She had been to the beach, the mountains, and shopping in San Bernardino, even L.A. But living in the East for several months had been a real eye opener. Yards and landscapes were green and lush, all without the need of sprinklers. Snow fell in the winter, and when it rained, it poured for days. Temperatures rarely exceeded eighty-five degrees. Most of those you crossed paths with would remain strangers forever.

Camm had tried explaining Trona to her East Coast friends. It was like trying to explain life on a different planet. As Camm looked over the dilapidated homes and trailers, the place now looked surreal. People lived their whole lives here and knew nothing else. Now, Camm was almost sorry she did know something else. She enjoyed being fiercely loyal to Trona.

She climbed out of the car and circled around to help J.R. get out. As she guided him up the hard dirt pathway to the house, she asked, "What does 'J.R.' stand for anyway."

The old man chortled to himself as if he was about to reveal a great joke. "It stands for what it abbreviates: Junior!" The answer caught Camm off guard. She knew it was significant, but didn't have time to figure out why.

Knowing from prior visits not to try the front door, Camm went directly to the side door. The old car that had been in the driveway was gone. A used but somewhat newer car was parked in its place. A light was shining from within the house. Someone was home.

Camm banged on the door loudly three times. She wanted the elderly Sarah to hear her. Surprisingly, the door opened immediately. In the doorway stood, not Sarah, but Miss Cathleen.

"Oh, it's you." Miss Cathleen peered out over the top of her glasses. Cutting off any reply, she said, "Come in, come in. There is someone here who wants to see you. Have your ears been burning?"

Camm stepped inside, gently steering J.R. into the small kitchen.

Miss Cathleen eyed the old man suspiciously. "And who is this?"

"Someone I want Sarah to meet." Camm glanced around

the otherwise-empty kitchen. "And who is it that wants to see me?"

If Miss Cathleen was suspicious of J.R., Camm was also suspicious of anyone wanting to see her. After all, half the town was looking for her.

"I want to see you," said a voice from the next room.

Before Camm could react, Martha ran into the kitchen and gave Camm a hug, her face tight against Camm's shoulder. "I'm so glad you came here. I've been so worried about you. No one would tell me anything after you disappeared."

Camm pushed Martha back by her shoulders and gave her a careful look. "I'm glad to see you, too, but how did you get here? I thought you would be in L.A. by now."

Sarah shuffled into the kitchen, but stopped in the doorway, bringing a hand to her mouth. She leaned against a wall. Looking expectantly at J.R., her eyes began to glisten.

"I ran into Martha in Ridgecrest," Miss Cathleen said. "I can tell you the rest later. First, where have you been? How did you get here? And who is this you have brought with you?"

"I know who this is." The voice was hesitant and small, but also sweet and clear. Tears now trickled down Sarah's cheeks. She held out her hands in J.R.'s direction.

"Al? Al, have you really come back to me?"

Camm was stunned. She looked at J.R. and saw tears flowing down his cheeks as well.

He held out his right hand and stepped toward Sarah. "Oh, my sweet, sweet Sarah. My dearest, my darling. I have finally found you. I have come home to you."

He took her in a tight one-arm hug and tenderly kissed her on the lips. They gazed into each other's eyes as he released her to reach up and gently stroke her hair.

For the moment, nothing more needed to be said. Even Miss Cathleen was wordless.

Camm had no idea that two octogenarians could provide such a touching, such a romantic, such an emotional scene. She felt her own eyes tearing up.

This whole time she had been hiding out with Alberto Samuel, Junior. The rightful owner of the Searles Mansion, and the last surviving keeper of its deepest secrets. He was still alive, and, after more than sixty years living in a cave, was now reunited with the love of his life.

Camm looked at Miss Cathleen. "Say hello to your father-in-law."

XXX

Scowling deeply, Mr. C walked along the second floor balcony. All his plans were falling apart and he was not happy. The excruciating pain in his feet and back did nothing to improve his mood. Each step felt as if he were walking barefoot on sharp gravel. To make matters worse, a sudden pain, like an electrical shock, would randomly shoot through his legs and lower back. Stress only increased the pain.

His pocket was full of Vicodin pills, but he knew he couldn't take one. He needed a clear head at midnight, and he needed the pain to keep him more wary and alert. Mr. C used pain to remind him of the tasks at hand and to help him push other matters out of his mind. Tonight, he would need all his mental facilities active if he was going to make it through the night alive.

He stared over the balcony rail at Agent Kline, seated at

the foot of the stairs below. Mr. C had counted on having Kline to help them work the grandfather clock at midnight. So many things could go wrong, and Kline was one of his best problem solvers. Now they would have to do the best they could without him. Bringing back those two knuckle-headed college boys from the overlapping dimension was turning out to be almost more trouble than it was worth.

They had tried to get Agent Kline to a bedroom upstairs, where he would be safe, but it had taken all their combined efforts just to get him up the spiral stone stairs and into the main hall. Once there, he hadn't wanted to move from the foot of the staircase. If anyone tried to move him farther, he became agitated. He was just too big and strong to force.

Right now, he was holding his hand in front of his face, turning it back and forth, looking at it as if it were the most amazing thing he had ever seen. He was silent, except for an occasional comment such as, "Mind-blowing" or "Fabulous, extremely fabulous" or even "I can see my bones and tendons. They're multi-colored!"

True, they had obtained phenothiazine as an anti-psychotic and valium as a calming agent, just in case, but they didn't have time to play nursemaid to Agent Kline. As long as he remained calm, there was no reason to put more chemicals in his system. He was calm as long as everyone left him alone, staring at his hand. For now, the best plan was to not agitate him.

Mr. C started down the large staircase, holding a pool cue in his hand. In spite of himself, he was using it as a cane. It didn't relieve the pain, but it helped him move faster.

He stepped around Agent Kline at the bottom stair. Hesitating for a second, he studied Agent Kline, who seemed more alert. "Agent, are you feeling better?"

Agent Kline did not take his eyes off his hand, but responded nevertheless. "I have the most fascinating fingers and thumb."

Mr. C didn't take the time to sigh, but moved on toward the giant grandfather clock. Electric work lights had been set up around the perimeter of the room, all aimed at the clock. A few agents, including Agent Allen, were standing near the walls, trying to stay out of the way, but available in case something should happen.

Agent Allen had the Smith and Wesson 500 conspicuously stowed away in a shoulder holster. Mr. C nodded in her direction. "I trust you know how to use that cannon?"

She looked annoyed. "I am a special agent with the FBI. I trained in the use of all hand weapons. I know what I'm doing."

Mr. C hoped so. It was one thing to know how to handle a standard revolver, but that Smith and Wesson 500 Magnum was basically hand-held field artillery.

Mr. S stood in front of the clock, looking over a checklist. He glanced up as Mr. C approached. "I think everything is in order. We should be ready to go. It's a good thing Agent Kline was so meticulous in keeping a written log."

Mr. C snorted in derision and waved a hand in the air as if batting away a pesky fly. "Everything is out of order, and we are ready for nothing. The rat is missing. Who knows where it is. Our clock expert is in a daze and sitting over there, right in the way of any confrontation that may arise in connection with a cross over. He is staring at his own hand and hopped up on enough LSD to send a horse into outer space.

"We don't know how this clock works, if it does work, or possible negative scenarios that will be generated from using it. And worst of all, without the rat acting as the guardian in the mansion, we don't know whether performing this transition will bring the giant snake or something even worse through to this side in the cross over. We should have brought more agents. It is difficult to see how we could be less prepared."

Mr. S smiled a grim smile and patted Mr. C on the shoulder with his bandaged hand. "Always the optimist. You are always the optimist." Mr. S scanned his checklist again. "It will be interesting to interview those boys once we get them back. They should be able to tell us quite a bit about the transverse side to this world."

Mr. C grunted, "If we get them back."

Mr. S ignored the comment.

It crouched behind oleander bushes a safe distance from the mansion and waited, hidden by the dark. Anticipating this night's work, it began to drool green slime.

It knew the mansion. It knew the worlds on both sides. It knew how to work with the transitions. It knew the mansion was no longer its prison. Things had changed. The devilish frame was gone. The cursed chain was gone. It had no intention of going back to its prison, not in the morning, not ever.

It knew about the snake. It knew more than the humans did about all transition creatures, and it knew the humans were ignorant. It could sense a transition was coming. And it knew how to interfere, how to cause them trouble. It would stay long enough to upset their plans. Then it would disappear before . . . just before.

Tonight, it would feed, maybe even on the despised one. She was back. It had followed her scent in the mansion. But if not on the despised one, it would feed on one who had caused it pain. It had been too long since it had tasted human flesh. Tonight, it would fill itself.

A thick green mist swirled from its nostrils with every breath. The overwhelming stench of sulfur and things long dead soon spread across the ground like the harbinger of death that it was. Putrid green drool ran down its long fangs and dripped to the ground.

Tonight it would feed!

XXXI

"**T**onight when all hands are up, there it will come. All will be fierce. All will be danger and death at last, even as at first."

Camm rubbed her tired eyes, and stared intently at Al Jr. He had started talking gibberish again. No one could put it all together, not even Sarah, who was sitting next to him.

"Death will be there, oh yes. Death will watch, but will not aid us, oh no. It will not." He closed his eyes as if to concentrate and continued holding tight to Sarah's hand.

Camm could see Al Jr. was struggling. All these years, his only companions had been dead bodies. Camm knew how little conversation that produced. How long had it been since he had actually spoken to live people? For so long, he had just spoken to himself. It had to be difficult for him now to communicate what he knew.

Al Jr. opened his eyes and squeezed Sarah's hand. "V. ready seer pans will be the challenge tonight, and death will watch, will watch with celebration."

Martha whispered to Camm, "What is he talking about?"

Camm rolled her eyes. "I've been listening to him for days. I still don't understand him."

Camm turned to Sarah, nodding toward the old man. "Do you know what he is saying? You were . . .you are his wife."

Sarah just shook her head and buried her face in Al Jr.'s shoulder.

Without disturbing Sarah, Al Jr. turned to look directly at Camm. "I have been watching. Oh yes, watching all these years. I observe you. I observe him. I observe death. You act good, righteous good, but it was taken away by fools. Tonight death laughs. When all hands are up, it comes back. Green and red will spill, will mix again. Tonight death feeds."

Camm glanced at Miss Cathleen, who only shrugged her shoulders. She did not understand the old man either.

Camm looked back at Al Jr. He nodded at Camm. "You understand. You go. You know it. It know you. You look at death. Death look at you. You go stop death when all hands are up."

A chill ran down Camm's spine. She did understand some of what the old man was saying. She looked at the clock; it was after eleven o'clock. She looked at Martha.

"When he says, 'When all hands are up,' he means midnight. Something happens at the mansion tonight at midnight. I believe that is what he is trying to tell us."

The old man nodded his head vehemently. "Yes, yes. You go. You stop fools. Time to stop death. Time to stop both, or red and green will mix again, very much so."

Camm released a weary sigh as she stood up. Turning to Martha, she said, "We need to talk. I have so much I want to tell you, but Al Jr. is saying I have to go back to the mansion first. I have to go right now, or I will be too late!"

XXXII

As midnight approached, Agent Allen grew nervous about the number of lights they had in the mansion. Or better said, by the lack of lights they had in the mansion. The main hall was brightly lit for now, but she remembered how easily the rat had extinguished the lights along the stone spiral staircase. Right now, they didn't even know where the rat was. It might be hidden in some secret compartment somewhere in the mansion, waiting for the transition.

How did Camm and Cal cope with the lights when they attacked the rat, she wondered. She wished she had asked more questions when she had had the chance.

Glancing around the main hall, the large fireplace at the far end triggered a memory. The morning that she had discovered

Camm and Cal still in the mansion after fighting off the rat, the fireplace had held the remnants of a still smoldering fire.

A fire? Was it harder for the rat to extinguish a hot burning fire than it was to block an electric light? Somehow that made sense.

Her memories sent her back to the first time she had entered the cavernous main hall with Camm. At the time, she had thought the mansion weird and otherworldly, even slightly interesting. Now it felt foreboding and sinister. With its black slate floor, fearsomely carved baroque woodwork, and grotesquely cut stone bricks, the mammoth room seemed taken out of an earlier and more primeval time. It had been designed as a place for evil things to happen.

There was no time to think more about the fireplace. The focal point now was the clock, whose hands pointed straight up, waiting for midnight to arrive. It was hard to believe the giant grandfather clock was a sophisticated piece of machinery. With its hangman pendulum, bizarre carvings, and enormous size, it looked like a sadistic piece of Salvador Dali artwork. She looked at her watch—only a few minutes to go. She wished she had thought about the fireplace sooner.

Misters S and C stood next to the clock. Mr. S watched the time on an electric device that showed him the exact time down to a thousandth of a second. Mr. C was reviewing notes on a small note pad. He held a pool cue in his left hand with the butt end down on the slate floor as if it were a shepherd's staff.

Agent Kline sat on the stairway, his legs splayed out in front as he reclined back on the steps above him, his large hand still out in front of his face. Everyone knew he should be somewhere else, but no one was big enough to move him against his will. It would be some time before all the LSD metabolized out of his body.

J.R. stood not too far away from Agent Allen, but he was no longer talking to her. She was glad about that. His split lip was thick and swollen with tape across the break. He needed stitches. She almost felt bad about that.

Mr. C had said little about the incident, except that J.R. would have to wait until the next day to seek medical treatment because they were already short on agents.

J.R. had not been happy.

The weight of the Smith and Wesson 500 Magnum hung heavy on Agent Allen's shoulder. Patting it, she smiled. At least there was one thing she could count on tonight.

Mr. S announced loudly to the whole room, "Sixty seconds, everyone, sixty seconds to midnight." With his announcement, as if it had been planned, all the lights in the mansion blinked once, twice, three times, and then went out. All the lights they had wired in the main hall, all the extra lights they had brought in, and every light in the mansion went out.

At first it was pitch black, while their eyes adapted to the sudden change in illumination. The only light now was the moonlight and stray light coming in through the windows from the chemical plant next door. Because of the evacuation, most of the rest of the town was dark. The available light was extremely dim. Everything in the hall was masked by deep, dark shadows.

At the same time, a gagging sulfur smell filled the hall. It was almost painful to breathe. And the temperature was dropping noticeably as well. The hall was beginning to feel like a sub-zero, arctic cooler. Even though there was very little light, Agent Allen could still see her breath.

For a moment, all was silent in the room. Then she heard Mr. C's voice. "This is great, just great. Where did we put those special-forces headlamps?"

Mr. S's voice filled the hall. "Ready everyone! Battle positions. Midnight is coming, with or without lights."

J.R. turned on his flashlight. It immediately dimmed, flickered, and then went out.

"Leave your flashlights off!" Mr. S commanded, his voice harsh. "Don't turn them on until we really need them."

All was quiet again until Agent Kline's deep voice rang out. "This is so cool."

Agent Allen wrapped her fingers around the handle of the Smith and Wesson 500 and leaned back against the wall to brace herself. Dark or light, she was ready.

Camm pulled up in front of the mansion in the purloined car. Martha was on her way back to Ridgecrest with Miss Cathleen to check in before her curfew. Camm had not gotten the whole story as to how Martha had come out to Trona with Miss Cathleen. That would have to wait until later.

Al Jr. had been left with Sarah in Homewood Canyon. Camm couldn't help but wonder if they were having a second honeymoon, in their late eighties. It was a funny, but nice, thought.

A half-moon was rising over the eastern mountains on the far side of the dry lake bed. It offered scant light, but in the darkness down the street, she could make out a few figures and images. Determining what those figures and images were was another matter altogether. Except for stray light from the nearby plant, the night was dark. The mansion was even darker. Camm knew that was not a good sign.

Even though it was dark, it was still warm. The sun had baked the pavement and dirt all day, and now heat radiated back into the air. The heat was dry, sucking moisture from her eyes, nose, and mouth. The desert night sky showed the stars clearly. On a night like tonight, the stars glowed brightly, but still provided very little light to see by.

Now that she was at the mansion, Camm had no idea what she should do. Should she knock on that massive front door and turn herself in? Should she reconnoiter around the mansion, keeping in the shadows? She waved her hand in front of her nose to disperse the sulfuric smell. The smell had gotten stronger and stronger and was now overwhelming. That also was not a good sign.

It moved. She saw it, a deep black shadow, looming large.

Something very large on four feet slunk across the street in front of her, moving away from the mansion toward the desert.

Then she felt it. She felt it in her head. She could sense the rat. There was no doubt. She could feel what it was feeling. She could feel the murky depths of its ugly mind.

She also could tell the rat had not reached out to her. It did not know she was there. Because of their previous connections, it seemed Camm could now sense the rat when it was close by and read its primitive, but foreboding, thoughts—not in words, but in pictures and feelings. Its inner being was as foul as the evil odor it exuded externally. Inside, it reeked of hate.

The rat was pleased with itself, as if it had played some clever joke. It was also moving away from danger. Not from the humans in the mansion, it wasn't afraid of them. It was moving away from some expectation of danger that was coming. Something not yet there, but imminent.

Without thinking it through, without even realizing what she was doing, or what she could do, Camm mentally struck out at the rat. *You miserable monster, what are you up to?*

As soon as she sent out the thought, Camm knew she had made a mistake. She did not mean to let the rat know she was there, but once the connection was made, the force of her hatred caused the reflexive thought to reach out and touch it.

The hulking shadow stopped in its tracks. The figure slowly turned toward Camm. Then, she saw them, two eyes reflecting the moonlight in a red glow. Camm's body went cold. Her intestines coiled into a tight knot.

Know you. Hurt me. Hurt you. Eat you.

Every hair on Camm's body stood up on end. And though her hands and feet felt as if they were in ice water, a film of moist perspiration broke out on her brow. Her hand instinctively went for the ignition. Before she could start the car, she heard something from inside the mansion. She knew that sound.

DONG!

The sound of the chime was so loud, it almost startled Agent Allen out of her skin. Of course, standing in the blackness of that immense hall did not help. Tightening her grip on the Smith and Wesson, she searched the shadows of the room for something. She wasn't sure what. *Did someone scream? Was the clock glowing green?*

Mr. S, noticing the glow, commented casually, "This is a new phenomenon."

DONG!

In spite of herself, Agent Allen jumped again. *Why is that chime so loud?*

As she prepared herself for the next chime, she noticed the front doors of the mansion were open. They had been closed before the chiming had started. She also noticed a haze or phantasmal appearance in the middle of the hall. Even in the darkness, she could see it was red and large, glowing from within.

DONG!

She could see the image of the two college boys forming near the large, hazy red object.

Mr. C shouted, "The car! They brought the car inside! They are trying to bring that stupid car back with them!"

Mr. S called out calmly, "Everyone stay near the walls. Stay back from the red thing now materializing in the center of the room. We think it's a car."

DONG!

As Agent Allen watched, she saw the front doors switching between opened and closed. They weren't swinging, just jumping back and forth between instantly open, then instantly closed. When the doors were open, the outside seemed to shimmer with a green, reflective shine that was moving and undulating.

The image of the boys became more substantial. One of them, the one with the long hair, was pointing toward the front doors. His mouth was moving, but Agent Allen couldn't hear what he was saying. She couldn't hear any sound at all, except the deafening chiming of the clock.

DONG!

Something seemed to move by Agent Allen, but it was more like a sensation or a very slight breeze. Green and white sparkles moved in the same direction, floating through the air in an undulating pattern. As the image became more substantial, it appeared to be a gliding wall, sliding silently by, just feet from her face.

DONG!

The images of the boys were substantial now, but one was waving his arms in an exaggerated fashion. The long-haired boy seemed to run from his position in the middle of the hall toward the front doors. When he did, his image disappeared.

DONG!

With this chime, the image of the car became solid, as did the image of the remaining boy. It was Cal. Cal was back in the right world.

At that moment, Agent Allen saw it. The boy and his car weren't the only things to come over from the other world. The snake, the giant Mojave Green rattlesnake had come, too. It was in the mansion with them! It was in the great main hall and was now heading for Agent Kline, who was still reclining on the stairs.

In concert with the chiming of the clock, the rat bounded toward Camm. With no time to think, all she could do was scream and lock her door. In two leaps, the rat was on the hood of the car, its dripping, drooling fangs mere inches from the windshield. It clawed at the glass, staring intently at Camm. The windshield seemed to screech in pain as the rat's nails scratched down its length. The rat's thoughts and intents were clear. It hungered and it hated. It could resolve both at once if it could only get at Camm.

The clock still gonged, but Camm had lost count. The rat swiveled its head back and forth between the mansion and Camm, trying to look at both at the same time.

With the next gong, its lips curled back, showing long, mossy-green incisors. It growled at the mansion. Camm could sense its fear. Looking back at Camm, fumes wafted from its nostrils with each breath. Its glowing red eyes burned deep into her soul. She could feel its hate.

Finally, the rat focused its attention on the mansion. Camm sensed the tide of fear within the rat was overwhelming the waves of hate that had been directed toward her. It feared to stay. If it ran, it would live to hate another day. Raising its head to the black night sky, it wailed a long, lonely, painful shriek into the hot, dry air. Then it urinated on the hood of the car, splashing thick, noxious yellow-green liquid all over the front of the car, even up onto the windshield.

Finishing its filthy task, the rat jumped off the hood and fled from the mansion. With just a few bounds, it had vanished into the darkness of the night.

Camm sat frozen to the seat of the car. Her hands were clamped around the steering wheel, her knuckles white. With extreme effort, she forced herself to take a breath, and then slowly released her death grip on the steering wheel.

Turning her head toward the mansion, she was startled to see the massive front doors were open. Something was entering the mansion—slithering into the mansion. She saw barrel-sized rattles, and the last few rattles at the end were smashed and broken. As she watched, a giant snake's tail disappeared into the inky black mansion.

As soon as the tail was inside, the doors instantly closed. One moment, the doors were wide open and the snake was passing through them. The next moment, the doors were closed. They didn't swing close, they were just closed.

What to do? What to do? Camm's mind was all a jumble.

Did she dare get out of the car? Was the rat still nearby? Was it waiting for her to get out, laying a trap for her? She could no longer sense its thoughts, but was that a trick?

If she did get out, what would she do? Go in the mansion? Call for help?

The fright of the rat's attack, the surprise of seeing the snake, the futility of not knowing what to do, all combined in one overwhelming ball of emotion.

Camm did the only thing she could at that moment. She leaned her head against the steering wheel and screamed. Then, she raised her head and shouted at the roof of the car.

"What should I do? Why am I so useless?"

It was a quick sprint to the newly appeared red Camaro in the middle of the hall. Agent Allen planned to use it for cover while she fired at the snake. Just as she arrived at the car, all the lights in the main hall, in fact in the whole mansion, came back on simultaneously, bright as ever. Before she had been blinded by darkness, now she was blinded by the many bright lights. Shaking her head and squinting, she tried to see something while her eyes were still adapting.

"Whaoooooo!" Agent Kline was pointing toward the snake, his eyes wide, his head shaking in wonder. He made no effort to get out of the way of the approaching gigantic snake. Instead, he sat up and leaned forward to see more clearly. "Truly mind-blowing! Beautiful!"

Her vision returning, Agent Allen rested her arms on the roof of the car and pointed her hand-held cannon at the snake's head. She pulled the trigger twice, aiming before each shot. The explosive force of the gun rattled her to the marrow. The boom was deafening. She was glad she had thought to wear the ear plugs.

For all her bravado to Mr. C, when he asked if she could handle the gun, Agent Allen realized now what he was talking about. The weapon was so large, so heavy, so powerful, it was almost beyond her ability. Almost. She would handle it because she had to handle it.

Two puncture wounds burst into the side of the snake where she had hit it at the base of the head. The snake was bleeding red blood, profusely, from both sides of its neck—the bullets had gone all the way through. The snake hissed a loud whistling noise in angry protest and pain. It rose up in a striking pose, its head even with the second floor balcony.

Taking quick aim, Agent Allen fired another shot up through the bottom of the snake's jaw. Conscious that she only had two shots remaining, she waited for a shot into the snake's brain. She couldn't tell if she had seriously hurt the snake yet or not, but she had at least drawn its attention away from Agent Kline.

"No!" Mr. C half limped, half ran toward where she was standing. He still carried the pool cue he had been using as a cane. "Don't kill it!" He shouted. "Just distract it. It will return to the other side on its own."

The snake lurched forward. Too late, Mr. S yelled, "Watch out!"

The snake struck at Mr. C, but with amazing speed for a crippled old man, he lurched to one side. The snake missed, but Mr. C fell to the floor on his side. Instantly, the snake struck again, this time clamping its maw around Mr. C's midsection, fangs piercing him through.

The snake lifted him into the air, high above the heads of everyone else. From below, Agent Allen could see Mr. C's feet sticking out one side of the snake's mouth, and his arms, shoulders, and head sticking out the other. Mr. C swore. His face screwed into a tight grimace—the pain he felt was palpable to everyone in the room. He still clenched the pool cue in his fist.

"Shoot it! Shoot it! Shoot it now!" Mr. S was running across the room, his finger pointing up at the snake. "Don't hit my brother!"

Agent Allen let fly the last two bullets in her weapon, carefully aiming up into the throat at the back of the snake's head. As deep holes blasted into the neck below, geysers of blood burst out on top of the snake's neck. Again, the bullets had gone all the way through.

At the same time, J.R. also began firing his .38 up into the snake's throat. His gun sounded like firecrackers compared to Agent Allen's cannon. Running underneath the snake's head, Mr. S was also firing his own .38 into the snake's throat from below.

The snake swung its head around and fled for the far side of the hall. Mr. C seemed to immediately understand his situation. The snake was trying to carry him away as it escaped the pain being inflicted from below. Lifting the pool cue high in the air, he plunged it down deep into the left eye of the snake.

The reflexive reaction of the snake was to toss Mr. C, slamming him against the second story wall. He slid down the wall, leaving bloody streaks, and crumpled onto the balcony floor.

The giant snake, with blood flying and pool cue still sticking out of its eye, raced for the back wall of the hall. As it slithered across the floor, it began to shimmer, and then to quickly fade. It dissipated into the wall as if passing through an unseen opening, disappearing completely as the broken rattlers, last of all, slipped into the wall, which became solid again.

For a second, no one breathed. Mr. S started at a dead run and bounded, as well as he could, around Agent Kline, who was no longer reclining, but sat on the stairs, staring at the back wall. Noticeably struggling, Mr. S hurried up the stairs to check on the crumpled body of Mr. C.

Agent Allen left the cannon lying on top of the car, and

tried to follow Mr. S up the stairs. Agent Kline grabbed her wrist as she passed, jerking her to a sudden stop. "Did you see that? Was there a giant snake in here? Did it eat Mr. C, or was that just me?"

Agent Allen gently released herself from his grip. "No, the snake was really here."

She quickly followed Mr. S up the stairs to see what aid she could provide Mr. C.

XXXIII

Across the street from the mansion were a couple sorry-looking salt cedars. Climbing out of the besmirched car, Camm hid behind those trees and watched the comings and goings at the mansion. Whatever had happened inside had caused a lot of commotion. A med-flight helicopter had landed, and medics had rushed a body out the mansion's front doors and flown away in a hurry. Black SUVs had been arriving in turn, and one had been dispatched away at high speed, colored lights flashing.

A second helicopter, black with no markings, had landed in the vacant lot next to the mansion, spraying dust and sand everywhere. It waited with the engine running as if on call. San Bernardino sheriff's cars had surrounded the mansion, and deputies were spread out across the yard, standing guard, as if to keep the crowds away. But with the town evacuated, there were no crowds, only Camm hiding across the street.

Camm had no idea what was going on, but clearly something big had happened. She watched the large black agent, who had been one of her Swift Creek guards, lumber out of the mansion and sit down. Other than Agent Allen, he had been the only agent friendly to her. She remembered his name, Agent Kline. He was now seated on the front steps, just outside the massive front doors, resting his head in his hands. Nobody paid him any attention, and he didn't seem to be aware of the commotion around him.

Throughout all the excitement, she had not seen Agent Allen. She hoped Agent Allen wasn't the one who had been taken away by the medics. After a while, the sheriff's deputies began leaving, apparently no longer needed.

Eventually, she saw J.R., the agent who had challenged her at the Jimenez house, come out the front doors. He escorted a tall figure, bound in handcuffs, with a law enforcement jacket draped over his head and shoulders.

At the bottom of the stairs, J.R. hesitated and turned his head as if someone had called to him. The tall, old white-haired man came out of the front doors, talking excitedly and pointing at the figure in handcuffs. Because of the noise of the helicopter, Camm couldn't make out what was being said, but J.R. was waving a hand and nodding his head in agreement.

Finally, the tall man went back inside. As J.R. turned to

continue on his way, the jacket fell off the shoulders of the tall figure in handcuffs.

Camm gasped. It was Cal! They were taking Cal away in handcuffs. They were keeping their promise to put them both in prison. Cal had made it back from the other side, only to be arrested and thrown in prison.

J.R. took Cal by the elbow and hustled him over to the helicopter where more federal agents waited.

This was wrong! This could not be happening. Camm could not let this happen. She needed to talk with someone. Agent Kline was still sitting on the stairs. She would talk to him. Stepping out from behind the trees, Camm's mind raced. What should she say?

Before she could begin her march across the street, a hand from behind grabbed her firmly on the shoulder and pulled her back.

Gasping, she spun around to see who had her.

Raising one eyebrow, Agent Allen said sternly, "And just where do you think you are going, Ms. Smith?"

Camm was both startled and relieved to see Agent Allen. "You're okay!" She grabbed Agent Allen in a quick hug, but then immediately released her.

"They're taking Cal! He's in handcuffs." The words caught in her throat. They brought him back only to take him away to prison, to who knows where. This is so unfair. I'll never see him again. I have to go with him!"

Agent Allen shook her head and gripped Camm by both arms, pulling her back behind the trees again. "There is nothing you can do for Cal right now. Maybe later, but not if you go with him. If you really want to help Cal, you must come with me."

Camm was confused. She didn't know whether or not she could trust Agent Allen anymore. "Where? Where are we going?"

"You'll see. I'm not playing their game. From now on, we are going to do things differently. You are coming with me. You are of no use to anyone if you go into lockup with Misters S and C holding the key. I need you with me. I need to know what you know, and you need to know what I know. Together we are stronger."

Keeping a tight hold of Camm's right arm, Agent Allen turned Camm away from the mansion and hustled her away into the dark Trona night.

Camm didn't get a chance to explain the monster rat had just gone this same way.

XXXIV

The bright desert sun burned down on Lenny with no mercy, waking him up from what had been a very short slumber. Seeing the snake enter the mansion, Lenny had fled from it, out the front doors of the mansion, which the boys had left open after driving Cal's car up the stairs and into the main hall.

Unfortunately for Lenny, he left the mansion before a full transition could take place, and he was still in the alternate world. The primitive one without food. As he rubbed the sleep out of his eyes and stood up, he noticed he was not alone.

Not only was he not alone, he was totally surrounded. He rotated 360 degrees and saw men standing all around him. Short men, all dark skinned, barely clothed. Their faces were painted in bright red and yellow. Their long black hair was braided and, in many cases, decorated with feathers. Lenny reached up and smoothed his long blond ponytail.

At first no one spoke. In wonder and confusion, Lenny surveyed all the men around him, looking for a friendly face. They all looked back at him with curiosity and animosity. One of the men stepped forward. He was older than the others and appeared to have more hair and body decorations. Perhaps he was in charge.

Lenny stood straighter and raised his right hand to shoulder height, with his hand open and palm facing forward. He said just one word. "Dude."

ACKNOWLEDGEMENTS

So many have done so much to help us in creating the *Dimensions in Death* series. We first must thank our wives whose editorial services and advice and inspiration were not only extremely helpful, but essential, to the completion of this book. We also want to thank our kids and grandkids. Not only are they a great blessing in our lives, but were key in helping us put this book together. We love and thank all of you, but want to especially mention Ambre, Amy, CJ, James, Eliza, Isaac & Katrina, Ephraim & Kimm, Caleb, Josh, Ben and other family & friends, especially Tammy Kenady, for reading along as we wrote and advising us on how to make the tale better. This book could not have happened without your patient support, encouragement and help.

We love you all more than you know. Thank you again.

Berk and Andy
Husbands, Dads, Grandpas,
and Storytellers

A. L. WASHBURN and B. W. WASHBURN are brothers, licensed lawyers and full time writers, residing in Colorado and southern Utah. Growing up in a large family in Trona, California, a small mining community not far from Death Valley, they spent many happy days in their youth roaming the wastelands of the Mojave Desert. After living in South America at different times, each came back to finish graduate school and start separate careers. Living thousands of miles apart, they worked in different areas of the law, while raising their own large families.

Each has authored legal materials and professional articles, but after years of wandering in the wastelands of the law, their lifelong love of fiction, especially fantasy, science fiction and horror, brought them back together to write a new young adult horror series, beginning with *Pitch Green* and later *Mojave Green.* They have found there yet remain many untold wonders to be discovered in the unbounded realms of the imagination, especially as those realms unfold in the perilous wastelands of the *Dimensions in Death.*

Connect with The Brothers Washburn at
thebrotherswashburn.blogspot.com